Praise for *The Cur*

"Hoppe offers a crime thriller about the difficulty of stealing famous art…an inviting story of a modern-day gentleman thief."
— **Kirkus Reviews**

"We think of an art thief as Pierce Brosnan, rich, handsome, too cool to come within miles of arrest. In *The Curse of Van Gogh*, Paul Hoppe gives us a more credible character: recently out of jail, burdened by family problems, forced to commit the world's biggest art heist by a billionaire who plans to kill him as soon as he delivers. Oh, and there's a curse. This is a nail-biter."
— **Jesse Kornbluth,** HeadButler.com

"I blazed through Paul Hoppe's fun, fast-paced, and thoroughly entertaining, *The Curse of Van Gogh*, knowing after only a few pages, that I should save it for some transcontinental flight. But, caught up in the perfectly drawn world of the high stakes, high commerce, and high egos of the international art market and its surrounding riff raff of forgers and thieves and wannabes, I was unable to stop myself. Dive in yourself. You won't come up for air until you reach the last sentence."
— **Pete Fromm, award-winning author of *As Cool As I Am* and *If Not For This***

"Centered on the downtown New York art world where greed and cool intersect, this thriller has a riveting plot that clicks right along. Sharply drawn, tightly composed, full of delicious details and sparkling dialogue. I loved it."
— **Bart Gulley, artist**

The Curse of Van Gogh

Paul Hoppe

SparkPress, a BookSparks imprint
A division of SparkPoint Studio, LLC

Published by SparkPress, a BookSparks imprint,
A division of SparkPoint Studio, LLC
Tempe, Arizona, USA, 85281
www.sparkpointstudio.com

Printed in the United States of America.

ISBN: 978-1-940716-15-2 (pbk)
ISBN: 978-1-940716-14-5 (ebk)

Cover design © Julie Metz, Ltd./metzdesign.com
Formatting by Polgarus Studio

This is a work of fiction. Names, characters, places, and incidents either
are the product of the author's imagination or are used fictitiously. Any
resemblance to actual persons, living or dead, is entirely coincidental.

DEDICATION

For Jane Prior

Her patience and spirit: priceless

PROLOGUE
THE CURSE

April 1, 1944
Stuttgart, Germany

Christian was hopping back and forth, trying to stay warm. The tarmac exhaled steam as the predawn light slid from pitch black to gunmetal gray. He could barely make out the wind sock, in silhouette, at the far end of the airfield. Even with his wool-lined three-quarter-length black leather coat tied tight, he was bone chilled. The coat was his bonus for enlisting in the Luftwaffe. He was young and restless and thought that being an aviator would get Anna, the prettiest girl in his hometown of Bamberg, to take notice. Still, he was freezing. The only sound was his breath as he exhaled. Eager for his mission to get under way, he stood next to his motorcycle, a Zuendapp KS 750, minus the sidecar and the usual Third Reich insignias. Instead it was camo colored from front fork to tail-pipe.

Christian pulled out the pack of Lucky Strikes he'd received from a Yank POW at the camp in Bamberg, not far from his parents' house. When he first enlisted he was assigned guard duty at the camp, but he still carried too much youthful innocence to be much of a ruthless guard. He actually felt sorry for the scrawny POWs, and managed to sneak some of his grandmother's apple strudel to some of the prisoners in exchange for teaching him English. The head POW, Colonel Grant, gave him a couple of packs of smokes as thanks for showing some civility.

He fired up one of the Lucky's he heard the low drone of an aircraft. Coughing out smoke, he quickly stubbed out the fag. The noise intensified and he began to feel a warmth flow through him. The adrenaline of his first real mission. He had been told this was a top-secret mission. Ordered by Reichsmarschall Goering himself, commander of the Luftwaffe, and second in command of the Third Reich. Only Hitler wielded more power.

Christian couldn't help but smile as he watched the Messerschmitt do a low fly by, and then circle to land at the military airfield ten klicks south of Stuttgart. It would be another hour before sunrise but the dew-covered runways were now clearly visible. The plane came in fast over the near end of the runway and floated less than a foot above the runway. A quick puff of smoke from the tires was the only indication it had made contact with asphalt.

While the pride of the Luftwaffe taxied back towards the hangar at the northwest corner of the airfield, Christian began pushing as hard as he could on the sliding door.

With the hangar door all the way open he stood at attention, in what he hoped was a perfect military salute.

The plane taxied straight into the hangar, the pilot shutting down the counterrotating four-bladed propellers. The back door popped open and out stepped General Stern in dress Luftwaffe uniform. The eager young corporal clicked his heels together in military etiquette. General Stern strode over quickly, telling Christian to rest at ease and asking him if he was, in fact, alone.

Yes.

And had he told absolutely NO ONE.

Yes, replied the nervous corporal, even though he'd whispered to Anna he was being sent on a top-secret mission. Her kiss had weakened his vow of secrecy.

The colonel barked a command and suddenly two more Luftwaffe officers stepped from the plane. They unfolded a long red carpet. They, too, clicked their heels, and then the second most powerful figure of the Third Reich stepped from the plane.

He was big, bloated, and pockmarked, and seemed to fall forward at the shoulders, as though an unbearable weight had been thrust upon him, pulling him down and forward. He walked slowly toward Christian, and the closer the rotund man got, the bigger the young corporal's eyes became. His mouth dropped in awe. General Stern laughed inwardly.

Suddenly Reichsmarschall Goering was standing a mere foot from Christian who had a sudden urge to pee but held tight.

Goering, with his gloves still on, shook Christian's hand. He apologized to Christian that he'd had to wait so long. Goering then asked about his family back in Bamberg. Christian limited his answers to one word replies.

Good.

Fine.

Thanks.

He was in such a daze he barely noticed General Stern handing the two-meter long tube to Goering. It was made of aluminum and the exterior was covered in camouflage canvas. The ends were tightly sealed. A strap connected each end so it could be worn over the shoulder like an oversized quiver.

Goering handed the tube to the young corporal who slung it over his shoulder so that it rested snuggly across his back. Goering then handed him a slip of paper with a name and address in Zurich. He instructed the young corporal to go directly to the address on the piece of paper. He was to hand the tube over to the man whose name was on the paper, and NO ONE else.

DO NOT STOP. Take only the back roads.

Once his mission was completed he was to report back immediately to General Stern from the first checkpoint inside Germany.

A quick salute, a heel click, and Christian quickly ran from the hangar, fired up his Zuendapp 750 motorcycle, and sped off.

Reichsmarschall Goering and his cronies reboarded the plane and toasted with an early-morning schnapps to celebrate, as the pilot accelerated the Messerschmitt and lifted off the runway. Goering and his men chuckled at the young soldier's eagerness, knowing he'd be shot as a deserter as soon as he reported in to General Stern.

The young corporal snaked quickly through the streets heading south, careful not to push the bike too hard on the roads still slick with dew. A ridiculous grin locked on his face from the adrenaline rush of meeting Reichsmarschall Goering. Wait'll his father found out. And Anna!

His route would allow him to avoid all roadblocks and sentry points. There were rare patches of snow still remaining in the shaded sections of the landscape, but the Loewenzahn and Glockenblume wildflowers were in evidence the farther south he rode. He crossed the Danube near Riedlingen and swung the bike to the left as he headed toward a smaller stream crossing, another one kilometer away. For a naive nineteen-year-old, life was good.

Motoring along a winding road on a beautifully built German bike, with the sun cutting through the clouds and the wildflowers showing life—on a top-secret mission for Reichsmarschall Goering!

Christian was a hundred meters from the narrow bridge when he first spotted the large Mercedes sedan coming in the opposite direction. There'd be enough room on the bridge for both, as long as he stayed well left. The car reached the bridge seconds before the rider. Christian turned his head slightly to take in the full length of the elegant Mercedes. In the back seat was a young woman in a wide-brimmed hat. She pulled the brim up to see the young motorcyclist. She smiled as he passed. He smiled back. The car continued but the head turn of the young corporal pulled the bike slightly to center. As he forced the bike to the left it hit a small piece of ice still clinging to the notion of winter.

The rider's reaction, fueled by a quick jolt of adrenal fear, was to pull back on both grips—the brake and the accelerator—at the same time. The bike wasn't sure which command to obey, so it fishtailed. Christian released the brake before the accelerator and the bike lurched forward, rattling across the end of the bridge. The bike, now in control of itself, flew across the final meters of the bridge. As Christian attempted to regain control he yanked the handlebar right, unaware of the rocks sitting along the road as a kind of natural curb between the road and the muck that had resulted from the spring thaw overflows. The bike, fighting the rider, stayed left, rolling across a couple of smaller stones before clipping an immovable one. The front tire flew up, the rider jamming on the brakes, causing the front wheel to jump skyward. Unable to hang on, the rider's natural forward momentum sent him off the bike like a missile. His trajectory was halted by a sturdy, low-hanging, oak branch. When he came to rest, chest against the earth, his head rolled to a stop a few meters ahead, sheared clean off by the unforgiving branch.

The container he was carrying fell away and opened on impact. The contents spilled open. Sitting next to the young headless rider was a partially unrolled canvas. It was van Gogh's *Self-Portrait with Bandaged Ear.*

Vincent seemed to be staring sadly at the headless young rider.

ONE

September 1, 1999

The area of lower Manhattan called Tribeca, where a lot of artists and writers live—those that can't afford the lofts of SoHo—had managed to maintain some of the grit and majesty of old New York. The buildings had that wonderful pre-war look: rock solid yet with a touch of splendor on the facade. The kind of buildings where Tracy and Hepburn lived, in their old black and whites. Where the doorman's name was Mac.

A few steps down from the ground floor of one of these buildings stood the Art Bar.

The first thing that catches a visitor's eye is the old-fashioned, long, cherry wood bar, beautifully varnished to a reflective gloss. The wall behind the bar, where the bottles reign in classic tiered fashion, is divided into three parts. The end sections are slightly smaller than the middle, and they hold old mirrors with etched designs in them, faded to a sepia tone, as though looking back in time. The center section is entirely consumed by a copy of Manet's *A Bar at the Folies-Bergère*. The strange thing is that the Manet is not a print. It's a full-scale reproduction—a forgery. And an excellent one at that. Only the best chemical art experts could distinguish between this and the original. Plus, it has the exact same frame as the original, hanging in the Courtauld Institute at Somerset House in London.

Across from the bar are several booths, each of which contains a jukebox selector ripe with new and old jazz/big band selections, all on CDs, the bar's only bow to the modern world. The Art Bar is a throwback to simpler times. The place still does a lively lunch business, mostly Wall Street traders, and in the afternoon the booths serve as the perfect start for many discreet trysts. Above each booth, on the wall, hung exact replicas of Magritte's *The False Mirror,* Matisse's *Dance,* and Toulouse-Lautrec's *At the Moulin Rouge.* Again, only the best experts would be able to distinguish these from the originals. Certainly not your average patron.

It was into this bar that the Asian stranger appeared. He was a stranger for two reasons. First, everyone in the bar was pretty much a regular. We're talking a dozen years' worth of regulars. And second, he was impeccably dressed for the afternoon crowd. Maybe it was the fact that he had just stepped out of an oversized limo, which stayed parked across the street with the engine running, or maybe it was the fact that he was probably the only guy in the place at this hour whose gold Rolex wasn't as fake as the paintings.

The bartender was at the other end of the bar going over the day's receipts with the owner when the Asian gentleman arrived. The well-dressed stranger stood a foot from the bar, waiting. He didn't remove his hat or gloves, which signaled that he wasn't here for the atmosphere. The bar was well known in underground art circles for being the place to get the skinny on obtaining high-quality forgeries. Just as in the real art world, this hidden community contained specialists in classical works, impressionists, modern, etc. Among the most elite forgers, the very best was

Barthold—Bart to his friends. He took his work as seriously as the original artists had, locating authentic, old canvases or similar materials, and creating oils that were true to the original time period, and understanding the quality and depth of brushstrokes that each artist called his own.

Bart was the only forger whose talent allowed him to cross time periods and artists with ease. He was equally at home with Donatello, Botticelli, Rubens, Monet, Picasso, or even Pollock. Barthold was an enormously gifted painter, as well as an art scholar, who knew the minute quirks of each artist, as well as every artistic detail of their paintings. Unfortunately, three failed marriages, a lunatic girlfriend, and an occasional problem at the "sugar" bowl, not to mention that he was one of the house regulars, meaning he was well in arrears on his tab, kept him more occupied as a forger than at creating his own work.

After convincing the manager that the lunch receipts were in order, the bartender walked to the other end of the bar where the stranger stood.

"What can I get you?"

"I'm trying to locate someone."

The bartender remained silent allowing the gentleman to continue.

"I'm trying to find a Mr. Sears. Tyler Sears."

No reaction from the bartender. The gentleman was expecting some kind of response so finally the bartender said, "He's around from time to time…. Is there a message?"

The gentleman seemed somewhat confused, but in true oriental deference he merely said, "If you could see that he gets this, it would be greatly appreciated." He reached inside his camel cashmere overcoat and extracted a card. It was 4x6, off white with blue pinstripe borders, with regal script. It was an invitation to an art opening. Not to just any opening, but to the posh inauguration of the new lobby of the Trans-Pacific building.

Trans-Pacific, a huge Asian conglomerate, had taken it upon itself to erect one of those new behemoths in Midtown—the ones where they destroy the entire neighborhood, cleaning it up, as the PR person stated in the *New York Times*, "in the name of modernization." What made this particular project noteworthy was the fact that the lobby had been designed as an art gallery. The idea was that new artists would be given the chance to exhibit their works on a rotating basis. This was the personal decision of the chairman of TP who was, himself, a collector, and an avid promoter of unknown modern artists. It was every starving artist's dream: a benefactor with deep pockets, a prime viewing location, and the chance for international exposure.

It was also the hottest ticket in town, and in a place like New York City that's saying something. It would be the perfect blend of high-roller biz, dethroned Eurotrash looking for a kingdom (or at least some diversionary fun), every major art dealer from London, Paris, Tokyo, and New York, and more wannabes than Elvis impersonators, although there'd probably be at least one of them there. The ultimate uptown melting pot.

And to top it all off, this invite included a VIP private reception on the seventy-fifth-floor boardroom, overlooking the world, prior to the main soiree in the lobby.

The gentleman looked slightly perplexed as he stared at the barman, but he hadn't moved since handing over the invitation. The bartender's only reaction was a barely noticed raised eyebrow.

"If you could see that Mr. Sears gets this it would be greatly appreciated." He slid the bartender two Benjamin's as a way of saying thanks. The barman pocketed the bills, tapped the invitation on the bar, and said, "I'll see what I can do about getting this to Mr. Sears." As the gentleman left, the only dilemma the barman faced was what to wear?

TWO

There's something wonderful about New York at night. The glitter, the thrill of the action, the excitement of the unknown, the danger. Tyler decided to use one of the crisp hundreds he'd received to cab it uptown. Cabs always gave him the feeling of being a tourist because he almost exclusively rode the subway. Seeing the city from underground, you can tell exactly where you are—not so much from the name of the stop, because after a while you don't notice the names. No, you can tell where you are from the quality of the mosaic on the walls, or even more telling, the music. The Brazilian group in wool serapes at Times Square, or the violinist at Lincoln Center, the folkies that inhabit the downtown stops, and of course, the hip-hop a cappella group at 161st Street. This is your real guide to the city Spalding Gray referred to as "a little island off the coast of America."

Heading up Sixth Avenue, Tyler always felt small. One skyscraper after another, all the way up on both sides. Overpowering yet insignificant. It's the most impersonal part of New York. No character, no charm, all business, no "there" there, not unlike his mother's second husband.

Looking out the window at the masses crisscrossing the city, Tyler was trying to figure out why Komate Imasu, chairman of

Trans-Pacific and one of the world's wealthiest men (fifteen billion and counting), would invite him to this shindig, and to his very private party upstairs. His art expertise?

Tyler had become something of an unofficial expert in obtaining previously "unavailable" works. He sometimes worked as a go-between when a buyer and a seller wanted to complete a transaction, far from the auction-based marketplace, usually to avoid the taxman. A guy with fifteen billion probably had a whole floor of tax lawyers working round the clock. The bigger question: How did Imasu know that he had just gotten out of Lewisburg Federal prison? Camp Fed to the campers. It wasn't like his release had made *The Post's* Page Six.

As the taxi neared the building he saw a massive traffic jam in front, courtesy of klieg lights, reporters, network cam-vans, and the rest of the hullabaloo that accompanies a full-blown Manhattan celebrity event. Tyler jumped out a half a block before the entrance so he could get a good view of the circus. It occurred to him that he could probably scalp his invite for a grand. But he'd never been to a private seventy-fifth floor of anything so he opted to keep his ticket. As he approached the entrance he got the feeling he always did whenever he was in the wrong place—queasy and uneasy. School often felt like that, or going to the country club for Sunday dinners with his mom and her number two.

He slid the invitation from his inside breast pocket, took a deep breath, and passed through the revolving door. The lobby was all it was reputed to be and more, except it wasn't a traditional lobby with the usual rectangular hallway with elevators situated off to the side, where no one notices the walls. This was different. This was designed like a maze, with a series of five-foot-high barrier walls that serpentined halfway into the lobby. An effect that forced you to look at the art as you made your way to the elevators.

He had expected not to like it. In fact, he was drawn in instantly; the surreal, oddly shaped walls, the lighting that came from every direction, and the mosaics on the floor were as beautiful as anything he had seen, short of Pompeii. And then there was the art. Both stunning and ridiculous, depending on your perspective. The Japanese pop art piece by Mashimo was the most bizarre. It always fascinated Tyler when cartoon characters' genitalia were as big as the Iowa State Fair's award-winning eggplant. And there was a Caunedo. Jorge Caunedo was considered the best young Cuban artist, championed by Castro. Jorge had smuggled his art (wonderfully surreal with a childlike optimism) out of Cuba, and then himself to Madrid. And there was the obligatory outsized Calder circling overhead. Tyler was in the middle of being mesmerized by Gulley's *Verve,* when a muscle-bound guy in a dark suit and black T-shirt with a headset plugged into one ear, approached him.

"Mr. Sears," said the baritone voice, "you're expected upstairs. Please follow me." The man's sheer size pre-empted Tyler doing anything other than obeying.

Tyler found himself following behind an enormous human barricade who led him to a private elevator. Tyler was about to say thanks but the baritone preempted him with "Enjoy the party," and the door slid closed.

In less than a minute, Tyler was emerging seventy-five stories up. It took his breath away. What a difference the top of the joint was. All business. A stark contrast from the downstairs lobby. The decor was Asian minimalist with an incredible 360-degree view of the New York skyline ablaze in lights.

The art up here was still modern but much more traditional. Twombly, Grooms, and the requisite Lichtenstein. Modern, but

14

banal all the same, although the Gaston Lachaise in the conference room was interesting with its twisted torso. At least, Tyler thought it was a torso as he bent his own body to try and get a sense from different angles. The overhanging lights had to have come from the boys at the Droog Design group from Holland, he was certain. Actually the crowd was almost as interesting as the art. Most of top-line New York society, with a mix of a couple of US senators, the mayor, the governor, and assorted politico gasbags. Tyler recognized several ex-members of the Clinton gang.

What really warmed his heart was seeing several ex-felons (himself included) swimming with the crowd. Tommy Bentoni, whose dad was still in attendance at Attica for racketeering, was rumored to be the go-between while pops ticked off the days. It was well known in art circles that Tommy's family was quick to overpay for hideous renaissance art pieces. But it was also rumored that his family had donated a large collection of Titians and Tintorettos to the Vatican, which is probably what kept the family in power and didn't hurt dad's chances for early release. Tommy was so southern Sicilian handsome it was scary. He had an ambiguous sexuality—he could be a girl's (or boy's) best friend and then seduce them the next moment. Tommy was the only kid who never complained about being molested by his local parish priest.

And there were a couple of "commodity" traders who sometimes worked out of the Art Bar; their trade was strictly South American, Bolivian marching powder, and emeralds. One of them eyed Tyler, and discreetly nodded acknowledgment. It's always fun to see a known drug/emerald dealer chatting it up with a US senator. And over in the corner, out of earshot, was ex-senator D'Amato whispering to ex-con Martin Siegal, each without their ex-wives. Everyone was dressed to the nines. Tuxes, haute couture, wearing Tiffany would be slumming it with this crowd. There were more Armanis in this room than at Giorgio's Lake Como villa at Christmas.

And of course, stunning women about every three feet or so.

New York City! What a country!

To be fair there were some good and decent people here. Tyler's favorite art enthusiast of all time, Thomas Hoving, was there with his very gracious wife. Tyler was surprised to see him, as he made most collectors nervous, with his ability to spot a fake from across the room. Even when he ran the Met, he never let the Park Avenue crowd get to him. He was always able to appreciate art in layman's terms, and always with enthusiasm. He never became an art snob. Plus, he had a wicked sense of humor. They'd met several years ago when the Feds brought Tyler in on an unsolved heist from the Metropolitan. Hoving proved much shrewder than the cops, and the insurance boys, at figuring out certain elements of the heist. He had an encyclopedic mind for art. But it wasn't just cold facts. He seemed to appreciate the passion and drive of the artists. He brought serious legitimacy to any art gathering. And even Hoving wasn't so jaded as to miss this shindig. He winked politely in Tyler's direction.

"Mr. Hoving, it's a pleasure to see you again."

"Thank you…. It's Mr. Sears, correct?"

"Ty is fine…. How've you been?"

"Quite well thank you. And you? Staying out of trouble?"

"Staying out of museums anyway," Tyler said.

Hoving chuckled. "Have you seen the Renoir sketches at the Frick yet?" he asked.

"Actually, I've been out of town for a while, but it's on my—" Tyler was cut off by a slight Asian gentleman, who approached him from the side.

"Excuse me, Mr. Sears, Mr. Imasu would like to say hello before the festivities."

"Now?" said Tyler, not sure what to say.

"Please sir."

Tyler excused himself from Mr. Hoving, whose eyebrows arched at the mention of Imasu, and followed the gentleman. The man pressed what seemed to be an invisible button, a door cracked ever so slightly and he slid into the wall with Tyler on his heels. They stepped into an office that seemed bigger than the conference room. The view was killer—as far as the Verrazano Bridge and beyond.

The office itself was extremely Spartan. To call it minimalist would be to say it was messy. It was, however, very peaceful and serene in its emptiness.

At the far end of the room was a beautiful Japanese screen, definitely Tokugawa dynasty. Next to that was a sunken area with silk cushions, and a steaming tea set that sat on a simple low table. The walls were completely bare except for the deep aubergine color.

Tyler removed his shoes as instructed.

They walked directly towards a low-slung, ebony lacquered desk. There was nothing on it except for the lone black orchid commanding attention. Tyler's guide paused, then stepped forward and leaned over a man who sat in a meditative fashion on the cushions next to the elegant tea set. He whispered something which Tyler couldn't hear, and then bowed as he backed up towards yet another door to exit.

The gentleman on the cushions rose slowly and bowed directly at Tyler. As he straightened up, his full, lean, five-nine frame was evident. Word on the street was that Imasu had a third-degree black belt in tae kwon do. It was also rumored that he'd killed a man in a sparring match over a business dispute—winner take all. This was running through Tyler's brain when the gentleman spoke.

"Sears-san, it is a privilege to meet you."

"Thanks," said Tyler, "and you must be… Mr. Imasu?"

Imasu bowed slightly with a sly smile.

"THE Komate Imasu, famous art collector… really?" said Tyler.

"You sound surprised," said Imasu.

Tyler looked around at the empty walls. "Where's the art?"

"Sometimes the absence of art helps us to remember its true beauty," said Imasu.

Tyler thought of his jail cell. Peeling paint on cinder block. Scrawled pornographic references. A seatless stainless toilet bowl.

"And sometimes the absence of beauty helps us to remember true art."

Imasu bowed ever so slightly at Tyler's philosophical touché.

Neither spoke for what seemed like a longer pause than necessary, so Tyler chimed in. "Thanks for the invite. The lobby looks terrific. All the up-and-comers will want to be there. You've done a great thing for the unknown artist. You've offered a shred of hope."

"Thank you Mr. Sears. From someone as knowledgeable as you, I take that as a compliment." Imasu paused as Tyler momentarily let the flattery go to his head.

"I hope you enjoy the party. I apologize for the private meeting, but I'm not a particularly social person."

"It's an honor to meet you but I am a bit confused… why exactly did I rate an invite?"

"Mr. Sears, I've admired your work from afar, and my sources tell me you're extremely knowledgeable regarding certain matters that require the utmost discretion,"

Tyler immediately thought that his illustrious host must want to buy or sell a piece away from the market. This was common practice in the high-end art world, especially as it related to well-known paintings, where the prices at auction were astronomically absurd. Except, that Imasu was known as an avid collector of modern works. Tyler was considering all this when Imasu interrupted his thoughts.

"Without delving into any details, I was wondering if you would join me for lunch… tomorrow perhaps?"

How do you say no to a man of his stature and power? A snappy retort was out of the question. His curiosity was piqued. He had nothing else on his calendar but his usual shift at the Art Bar. "I think I'm free tomorrow."

"Excellent, I'll send a car at noon."

"That's okay, I'll get here on my own."

"I insist," he said.

"I insist not… you've already been too generous," Tyler replied.

"As you wish," said Imasu.

A final humble bow by both, and Tyler exited Imasu's office. As soon as he stepped into the small hallway an elevator door opened. He got in only to realize there were no buttons. The door closed and with almost imperceptible motion, it descended. Tyler's brain was spinning. Lunch. Tomorrow. With Komate Imasu. What was this all about?

As the elevator opened on the main level, the party was in full swing. Manhattan Transfer was supplying the noise. The sights were pure New York. Half the people were trying to look important, the other half were. Haute couture was the dress code. Tyler's antennae were screaming *BEWARE* but the noise and flashing lights of the party were distracting him.

His brain: *What was up with that "join me for lunch"? Why couldn't he just talk to me now?*

He was still turning this over in his mind when a female voice pulled him out of his trance.

"Tyler?" a woman's voice said.

Tyler turned toward the voice.

"I'm sorry... ?"

A woman was standing directly in front of him, not smiling. Not just any woman. The memory hit him like a cyclone.

As she came into focus his brain began to flood with images of Paris. The Musée d'Orsay, the late-night strolls around the Palais Royal. Saint-Germain neighborhood. The Seine. The Kiss. That KISS.

"What happened to you?" was all he heard. Imasu's hold on his brain faded quickly. She was five-five with a gorgeous face— serious cheekbones and killer Irish eyebrows. Her hair pulled casually back, held in place with a cloisonné hairpin. Her trim, slightly muscled arms gave notice through the tight-fitting cashmere V-neck. And legs hidden by a three-quarter-length suede skirt with a suggestive slit halfway up the side. A pair of Italian black leather boots finished it off.

That KISS. His brain was reeling.

"I'm sorry, I'm a bit confused?" Tyler said, only half lying, staring straight at her.

"Paris, three years ago. I was studying at the Sorbonne, and you were... well you were taking advantage of an innocent graduate student."

He had first seen her staring at *La Nuit Etoilée* by van Gogh at the Musée d'Orsay. He was in Paris killing time before leaving for Madrid. That was almost four years ago.

"Lucy. How are you? What are you doing in New York?" Tyler leaned in to kiss her cheek but she pulled away.

"How am I? Three years later and that's all you have to say?"

It was just before he had left for the Prado job, which had gone completely belly up and cost him the last three years of his life. And now here she was. Slightly different hairstyle but the same woman.

"Lucy, I'm really sorry, I didn't mean—"

"Didn't mean what? Didn't mean to sweep me off my feet in a whirlwind romance all around Paris, and then leave me waiting at Willi's Wine Bar? For over two hours. And then nothing. Not a phone call, a note, *nada*. And now three years later you—"

Tyler interrupts, "You waited two hours? Really?"

The look on her face turned nasty.

Tyler quickly tried to recover.

"I'm sorry. Really I was—"

"You're sorry? I felt like a fool. Sitting there. And you're sorry?" She shook her head. "What happened to you? Being stood up is one thing, but you vanished off the face of the Earth. I even called the US Embassy to make sure you weren't hurt or in a hospital. Honestly, I've had some cheap dates in my life, but no one has ever just disappeared before. That was a first, and, I might add, a last."

His brain flooded with images. A skipped hotel check, and the long evening TGV ride to Spain. He was close to broke at the time. He started to grin, remembering sneaking out through the kitchen of the Hotel Daniel on the Champs-Elysées. It was definitely her he'd dreamt about in D Block, cell 24. And as time in a jail cell faded his memory, he had come to believe it was mere piecemeal fragments of different women he'd known, too much dreaming and a few too many *Playboys,* all blurred together. The horrible aftermath of the Prado job still pained him. He'd been turned out by a guy he'd paid a million euros to. Things had gotten crazy after that, with the extradition.

Lucy had become a distant memory. Collateral damage to a series of bad judgments.

He couldn't believe he'd done a runner on a woman like this. Tyler, like all men, had done some really stupid things when it came to women.

"What's the matter? Cat got your tongue?" she asked, not exactly friendly.

Not sure what to say, he thought he'd try honesty, sort of. "I'm really sorry. If I told you what happened you wouldn't believe me."

She hadn't thrown her drink at him or walked away, so he took this as a positive sign.

"How about another chance? Dinner, and I promise to be there," said with as much charm as he could muster.

This time she laughed out loud.

Gorgeous teeth. The better to bite me with, he thought.

As she stopped laughing she was shaking her head. He took this as a bad sign.

"I don't think so," she said.

"Why not... I can explain. Please, let me make it up to you."

"No."

"But I didn't even know how—"

"No."

If nothing else, she was consistent.

He hit her with his best boyish grin.

"Knock off the Tom Sawyer grin. I fell for it once. I learned my lesson."

"Please. I'm begging. You want me to get on my knees?"

She started smiling. Tyler started to kneel. She didn't stop him. With one knee on the floor he looked up at her.

"Just one more chance. Please."

She started laughing.

"You're even crazier than I remember." She pulled him up off the floor. Then, she slipped her hand down inside the slit of her skirt, near the top of the right boot, and withdrew a business card—the way a magician might show the ace of spades. A classy move, but the best part was getting to see The Leg.

"Can I call you?" he asked.

"You're a big boy, you can do whatever you want," she said.

And with that, she turned and disappeared into the crowd.

Riding home alone in the cab, Tyler kept reading her card as he passed under the streetlights.

Lucy Phillips
Assistant Curator
Guggenheim Museum SoHo

Great leg.

THREE

Tyler traveled uptown to the same destination he'd visited the night before. But this time he was underground, taking the N train to 50th Street, and walking back down Fifth Avenue the few blocks.

The area was awash with models, advertising execs, and Haitian vendors hawking bogus Rolexes and Guccis on competing street corners. Tyler walked past his old friend Julie's small antique shop at 49th, just off Fifth. She was a purveyor of high-end English antiques: a cane stand from a nineteenth century men's club at twenty-five large, an ivory backgammon set for eighteen thou, basic around-the-house stuff for people with way too much money. Spoiled rich kids, and rock star stuff. Over the years Julie and Tyler had become invaluable friends and it'd been awhile since he'd seen her. Hell, it'd been awhile since he'd seen anybody. As he walked past her shop, he noticed the place was locked up tight, the lights off. She was probably in England on one of her buying jags, or maybe she headed to Antigua where she kept a small storefront for the wintering colonials. The good life. If she weren't seriously taller than he, he would have asked her out years ago—but instead, they remained friends.

The Trans-Pacific building didn't have quite the pizzazz it had exuded the night before. Minus the news trucks and klieg lights it looked like just another of the boring behemoth's that lined Sixth Avenue. Tyler entered off 49th Street and headed towards the security desk. The guard was reading the *New York Post*, one of Murdoch's many rags. Tyler couldn't figure out which was more embarrassing, the paper itself, or the fact that Murdoch considered it journalistic. The guard glanced up as Tyler told him where he was headed. He grunted and pointed a stubby finger towards a far bank of elevators.

Several elevator occupants were making comments about the lobby, some good, some bad, some just plain ignorant. The receptionist on the seventy-fifth floor told him to go down the hall to the left. As he approached the second receptionist he said, "Hello, Tyler Sears to see Mr. Imasu."

"Yes sir. He'll be a few minutes. Is that alright?" she asked.

"And if I said no?" he asked.

She giggled nervously and pointed to a lounge area, preset with a full tea tray.

"I hope you don't mind, but Imasu-san thought you might like some tea."

Tyler realized the room behind him was the conference room from last night. Somehow it looked different. The whole place had altered, from fun and festive to busy people, ringing phones, business being done. Literally, night-and-day differences.

Tyler studied the tea set. He guessed fifth-century Yamato dynasty. If nothing else, the guy had style. He considered nicking one of the teacups as a Christmas present for his mom, but he knew she'd probably just give it to the Goodwill like all the other gifts he'd given her. And the idea of the Goodwill selling a ten thousand dollar teacup for five or ten bucks made him wince. Tyler appreciated that he was drinking from a museum-quality tea set. It reminded him of the Richard Wilbur poem, "Museum Piece."

> Edgar Degas purchased once
> A fine El Greco, which he kept
> Against the wall beside his bed
> To hang his pants on while he slept.

As the receptionist poured the tea he smiled at her. She smiled back.

"So how do you like working for one of the world's richest men?" Tyler asked.

"Sorry?" she smiled apologetically.

"How do you like working here? Is it fun, boring?"

She started to giggle again.

Tyler was beginning to wonder if things were getting lost in translation.

"He very nice man," she finally said.

"Do you ever get to ride on the company jet?" he queried.

Clearly this made her nervous. She smiled delicately, not sure what to say or do.

"Thanks for the tea," Tyler said.

"Tea thanks you," she said.

Definitely lost in translation.

"I'll call you if we go for a ride on the jet," he said, as she backpedaled away from him.

While Tyler sipped his tea, the steam rising from the cup, he kept wondering, what exactly he was doing here. What could Imasu want? He thought about how great it would feel to call Jerry, his parole officer, and tell him he just scored a legit job working for one of the wealthiest men in the world as his personal art expert. That would make Jerry's toupee slide right off. Usually they expect nothing more for their "clients" than a job at the local supermarket as a bagger, or at a fast food joint mopping the floor and being damn glad for it. At least that's what Jerry had been telling Tyler for the last month when he called weekly to check in, as per his early-release conditions.

Jerry wasn't thrilled about the job at the Art Bar. He told Tyler that it would just lead to hanging out with undesirables. Tyler thought the people Jerry hung out with at his local church were the undesirables. It reminded him of Tom Sawyer's Aunt Polly, scolding Tom relentlessly and telling him that his pal, Huck, was a "no good" and would end up in hell like the rest of his kind. As Aunt Polly rambled, on Tom pondered whether he wanted to spend eternity with Aunt Polly and her friends, or whether he'd rather hang out with Huck. A no-brainer.

As Tyler was considering young Tom and Huck, the cutie behind the desk came back to tell him that Mr. Imasu would see him now. She escorted him to the door, pressed a button, and the door swung open. No doorknob. Tyler realized the door was some sort of thick-grade steel, Kevlar-coated, bulletproof material.

When Tyler entered, Komate Imasu rose from his desk to greet him with a phalanx of yes-men moving just behind him. The office was the same as last night, only now the art was back on the walls. Tyler sensed that Imasu didn't want to be too long without his treasures.

Imasu extended his hand, as did Tyler. Which was followed up by a polite bow.

"Sears-san, how nice to see you again."

"Pleasure is mine," Tyler said.

Today Imasu looked more corporate, still serene, but with an edge. He was impeccably dressed in a delicate navy wool suit, most likely handmade. Tyler guessed a Shanghai tailor, as it was well known that even Savile Row was sending their goods to Shanghai for completion. The old English tailors were dying off and no one was willing to put in the time to learn the trade anymore; plus, the Shanghai gang would work for half the price and the quality rarely suffered. The tie was a silk cream-colored Hermès classic.

"Please Mr. Sears, let's sit." He motioned to the sitting area, and of course more tea.

"I see you couldn't go long without the art," Tyler said, turning his gaze to the pictures on at the walls.

Imasu smiled, the way a father looks at a favored child. "I hope you enjoy it."

"Between that and the view, it's quite a contest."

Ms. Giggles walked in with lunch. Sushi, beautifully laid out: yellow fin, perch, and shark, interspersed with maki and tiny versions of California rolls. But first, they slurped a couple of miso soups with seaweed, in true Tokyo street fashion.

Tyler didn't know whether to be nervous or to laugh out loud, sitting here with one of the richest men on the planet, noisily slurping soup. There was something Zen-like about this guy. Imasu certainly didn't exhibit the tension one would expect of a man who ran one of the most powerful companies in the world.

How wonderfully odd, thought Tyler.

Imasu interrupted his slurping. "Do you enjoy sushi, Mr. Sears?"

"In certain settings, yes."

He looked at Tyler quizzically, as though to ask if this was one of those settings.

"I'd say sitting seventy-five floors above Manhattan with wonderful art and a forever view qualifies as one of those settings."

Imasu smiled, and with a deft move of his chopsticks he swept a piece of yellowfin from the plate to his mouth. It reminded Tyler of the way a cutthroat trout takes a size 14 elk hair caddis fly on the Yellowstone River at dinnertime. Tyler followed suit with a delicate piece of perch, but suspected he looked more like a grouper chowing down on chum. It had been quite a while since Tyler had seen, or used, a set of chopsticks. They weren't exactly prison issue. Tyler made the mistake of starting to relax.

"Mr. Imasu, this is an excellent meal."

"I'm glad you're enjoying it Mr. Sears. Tell me, is your brother doing better?"

This question caught Tyler so off guard that he answered without realizing it.

"He's fine. Thanks for asking. I'm curious—"

Imasu didn't let Tyler finish. "And how's your mother doing? Enjoying the south of France?"

Tyler stopped eating and sat back. Where was Imasu going with these questions about Tyler's family? He hesitated. Imasu just stared at him.

"Mom's good, thanks for asking." How the hell did Imasu know that Tyler's mother was in Nice? Suddenly Tyler was sitting straight up and the look on his face spoke volumes.

"Why did I invite you to lunch?" Imasu queried.

"That, and—"

Imasu raised his hand as if to say "let me explain."

"Mr. Sears, you are considered to be an expert in your field."

Tyler was past the point of flattery. And the questions about his brother and mother were still lingering in his brain, like a mental hangnail.

"Your knowledge of art is second to none, and my sources tell me you have excellent instincts."

Tyler was starting to get goose bumps, and not in a good way.

Imasu smiled and continued. "It's your unique ability at acquisitions I wish to employ," he said.

Tyler suddenly felt ill. There was no way he'd steal again. *Nada.* Out of the question. Ain't happening. "What exactly did you have in mind?" he asked carefully.

"A specific acquisition," Imasu stated. "One that requires your unique abilities."

They both sat very still for a few moments until Imasu reached around behind him, and produced an envelope, the 12x9 variety. He handed it to Tyler without a word.

Tyler took the envelope, realizing this might be a mistake. He proceeded to open it, which was definitely a mistake. He found himself staring at a copy of what was probably the most famous painting of all time. Volumes had been written about it. Songs honoring it. Hell, even Tyler's cellmate could probably identify the damn thing. Imasu sat motionless while Tyler stared at the picture. And then Tyler's eyes shut and all was a blur, as he felt himself blacking out.

When he regained his equilibrium, Imasu was tapping him lightly with the chopsticks, saying his name over and over.

"Sears-san, Sears-san are you alright?"

Tyler blinked, startled, he sat upright and the picture dropped to the floor.

Vincent van Gogh's *Starry Night* stared up at Tyler Sears.

FOUR

Tyler was in a bad daze as he wandered aimlessly out on the street. Imasu wanted him to lift *Starry Night*. Ten million bucks for the job! A job that should take less than ten minutes, but would require months of planning. The guy was crazy, completely mad, thought Tyler, as he turned left onto 53rd and instinctively headed toward the MoMA. And he hadn't said no. Not yet at least. You don't exactly say NO to a guy of Imasu's reputation. "No" came only after serious deliberation, and then it was a dicey proposition. It didn't help that Imasu had mentioned several jobs Tyler had pulled (successfully), that no one else knew about. One of the jobs had been done with total anonymity. Who the hell were his sources? Even Interpol didn't know it was Tyler. But the thing that really gave Tyler the shivers was when Imasu had "inquired" about his brother Alex, and his mom. A veiled threat?

His brother, Alex, was a difficult issue for Tyler. Alex had always been the shining star of the family. The perfect older brother. After college, Alex was sent on assignment by the *New York Times* to cover the Middle East peace talks. The youngest person ever sent on such an assignment by the *Times*. He'd spent two years living in Palestine, witnessing daily atrocities from both sides. No one heard from Alex for over a year. He never really recovered from the horrors he'd witnessed. Post-traumatic stress disorder the doctors called it. It pretty much killed Tyler's father, watching his champion son deteriorate from hero to zero, from such lofty heights and dreams. Tyler was now responsible for his brother's welfare, paying the clinic bills, as well as lying about it all to his mother, telling her to hope. That Alex was doing fine. Compared to what, Tyler always wondered. A piece of asparagus?

And his mom. Distraught by her eldest son's decline and then devastated by the sudden death of her husband from a massive heart attack, she remarried and divorced within a year, and was now living in the south of France with a Pepé Le Pew character she'd met on a tour of Provence towns. She never got over the man of her dreams leaving her to deal with life on her own. The south of France escapade was the final act of escape from the painful reality she faced stateside. One son in some kind of clinic, and the other who knows where? It was all too much for her, so she toodle-ooed off to the land of poppies, lavender, and silky wine. Côte d'Azur.

What else did Imasu know? A swirl of ugly thoughts rolled through Tyler's head as he approached MoMA. He flashed his member's pass at the clerk and headed for the interior courtyard, a slice of peace amidst the madness of Manhattan. As he sat staring at the Rockefeller Sculpture Garden, a sense of calm came over him. And finally he began to resuscitate. Jesus, stealing art was one thing, stealing a van Gogh—it just wasn't done. Forget that you'd never get away with it; there are certain artists that remained untouchable even in the underworld of art. Even the mob had the good sense not to touch van Gogh. They knew about the legendary Curse of Van Gogh and its legacy of tragedies over the years, and carrying the Sicilian gene markers, they were too superstitious to mess with anything that might have a curse attached.

As far back as he could remember, Tyler had heard rumors that people who possessed van Goghs became possessed, or died a horrible death. Ever since Vincent's death, which was slow and horribly painful—a self-inflicted gunshot wound to the stomach and liver, turning his own blood toxic with bile. It took two and a half agonizing days for his body to poison itself to death. Vincent's friend and physician, Dr. Gachet, attended him as he lay dying; and a year later, the good doctor himself was put to rest. Ironically, Vincent had paid Dr. Gachet, for earlier treatment, by painting the physician's portrait. And the rumor of the curse was that ever since Vincent's death, those who possessed his paintings somehow suffered a horrible fate. Vincent's brother, Theo, his biggest supporter, and possessor of all of Vincent's work, died within months of Vincent's death. The Nazis involved in selling several of van Gogh's works (stolen during the roundup of the Jews in the ghettoes) were said to have met gruesomely freakish deaths. There was the well-known urban legend of the young Nazi motorcycle rider who was carrying a van Gogh to Zurich for transfer to a Swiss dealer in order to supply Hermann Goering with needed retirement funds.

The punchline: his beheading in a freak accident.

Funny, not very. Even in modern times the myth of the curse persisted. The Japanese businessman, Ryoei Saito, who wildly overpaid for *The Portrait of Dr. Gachet*, died within a year of spending $82.5 million for the painting. Worse, he had the painting stored away in an airtight vault while he was designing a house specifically to hang the work of art. He never actually laid eyes on the painting.

What a pity.

What a curse.

What an artist.

Tyler's mind was spinning on the curse as he looked up at the back of Pei's distinctive cleft atop the AT&T Building, almost oblivious to the autumn sun and the sharply angled shadows it was casting. He headed back inside as the late afternoon autumn chill moved in.

If he did steal the painting, it would end up in Imasu's private hideaway until he died, whereupon the family might admit they had it (if ever), and return it to the museum (unlikely). He pictured the downside: Tyler getting caught, the painting returned to the museum with great fanfare, and Tyler facing strike three (third felony), life imprisonment! He'd be looking down the wrong end of twenty to life. His Depends years would be just around the corner. He'd be an old man, with nothing left to justify the time spent inside.

And if he did get caught, he'd run the risk of Imasu siccing the Yakuza on him, making sure he never talked. The Yakuza had a reputation for allowing you to live, but taking away your ability to speak.

Yakuza translated roughly meant living death. His tongue did an involuntary roll around his mouth.

A grim look spread across his face as the various realities set in. The last, and least palatable scenario was being chopped up with a nine-inch Ginsu knife, and floated down the Hackensack River. This notion made him shudder.

He meandered up the MoMA staircase he muttered, "Nahh, it just ain't worth it. But how do I get out of this without getting killed, or worse, heading back to prison?"

When he stopped muttering and looked up, he was staring at the original *Starry Night.*

FIVE

The next morning, before he headed for his lunch shift at the Art Bar, Tyler spent the better part of the morning at the New York Public Library on Fifth Avenue in the research section, combing the internet for information on Imasu. He did a thorough background check in hopes of discovering that Imasu wasn't as bad-ass as his reputation claimed. Most of what he found were innocuous press releases sent out by Trans-Pacific Corp. Biography, family, civic activities, the usual PR fluff. Digging further, he discovered several sites set up by disgruntled employees and the usual conspiracy nuts.

Trans-Pacific Corp. had an inordinate amount of employee accidents, some resulting in death. Triple the number for a company of its size and stature. Union leaders accounted for a large share of the accidents. Three of the guys who had suffered untimely deaths were environmental activists and all three had died just prior to Trans-Pacific securing huge logging contracts from the Malaysian government. The deaths were investigated internally, with no outside police involved. Tyler knew this was due to huge payoffs, typical of the Asian culture.

The most disturbing story was about Trans-Pacific's biggest competitor. It seems the family that ran the company had all perished in a freak fire while on holiday in Thailand. In the ensuing chaos at the rival company, Imasu had emerged as a white knight, willing to buy the entire company. As for the family that perished, their deaths were ruled accidental by the Thai authorities. The bodies were burned beyond recognition so autopsies were out of the question. Case closed.

His options seemed limited to dead, or dead.

I'm fucked.

Unease crept up his spine as he headed downtown. He'd have to get out of this deal, and as far away from Imasu as possible, without taking a bullet for the home team.

His mom was actually pretty handy at getting lost, as proven by her near disappearance after his dad's death. But keeping his brother safe was a whole different matter. He'd have to contact the clinic in Arizona to check about security.

The Art Bar was an easy ten-minute stroll from Wall Street. Lunchtime drew the business crowd who talked shop, but with discretion. At lunchtime, financial information moved faster than the waiters. Tyler probably knew about more M&A deals than the stiffs at Sullivan & Cromwell. Just before he went in for his last stretch in the joint (courtesy of the botched Prado job), he'd overheard a female investment analyst, eating lunch at the bar with a male colleague, discussing the merits of the internet, and how it was the next NEXT BIG thing as she put it. She mentioned a Japanese holding company that had invested heavily in a couple of portals, business-to-business players, and a wireless outfit out of San Diego, all unknowns at the time. The holding company was publicly traded, but only on the Tokyo Stock Exchange. Her male colleague seemed skeptical. He seemed more interested in trying to figure out whether she was a thong kind of girl, or more of the cotton-panties type.

So just before Tyler headed to his 6x9 "shared studio apartment" at Lewisburg, he called his banker in Zurich and told him to invest a chunk of his dough in said holding company. Three and a half years later his money had increased by a factor of twenty. Decent money for doing laundry and working in the library for a stretch. A big chunk of that profit went to his lawyer to secure his early release.

Easy come, easy go.

The remainder he had set aside for his brother's care in a special trust. While he was away, she, the source of his good fortune, had become the fastest-rising star on Wall Street, and the internet was suddenly the talk of the town. She made partner (one of the youngest ever), and had become one of the seers of the internet. This he learned reading the *Wall Street Journal* in the joint. It was the only paper that didn't have greasy fingerprints all over it. Unlike the *National Enquirer* or *Soldier of Fortune*. He was always stunned at how many jerk-offs in the joint knew who Roseanne Barr was married to, but not who Alan Greenspan was married to.

As Tyler cut lemons and limes at the bar, he tried clearing his head of Imasu. The walk from MoMA to his hovel near Union Square hadn't done it, nor had the double Jack Daniels, with a beer back the previous evening. His hangover did speak to the later difficulties he'd had arguing with his friend—Jack Daniel's.

His throbbing brain stem was trying to decipher why one of the biggest collectors of contemporary avant-garde art would want a masterpiece he'd never be able to show? Sheer madness. It was van Gogh's best-known painting. Hell, it was one of the world's best-known paintings. As high profile as it gets. The damn thing was on coffee mugs, T-shirts, even place mats. How degrading for poor Vincent. He sold only one painting while he was alive, and now his most famous image—the swirls of blue-black night sky that appeared like the ocean roiling, the weirdly rotating moon, the stars exploding like fireworks—was everywhere.

Tyler had to figure a way out of this, carefully. The whole idea was lunacy—the painting, the buyer, the museum, the publicity, and of course the Curse. At heart he really didn't want to steal again. It made him feel ill even to contemplate. His hangover wasn't helping matters. He felt trapped. With a theft like this, the Feds and Interpol would come down hard on him, his family, and friends. His mom would kill him, or worse, it might kill her. Tyler couldn't afford to take the chance. He couldn't shake Imasu's query about his brother and mother. His life was one thing, but risking theirs was out of the question.

Lunch was moving into high gear. Lots of noise and action, with unstable data flying everywhere. No Evian for this crowd. The martini lunch was alive and well. Tyler nicked his finger. Drew blood. The lemon juice in the cut intensified the sting. He poured a quick shot of vodka, set it below the bar, and stuck his finger in it.

Maggie, Tyler's favorite waitress, and a dear friend, was moving on autopilot. She moved effortlessly as though she were standing still, but actually moving just shy of the speed of sound. Her grace under pressure was a thing of beauty. The smile never left her face as she delivered drinks and armloads of plates, and put up with the daily gawkers. She stood at the edge of the bar.

"Trying to get your finger drunk?"

Tyler looked up and tried a smile.

"Dinged my finger cutting lemons."

As she was loading drinks onto her tray at the bar, she said, "Ty, A-OK?"

"Yeah, it'll be fine."

"Not your finger, I meant you. You seem… a bit distracted today." As she slid her tray off the bar she whispered, "How bout a joint after work?"

With her beautiful green eyes and her smile, it was impossible to turn her down. Almost.

"Let me get back to you on that one," he said.

She winked and toodled off.

The rush of the lunch crowd lasted from 11:30 to 2:30. It was a great escape from Tyler's more-pressing problem—what to say to Komate Imasu? The billionaire had given him till end of business to respond. He had less than four hours to figure out what to do. How many people had ever said no to Komate Imasu? And more important, were any of them still alive?

As things started to wind down, with only the hardcore trying to stretch the long lunch concept, Tyler felt his time running out. There was no way he was going to steal van Gogh's *Starry Night*. He needed an alternate plan. An alternative to death, or worse, life imprisonment.

This wasn't what he remembered telling his fourth-grade teacher, Miss Harding, when she asked what he wanted to be when he grew up. His recollection was Indian chief, or something along the Wild West lines.

As he tallied up the day's receipts and was wiping down the bar, the phone rang.

Mary, the bookkeeper yelled, "Hey Ty, it's for you." He was half-expecting Max, the boss, calling for the day's tallies. Instead it was a woman's voice with a Japanese accent.

"Mr. Sears, Imasu-san was hoping you might stop by later today, if possible."

He didn't panic, though his palms did get sweaty as he held the phone. He stalled. "Actually, this afternoon isn't good for me. Tomorrow would work much better, if that would be okay with Mr. Imasu?" He couldn't believe he just asked her that, but like mom always said, "What's the worst they can say, no?"

There was a long pause and when she punched him off hold she said, "Imasu-san said that would be fine, he also rather busy this afternoon. So same time tomorrow, but he insists it be tomorrow as he leaving tomorrow night."

Tyler's hand was covered in sweat as he clicked off the receiver.

Maybe the giant asteroid will finally crash into Earth was all Tyler could hope for.

As the dinner crew arrived, Tyler found Maggie in the back, in the wine cellar/cleaning closet, sitting on a couple of cases of Pommard, counting her tips.

He watched her count. "Good day?"

"Shh… I'm almost done," she said, totally engrossed in her counting.

"Seventy-eight, seventy-nine, eighty, eighty-one and five makes eighty-six. Two hundred and eighty-six bucks. Not bad for a three-hour shift."

"No offense Mags, but I think your smile has a lot to do with it."

"Really? Not the snappy patter?"

Tyler smiled as he shook his head.

"The smile, and that schoolgirl pleated-plaid mini make men weak."

She laughed as she rolled the bills into a tight wad and dropped it in her black bicycle messenger bag. There was something wonderful about a cash lifestyle, and the way it affected people. You could feel the weight of your wealth as you walked. It had heft. It made you existentially rich. At that moment you didn't care about health insurance, mortgages, 401Ks, or much else. There was cash in your pocket. With cash you could make the rent (hopefully), buy groceries (maybe), and a round of drinks (definitely). It always amazed Tyler how many people lived that way. And of course no one ever reported cash to the Internal Revenue Service. The IRS tried to keep track, but cash moved so quickly, they had to rely on peoples' honesty in reporting. And if there's one place where everyone, universally, will lie, it's to the IRS. Good and decent folks, like Tyler's Aunt Mabel, found the IRS so repulsive that even she fudged when it came to tax time. Now imagine a single woman, working as a waitress, living from tips to tips.

Ca$h is King.

Tyler and Maggie skipped out the back door and headed north up St. John's, cut over to West Broadway, and then along Prince Street, past the galleries of SoHo until they were at her loft. She had the back of the building facing south on the top floor. As free-spirited as Maggie was, she was nobody's fool. Ten years back, when she was at the height of her modeling career, she took the money she made and bought the loft. Back then, property was still reasonably priced. With killer views its value had increased fivefold since she'd bought it.

They went up five flights in the cranky old service elevator, with its steel door that required some serious muscle to open—muscles Maggie had acquired through a regimen of constant yoga.

The place was furnished in what could only be described as shabby chic. Comfort was her main priority. The oversized chairs were stuffed with down. Her only homage to true decorating was the light-gray suede couch she'd bought in Milan on one of her Euro modeling trips. It was in itself a work of art.

There were no walls as such; it was just one huge space that could be converted to smaller spaces depending on the occasion. The furniture and the three-quarter walls were all on a mobile system so things could be rearranged at a moment's notice.

She also had a large outdoor deck facing west, with high translucent walls surrounding it. This was extremely private. It was her nude sunbathing area. Nude sunbathing was a pastime she'd acquired on the beaches of Australia. Her bed was on rollers so she could slide it out on the deck during summer months and sleep amidst her wonderful garden of climbing roses, sage, and lavender. There were also a few potted ficus trees growing around the perimeter of the deck. The cool autumn breezes were just settling plant life into their dormant state.

While Tyler was taking all this in, Maggie went to change. With the three-quarter walls they could easily converse as she put on a fresh outfit.

"Hey Ty, you okay? You were covered in sweat by the end of the shift."

"Great view," Tyler said, trying to change topics.

"Yeah, I love it, especially on those clear days when I can see all the way down to Lady Liberté, and out the harbor," she continued. "Ty, help yourself to a drink, there's stuff in the fridge, and there's a bottle of Patrón in the freezer."

He headed towards the professional kitchen Maggie had installed. She loved food. She had taken cooking classes in Italy when she was between modeling shoots. Her homemade pizza was *squisito!* Plus, she knew how to whip up real gelato. Maggie was blessed with the perfect metabolism. She ate the same quantities of food as a sumo wrestler, and still, at age thirty-two, looked as good as anything in the Victoria's Secret catalog.

Tyler was pouring a shot of Patrón into each of the iced shot glasses just as Maggie came around the corner licking a joint closed. For a split second Tyler's brain wondered what Imasu was up to. Then it was gone as he moved on to the moment in front of him: a beautiful woman, a joint, and a shot of Patrón.

Living well IS the best revenge.

With the joint fired up, his worries began to slip away. They moved to the couch with their drinks, and a plate of homemade chocolate sambuca cookies. Tyler's brain flashed on his recent release. The cell, the number, the horrors, all seemed like a far away fog. The fact that you could never forget was all the more manageable when you were sitting opposite a cool chick who just wanted to have a little fun. Tyler had known Maggie since his misspent youth. They had met years before, at a summer party on Fire Island; they were the only two straight people at the party. They had quickly become close friends, never quite closing the deal. Either he was in a relationship, or she was, and their breakups never coordinated. Maggie was the one who gave Tyler honest advice about women, and Tyler was there for Maggie when the jerk(s) she was involved with did something Neanderthal or toady.

She was wearing baggy sweatpants and a nearly sheer cotton/linen tank-top with nothing underneath, which only added to the equation.

Everything seemed to loom larger, the sky, the buildings, the windows, her breasts.

She brought Tyler back to semi-reality. "Get much action in the joint?" she asked with an easy grin.

"Just with my wife Lefty," Tyler said as he held up his left hand and wiggled his fingers.

"I managed to avoid being someone's bitch, if that's what you mean."

"Sorry. Do you mind me asking?"

Jail is a strange place. No matter how many stories you hear, or how many questions are asked, unless you've been there you just don't get it. Tyler figured it's the equivalent of childbirth for women. A nightmare while it's happening, but when it's over it's like it never happened.

"So how does a good looking guy like you end up in the safety zone, on the inside?" she wondered.

Tyler laughed. "Safety zone? Is that what you call not ending up as someone's "wife"? Money. It's always about money. I bought a lot of protection. I'm close to broke now, but at least I'm not *il castrato*. Plus, I worked in the library where I helped a lot of guys—black, white, and Hispanic—pass their GED exams, and for that I got special treatment. Which is a nice way of saying they left me alone."

"You're a clever boy, Tyler Sears. Always working the angle."

"Not clever enough… ," he replied, his face showing the strain from bad memories. But by then the dope began to work its magic.

His grin was coming to full blossom, as the bad of the last three years faded. As he sipped his drink he was thanking his lucky stars. His brain was downshifting as the tension of his imminent meeting with Imasu was slipping away. That, coupled with the exhaustion of his time in the joint, was all working together as Tyler's brain went into slo-mo. He tried to say something but it all came out garbled. They both laughed.

"Ty, you alright?" she asked.

His grin was infectious.

"Sit tight. I'll get you some water." She jumped off the couch and skipped over to the fridge.

Tyler watched as she headed towards the kitchen, exhaustion grabbed him. His eyes rolled back and he fell, face first, onto the pillows on the couch.

"Here, this should help," she said as she returned with a bottle of water. She looked down at him sprawled asleep on the couch. She rearranged the pillow so he'd be more comfortable and threw a down comforter over him. She slid into the Eames chair and opened her novel, *As Cool As I Am*. She watched over Tyler while the noises of New York City honked below.

The perfect end to a perfect day—except they were oblivious to the person who had been watching them, through binoculars, from across the rooftops.

SIX

The next morning, Tyler awoke to Maggie making noises in the kitchen. He could hear the oven door open and close. Her footsteps were moving towards the living room.

"You feeling better?" she asked.

"Better than what?"

"I don't know. You just seemed tense yesterday."

"Prison will do that to you."

"Up lazy boy. It's time for breakfast."

Tyler wandered into the bathroom, splashed cold water on his face, and joined her in the kitchen. Sitting on the table was a breakfast burrito, jalapeño cornbread (made from scratch), fresh squeezed juice, sliced mango and strawberries, and a large pot of green tea. The morning sun was just peeking through the autumn clouds.

They ate, and barely spoke for a good five minutes. Tyler hadn't realized how hungry he was. His strength was returning with each bite.

Life was good.

"What did you mean, what you said before?" Tyler asked with his mouth full.

"About you being tense?"

Tyler nodded as he slid another slice of cornbread into his mouth.

"You tell me. Everything okay?"

"No complaints, not a one," he lied.

Maggie knew something was up, but she also knew not to press. "I'm just concerned. I know it can't be easy being back out. I worry for you," she said as she wiped the cornbread crumbs from the edges of her lips.

"I appreciate your concern. Things aren't bad, considering I'm nearing thirty-three and mopping up drunks' spilled drinks. But at least I'm out of that shithole prison."

"Are you really that old?" she asked in mock disbelief.

"Ouch, I was hoping it wouldn't be an issue?"

She smiled.

There was a wonderful ease with Maggie. She let you forget a lot of wrongs, and made you feel right. The problem was, she never let anybody get close, really close. There was too much damage done when she was younger, too many predators. So now she played it alone.

Her game.

Her rules.

Tyler gave her a reassuring grin.

She walked around the table, sat in his lap, and gave him a tight hug. "Just be careful, okay?"

He just held her.

Tyler decided to walk home. It was still early and Manhattan was just coming alive. Even though he'd been living in New York since he dropped out of Reed College, he still found the city electrifying, the energy level a kind of swirl of cocaine, sugar, and a doppio espresso. He wandered along 14th Street, cut across Union Square and stopped at the newsstand to pick up the *New York Times*, *Newsday*, and *ARTnews*. Ten minutes later he was sitting in a lounge chair on the roof of his worn-out four-story walk-up apartment at 18th Street and Irving Place, across the street from Pete's Tavern. In the Arts section he read that the mayor was in some kind of brouhaha over restricting an art exhibit in Brooklyn. An artistic photographer, who had decided to push the boundaries of good taste, was exhibiting some rather graphic homosexual images. If the mayor had just kept his mouth shut, the show would've attracted probably a tenth of the viewers. But Mayor Bullhead had to make a stink, and suddenly everyone's a critic. This from a mayor who has been photographed dressed in drag.

Go figure.

He flipped over the front page of the Arts section to read below the break and the smaller headline hit him like a Mack truck. His eyes focused, and he started reading. He couldn't believe it. He grabbed the *ARTnews* and saw the same story with a bit more detail. In that moment the planets lined up; the tectonic plates made a subtle shift, and for the briefest of moments he was released from the gravitational pull that weighed so heavily on him. His solution to Imasu was staring back at him in black and white. An idea so outrageous that no one, no matter how rich, would dare it. Suddenly, he was excited about his return visit to Imasu's office. Tyler believed his freedom from Imasu was imminent. And this time he'd be in the driver's seat.

SEVEN

The same cute, giggly Asian woman welcomed him back to Imasu's office. Same routine with the tea. Tyler decided to forgo the snappy patter and just enjoy the tea in silence. His adrenaline was pumping. He knew he held the key to checkmate, in one swift move. His gambit was based on the idea that NO ONE was that reckless—Imasu was a lot of things but reckless wasn't one of them—and that reason would prevail. And in less than half an hour he'd be free of Imasu. Tyler was convinced no one would dare a bet with such long odds.

An assistant approached and signaled for him to follow. They walked through the anteroom with its matching sixth-century Buddha sculptures and into Komate Imasu's main perch. Today was one of those glorious late-autumn days when the sun was on full bore, with a classic swirling breeze that felt like it'd knock you over given half a chance. Only up here, in this airtight aerie, there was no breeze, just the glint of the sun reflecting off all the other glass-sided inert giants that lined Sixth Avenue. The knockout view was still there. The Hudson glittering away. Spectacular at worst.

Imasu was nowhere in sight. The assistant politely guided Tyler into a chair and told him that her boss would be with him momentarily. Imasu entered from his side office. He was accompanied by yes-men in tow, in his case *so desu*-men; Tyler had done a quick read of Japanese business phrases in preparation for this meeting.

As Imasu reached Tyler he turned to his entourage, raised his hand slightly, and said, *"Imashimeru."*

They all bowed and departed silently.

Imasu bowed to Tyler. *"Heiwa,"* peace he said.

Tyler returned the bow and said, *"Doyo ni."*

At this, Imasu smiled.

"Sears-san, you've been studying."

"Common courtesy in the presence of an elder," Tyler replied.

In Imasu's culture, great respect is paid to elders, as opposed to in American culture where anyone over sixty is usually thrown in the dumpster and left to rot quietly, forgotten, and out of sight.

"I commend your manners, and wish that your political leaders were half as gracious as you."

Mom would have been ecstatic to hear this, Tyler mused. He figured he'd continue the stroking, and bowing said, "It was you who were gracious in allowing me the extra day to come to a decision." Blah, blah, blah, thought Tyler, trying to keep his elevating pulse in check.

"And I hope the added time helped you come to a positive conclusion."

"Well actually I have good news. And bad."

Neither spoke as they stared at each other for a few seconds. Imasu had that air of authority that extremely successful men have. Steely authority. He sat stone still waiting for Tyler to deliver the news.

"I thought a lot about your offer. And there are many problems I believe too difficult to overcome to bring everything to a successful conclusion. So, as generous as your offer is, I am afraid I must decline."

Nothing changed in Imasu's face. Maybe the eyebrow moved a millimeter, otherwise nothing. This guy was scary. Tyler tried to imagine playing poker with him. He figured he'd get cleaned out in three quick hands. He waited, motionless, until Imasu leaned forward.

"Well, unfortunately, I have some bad news for you," Imasu said as he pushed a small button next to his chair.

A small side door opened and one of his yes-men entered carrying an article from a French newspaper. All Tyler could understand was the photo, which showed a car that had run head-on into a tree. Tyler stared at the photo.

"My condolences to your mother."

Tyler's pulse flew off the radar.

"Thankfully she's okay. In fact I thought you'd want to speak to her." Imasu's assistant handed Tyler a small mobile phone.

Tyler reluctantly reached for the phone. "Hello?"

"Hi honey, how are you?"

Tyler ignored her pleasantries. "Mom, where are you? What happened?"

"Something about the brakes failing. It was just one of those freak accidents. I'm fine now. Luckily it was just a few scratches, and I sprained my wrist so they've wrapped it."

"Who's they? Where are you?"

"I'm in the local hospital in Nice (which she pronounced "nice"), but luckily your friend had his doctor visiting the area. So he's making sure the doctors are taking good care of me. Here comes Doctor Kazuhiro now. I gotta go Tyler. Call me later. Bye, bye."

"Mom. Wait!"

She'd hung up.

Tyler just stood there unable to blink. His brain was raging but he knew not to lash out unless he was looking forward to a double tap from a 9 mm. Finally he snapped the phone closed and just dropped it on the floor. He was feeling trapped. He looked down at the floor trying to get his bearings. He looked up at Imasu.

"If you have anything to do with harming my brother, or my mother, then all deals are off. You decide right now. Make the necessary calls, or I walk."

Tyler didn't move, nor did Imasu. Finally Imasu reached in his inside jacket pocket. Tyler was thinking he was about to call it a day, a life. Instead Imasu pulled out his phone, punched in some numbers, said something in Japanese, and then returned it to his pocket.

"For now, your brother is spared. And your mother will be fine. I will not stand for any more of your insubordination. Are we clear?"

Tyler just stood there.

"You owe me. You do this job and you're free."

"I'm sorry? I owe you. Owe you what?"

"Sears-san, it was I who got you out on early release. Did you really think you got out because you were a model prisoner? You got out because I paid for your freedom. Your greedy warden cost me an extra hundred thousand. And now you will do as I say. Understood?"

Tyler was being bombarded with emotional information. Imasu was the one who got him out? The gorgeous view out the window was becoming a blur. The last three years were becoming a blur. The parole hearing. The snarling warden. The condescending parole board. The guard, Captain Happy, as the cons called him, with his ever-present sawed-off 12 gauge, safety off. All of them sitting in that small windowless room. The chairs and table bolted to the floor. All that money he'd paid to his own lawyer. All that shit, and all of it a foregone conclusion. Tyler's courage and bravado were slip-sliding away. It was all he could do not to scream. Sweat was starting to slide down his backbone.

He tried to regain his composure.

"It was you, Komate Imasu, who arranged my early release?"

"That is correct Sears-san."

"As grateful as I am for your generosity I must reluctantly decline your proposal," Tyler said as quietly as possible.

Imasu said nothing. He reached for his phone and started to dial. He stared at Tyler and waited. Tyler put his hand up silently asking Imasu to wait.

"Imasu-san, *Starry Night* is too risky. Too high profile. It carries too many myths."

"Sears-san, don't tell me you believe those silly rumors about all the lives ruined by those who possess a van Gogh?"

Tyler tried to smile.

"Next you'll tell me the real *Mona Lisa* is sitting over the fireplace in some mobster's home in New Jersey. Please, Sears-san, I never figured you for someone who believed silly urban myths."

Tyler looked directly at Imasu. Here was his opening. He knew it was now or never. Time to roll the dice.

GO BIG, or go home.

He took a breath and swung for the fences.

"Imasu-san, the problem with your proposal is that it's too high profile. Too risky, but it got me thinking. If one is to go in that direction, then why not go all the way? If what you said is true, then let me repay your generosity in kind."

Imasu's look changed as curiosity spread across his face. "Please, continue Sears-san."

"Permit me to make a counteroffer."

Imasu nodded.

"Why bother with a single masterpiece when you can have a complete masters collection?"

On this, a smile crept across Imasu's face.

Tyler had clearly captured Imasu's attention. It was time to jump from the high dive.

The Big Bluff.

Checkmate.

The Fallen King.

"Continue Sears-san."

"In lieu of a single piece, I propose to acquire a dozen extraordinary paintings, a complete masters collection." Tyler handed Imasu the article from *ARTnews* magazine.

THE 100 GREATEST PAINTINGS OF THE LAST 1000 YEARS
An end-of-millennium showing at the National Gallery of Art in Washington, DC from November 21 through January 31, 2000. A complete retrospective from Giotto to Pollock.

"If you read the fine print you'll see they are planning to include a dozen impressionist and postimpressionist paintings."

Imasu's eyes narrowed as he tried to fathom what Tyler was saying. "And your plan is… ?"

Tyler knew he had him. The hook was set. Now to reel him in with a counteroffer so outrageous that even Imasu would never agree.

"The plan is mine to know, but for you it means an entire masters collection: Monet, Cézanne, Renoir, Gaugin, and yes, van Gogh."

"And how much will this cost me?"

"A hundred million dollars, US, half up-front, wired into a Swiss account within twenty-four hours, the remaining half in cash, upon delivery, plus five hundred thousand cash, now, in unmarked, non-sequential small bills, for immediate expenses."

Tyler almost forgot to breathe.

Imasu placed his fingertips together and tapped the forefingers. His brain was working quickly. Either he took the bait, or Tyler feared he was about to be thrown from a seventy-fifth-story window. Either option was a frightening concept. Who was he fucking kidding? Stealing a painting was one thing, but a dozen was sheer suicide. The time factor alone was impossible to consider, much less the transport factor. Nobody could walk out of there with twelve of the most famous paintings of all time. And if he got caught... shit, he didn't even want to think about it. But there was NO way the guy would consider parting with a hundred million dollars to someone he met yesterday. A two-time convicted felon. The whole idea was too absurd even for a guy as rich and powerful as Imasu. Tyler had him boxed in. He'd already said no to Imasu's offer, now he just needed Imasu to politely refuse his counteroffer and it would be a stalemate. No harm, no foul. Then all he had to do was get out of the building alive.

STAY COOL! Tyler's brain was screaming. *Slow the breathing. Stay calm.* His adrenaline was seizing control.

Finally Imasu spoke. Actually it was only a few seconds later, but it seemed like an eternity. "You've thought this through, Searssan?"

"Completely."

"You'll use my men for assistance."

"No, and it's non-negotiable."

"With all due respect Sears-san, you're in no position to negotiate. A deal this large requires I keep an eye on you, my money, and my paintings. You will use my men."

"Imasu-san, van Gogh's *Dr. Gachet* sold for $83 million. One painting. I'll deliver you twelve. I will use your men, but I design the job by myself. I will not tell your men, or you, the plans until the day before we actually execute them. Also, no harm will come to my brother or my mother. Those are my conditions."

Imasu got up and walked over to the window. The New York skyline was glittering. He barely noticed. The silence was deafening. Tyler tried slowing his speeding pulse. He stood stone still.

Imasu reached into his pocket and pulled out his cell phone. He punched a few keys and spoke quickly and quietly. He closed the phone and returned it to his pocket. Finally he turned toward Tyler.

Tyler was not sure what was happening.

Imasu extended his hand and said, "Sears-san, we have a deal." Without realizing what he was doing, Tyler shook hands with Imasu.

"Good" Tyler said. "Very good."

Tyler could feel his brain crashing. He and Imasu continued to shake hands. Neither man would let go. It was as though they were sealing their fates beyond a simple transaction. They would be forever linked through this shaking of hands. The energy surging between them was startling. Tyler was beginning to realize Imasu's real power, and why he was so feared.

Just then, a door opened and in walked the geisha-receptionist. This time she was carrying a tray with two Baccarat champagne flutes filled with a rosé champagne. She set down the tray and exited without making a sound.

Imasu handed Tyler one glass, raised the other one, and said, *"Tetto tetsubi,"* roughly translated: through and through/start to finish.

"T'subi," Tyler responded trying to hide the fact that he was in shock. Little did he know how telling that comment would turn out to be.

Imasu smiled.

Tyler was scared shitless. "Well, you're certainly in a pickle this time," his Mom would have said. He put down his glass.

Imasu said, "Good luck, Sears-san."

Tyler had just agreed to steal twelve of the most valuable paintings in existence and Imasu had agreed to buy them, at what Tyler knew to be the highest price ever paid for stolen art. He was too shell-shocked to speak. His big bluff had backfired. Now what?

Tyler wandered past the geisha/receptionist. The elevator door was open and there were two full-size Japanese men waiting on either side of the door. They nodded imperceptibly as if to say, "You first."

They all got on the elevator. No one spoke. Tyler was still speechless and it was clear that chatter wasn't part of their MO. The one on Tyler's left was the taller of the two. He had a broad face with perfectly styled jet-black hair. He was close to six feet tall. His eyes were as black as his hair. His small nose looked out of place with the rest of his overpowering features. His eyebrows alone looked as if they could kill.

The one on Tyler's right was younger, with a bald pate, and a small gold hoop earring. He was a shade shorter than Tyler, with a rounder face, so he looked like a cross between the man-in-the-moon and a basketball. Although Tyler doubted anyone ever told him that. His face was expressionless but his body was tense. Tyler felt that the man could snap at any moment.

As they exited the elevator, the older one silently indicated the direction they were headed. They took a sharp left, went behind the bank of elevators and out a side door. Sitting directly in front of them was a black stretch Mercedes limo. The taller one opened the door, while raw nerve got in the front passenger side to ride shotgun.

Tyler slid into the back seat, the door closed, and he heard some muted Japanese spoken as the car slowly pulled away from the curb. It was headed up Sixth Avenue and entered Central Park.

Tyler wondered where the hell they were going. Sitting next to him on the seat was an Hermès carbon fiber attaché case. Tyler eyed the case. His initials were engraved just below the Hermès logo. He glanced forward to see if anyone was watching, but the divider was up. Slowly he turned the case, and one at a time slowly opened the platinum locks. He took a deep breath, and as he exhaled, he carefully opened the case. What he saw paralyzed him momentarily—and then he sat back and began to laugh like a crazy person.

EIGHT

The next day Tyler awoke with a horrible sense of dread. A mental hangover. Far worse than the one Uncle Jack had whacked him with a couple of days back. He sat on the edge of his bed. The throbbing in his head intensified. He still couldn't believe that Imasu had agreed to his outrageous counteroffer. He headed into the bathroom and leaned into the mirror. Not pretty. Grabbing the aspirin bottle he popped the top off which flew through the air and did a perfect Olympic spinning dive and landed in the toilet.

"Well done. Yet another reason to keep the seat down."

He poured out a handful of aspirin and used the bathroom faucet as a drinking fountain. When he came back up for air the view in the mirror was worse. Water stains covered his T-shirt.

He decided a morning run along the East River might revive him. It helped. After a gluttonous breakfast he called his parole office, Jerry, told him how great things were going, and no he hadn't had a drink since he got out. Why was it that the parole officers were always so worried about drinking, when most guys in the joint used liquor as a sedative against the heroin? Tyler told Jerry he had some solid leads on potential jobs in Washington, DC, and promised he'd be back within the week to update him on his progress.

After he hung up on his call to Jerry he realized that in the madness of the last forty-eight hours he'd forgotten to call Lucy Phillips. Standing a woman up once is allowed, but twice is unforgivable. With women it's usually two strikes and you're out. The key here would be to go on the offensive, and quickly. It was 11:30 so he might just pull it off. He hustled over to her downtown office, and at 11:52 he was standing at her door. It was a typical downtown office. Simple, no view, small window set high against a wall of exposed brick. The desk was a built-in "L" shape with all the usual conveniences, phone/fax, computer, and some odd-looking scanner devices that they hadn't yet acquired at Lewisburg. The walls were painted cerise. The only difference between this and any other office were the assorted canvases lined up against the wall. From where he stood he could see a Kenneth Noland, an Ellsworth Kelly (no relation to the notorious Ned Kelly), and a Frankenthaler. Not bad to have lying around the office. They sure beat the autographed baseball that sat in most offices.

Lucy's back was to Tyler and he observed her quietly. Her hair kept back by a pair of black Persol frames. What a mane. She was wearing a light-gray cashmere sweater and a pair of Missoni jeans.

Before she could turn around Tyler said, "So, you ready for lunch?"

Taking her time, she swung her chair around. "You're a day late, and I'd be willing to bet at least a dollar short."

No smile.

Tyler tried to give her his best quizzical look. She looked even better in daylight. Her brown doe eyes, the delicate nose, the high cheekbones. She looked as good as any peppermint-stick ice-cream cone he'd ever had. "I thought we were supposed to have lunch today at noon... you mean you forgot?"

"Very funny lothario. It was yesterday. And in my league you're out on two strikes, so if you'll excuse me...."

"Don't you think you're being a bit harsh?"

"Harsh! Three years ago I'm stupid enough to fall for someone I don't know from Adam, and he pulls a runner, and leaves me stranded at some bistro. No note, nothing, *nada*. And you expect me to jump at the chance to have lunch with you—"

"Was it three years?"

"Three years later you show up again, flash your Tom Sawyer grin, and I'm supposed to fall for it? Dream on."

"I'm really sorry.... I had a meeting with Komate Imasu, and I was unable to call you."

"You expect me to believe that's why you missed lunch?"

"That's the truth."

"No."

"No what?"

"No I don't believe you, and no I won't have lunch with you. Not now, not never!"

"That's a double negative, so you will?"

"No! Past, present, and future. Now, Mr. Grammarian, if you'll excuse me."

"I'm really sorry. Please? I hear Lucky Strike's has an excellent grilled salmon and arugula—"

"What part of N-O don't you understand?"

As Tyler continued to wear her down he sensed someone standing behind him.

A tall, thin guy, wearing black engineering specs was tapping on the door. His Adam's apple was prominently displayed against the plaid shirt that was more seventies than hip. Tyler was looking at the original ninety-eight-pound skinny weakling as an adult.

"Excuse me," he said as he peered around Tyler, "Lucy, are we still on for lunch?"

Here was his chance. Tyler said, "Actually Miss Phillips and I—"

Lucy cut him off. "We were just finishing our meeting.... Yes, lunch would be great Henry. Give me five minutes."

"To the deli?" Henry asked.

"Actually I hear Lucky Strike's has an excellent grilled salmon and arugula salad, and Henry, my treat." She smiled sweetly.

Barney Fife's eyes lit up.

"Wow, that'd be great. See you in five minutes."

And with that he was gone, and so were Tyler's chances at redemption. He stared at her in stunned silence. She was grinning.

"Your mouth's open," she said smugly.

"You're going to lunch with Barney Fife?" Tyler asked incredulously.

"He's on time, he always pays, and his manners are impeccable. Now if you'll excuse me." She started tidying her desk. And then she did those simple things that women do before they go out in public. Comb hair, check makeup, apply lipstick, the basic tune-up.

NINE

Tyler felt as if someone had kicked him in the gut. First, he stupidly dares himself into the heist of the century, and then he loses the girl to the president of the math club. Depressed, he wandered around SoHo. His phone beeped. There were too many numbers for it to be local. He punched the MSG button. A recorded voice message with a Swiss accent said, "You have received a message from the International Bank of Zurich. Please enter your security access code."

Tyler punched in a series of numbers. A computer-animated voice spoke next.

"You have a deposit of 5-0-0-0-0-0-0-0 in US dollars as of 1-0 minutes ago. Press 4 to repeat the message. Press 5—"

Tyler hit 4.

"You have a deposit of 5-0-0-0-0-0-0-0 in US dollars as of 1-0 minutes ago."

Tyler stood shell-shocked. He just stared. All noises muted. Everything blurred. His mind was racing, and in all the wrong directions. He'd just won the Powerball lottery of a lifetime. The brass ring. The dream of dreamers. But at what cost? A strange smile crossed his face. It was the one death row inmates had on the morning of their last day on Earth.

"Shhhiiitttt" was all he could muster.

He was doomed. His brain fell into that delirious point of euphoria knowing the end was near, and there was nothing he could do about it. No way in. No way out. Here he was with more money than he'd ever imagined, and he probably wouldn't live long enough to spend it. Be careful what you wish for, his Mom used to tell him.

He dialed a number.

"Where are you?" Tyler asked.

"None of your business. I'm hanging up—" said the voice.

"There's money. Good money," Tyler responded.

"My studio, off Canal."

As Tyler turned onto Canal Street, with its discount camera, luggage, and whatnot shops, he noticed the sky was changing from bland overcast to ominous. Halfway down the street he came to a service alley that dead-ended. He stopped about twenty yards from the end of the alley at a doorway. It was steel with a thick mesh window that looked into a void of darkness.

Tyler rang the large, faded red buzzer next to the doorway. The little speaker crackled.

"Whaaatt?" The voice was almost inaudible.

"It's me, Ty."

A buzzer sounded and Tyler pushed open the door. He stepped into a warehouse-sized space that was dark and dank. To his right was a service elevator. It was clear that Tyler had been here before as he waited patiently for the elevator. It was too dark for him to see the hidden cameras watching his every move. They had night filters on them so even in total darkness the cameras could still detect movement.

The elevator clunked to a halt, and Tyler pulled on the strap at the bottom of the gate and the door swung upwards. He stepped in and pulled the door shut, and the elevator ascended. As it reached its destination he saw the first shafts of light filtering down. Again, he swung the door upwards, and stepped into what looked like an art warehouse. Canvases were stacked everywhere. The thick smell of gesso and oils hung in the air.

"Up here," came a voice from above.

Tyler went up the staircase and found Barthold working on a canvas. It was Degas's *Ballet Rehearsal.* It was half done. The sketch lines were still visible on the canvas. The rendering was startling in its exactness. Behind Bart, in the corner, was a small ceramic oven that he used to heat the oils, which gave his paintings the aged look of the originals. Bart was sitting on a stool analyzing his work, with the ubiquitous cigarette hanging from his mouth.

Tyler moved next to him and stared at the painting. "Not bad," he said.

Bart snorted. "Not bad! It's fucking perfect."

Tyler laughed. It was fucking perfect. He loved Bart's confidence. For all of Bart's personal demons, his ability as an art forger was second to none. "Private collector?" he asked.

"No. Actually an insurance company requested it for an exhibit they are insuring. A retrospective of Degas, and Renoir, showing in Saint Petersburg. They're a bit worried about thieves so they decided to hang a copy and keep the original in storage. They figured no one would know."

"Doing any of your own work?" Tyler asked.

Bart nodded his head past the canvas in front of them to an easel on the left. Tyler walked over and took a look. It was a visually stunning view of the Palisades falling into the Hudson River. The depth and colors together gave it an eerie feeling. But the river was so placid that all seemed well in the world. It was mesmerizing.

"It's the *Palisades in Winter*," Bart said.

"Is it for sale?" Tyler asked.

"No. I owe Luca, my tailor, serious dough for the last year's suits and shirts, so I told him I'd give him that when I finish it."

Bart was always immaculately dressed for a painter. No blue jeans and T-shirts for him. He tended toward gabardine slacks, custom-made shirts of Egyptian cotton and always a hand-tailored vest.

"When will it be finished?"

"Whenever he delivers the next batch of shirts, and the winter suit I've been waiting three months for. I'm kinda hungry. You want lunch?"

"That'd be great," Tyler replied.

Bart strolled over to the fridge near the ceramic oven and pulled out two sandwiches wrapped in butcher paper, along with two bottles of beer.

They headed upstairs and through the door to the rooftop. Bart had created a fake beach on the roof, complete with giant rubber palm trees, a kiddie pool that served as a cooler during summer parties, and a ton of sand, literally, that he'd had delivered during his crazier days. And of course beach chairs. He'd also recently had a heat lamp delivered, courtesy of Max, the owner of the Art Bar.

They sat with their deli sandwiches on the faux beach staring out at the Twin Towers and life beyond. "Surfin' Safari" played on the CD player in the background.

"How's things?" asked Bart.

"Things are good and looking up," said Tyler.

"I ran into Max and he said you were taking a leave of absence. Freelancing again?" Bart asked.

"Something like that. I'm helping out a collector on a project," Tyler said.

"And you need my help," Bart said as a statement of fact.

"Eventually, but now, more your counsel."

"You want to know if it's a fake?" Bart asked.

Besides being one of the premier forgers in the world, Bart was also capable of detecting fakes, no matter how well done. Being a master forger gave Bart indelible insights into that world. An expertise that the insurance boys, and museum directors, coveted. Which is why Bart was on retainer to Sotheby's, as well as Lloyd's of London.

They sat in silence for a while as they ate and drank their beer. The heat lamp above their beach chairs kept the cool autumn air at bay. Tyler was trying to decide exactly how much to tell Bart. "When I need your help, I'll need it immediately. And you'll be well compensated. Very well compensated."

This was always good news to Bart. He pulled out a blank card and wrote a phone number on it.

"This is a private cell number. You can call it anytime from any phone. It has a built in scrambler so no eavesdroppers can listen in, nor can they establish where the call originates or where I am."

"Thanks, that's perfect," said Tyler.

"Dare I ask who the buyer is?"

"A wealthy Asian businessman."

This information made Bart sit up in his chair.

"I hope to God it's not Komate Imasu," said Bart.

Now Tyler sat up in his chair.

"Why?"

Bart was peeling the label off the beer bottle using his thumb. This was his way of pondering an awkward situation. Tyler had seen Bart do it many times over the years when he was sitting with a woman at the Art Bar.

"About two years ago he hired a friend of mine to help him *locate* a piece... privately. Everything was going according to plan until payday when suddenly my friend disappeared, and wasn't seen again until about six months later—when his decomposed body was discovered by some kids in the marsh swamp, over near Fort Lee."

"God, what happened? Did he try to rip off Imasu?" asked Tyler.

"Not the way I heard it," Bart said. "Imasu just doesn't like loose ends."

Tyler felt his voice moving into a higher register. "What about the cops?"

"They didn't know the connection between the dead guy and Imasu, and none of us who knew were going to say anything," Bart said. "Just be really careful if Imasu's your guy. And Ty, don't call me if he is."

Tyler sat, stunned. "So the rumors about Imasu are true?"

"And then some." Bart leaned forward in his chair with a serious look on his face. "Those guys he has hanging around. You seen them?" he asked.

Tyler nodded.

"Those guys are all Yakuza. And they are some seriously fucked-up gangsters."

Bart's comment caused Tyler to freeze. Unblinking.

"Hey Ty?" Bart finally said.

Tyler snapped out of his spell.

"You gonna finish your sandwich or what?" asked Bart.

Tyler had suddenly lost his appetite and handed the rest of his sandwich to Bart.

They sat in silence, the wind swirling around them overhead.

TEN

His brain was still in freeze mode from his chat with Bart, but the smell of hotdogs made his stomach rumble. Tyler was standing in front of Nathan's Famous on Seventh Avenue, near Madison Square Garden. He swallowed down a chili cheese dog. Not exactly the lunch he was planning on. He watched the harried masses crisscrossing 34th Street and wondered what they were pondering as they hurried to get to their destinations. Tyler doubted it had anything to do with Aristotelian thought. Or pulling off the heist of the century. No, people's concerns, if you stopped them and asked, were the mortgage, the kids, money, the wife, money, the ex, the girlfriend on the side, all the things that should make us smile but instead give us ulcers.

Shame.

It was amazing how philosophical Tyler had become while sitting in the joint. A result of too much time on his hands. And NO ONE in the joint wastes a second feeling any remorse for their crimes. Although Tyler had come to the firm conclusion that he'd never steal art again, that resolution was quickly evaporating, thanks to events that were quickly zooming out of his control, sucking him into their vortex.

Most cons agonize over how they got caught, and swear it won't happen again. Never about remorse. Tyler, staring at the cinder-block walls and always keeping an eye out, had read the classics, and then he read them all over again. Some guys pumped iron voraciously, others plotted their next crime, and a few that actually planned ill-fated escapes. Tyler's aversion to dodging bullets had kept him cozy in his cell, and reading. Now his thoughts were consumed by thoughts of the Yakuza. Imasu was playing for keeps.

After inhaling the chili cheese dog, he jaywalked his way across the street to Penn Station. It was funny how everyone talked about "The Garden" as though Madison Square Garden were some kind of architectural wonder. Actually it had a kind of a retro World's Fair look to it. Certainly not timeless. Tyler wandered around the backside of the Garden trying to distract himself from thoughts of Ginsu-knife annihilation. What everyone missed, or seemed to ignore, was the Post Office on Eighth Avenue. Now that was a beautiful, old pre-war building.

Sadly, most people tend to miss Farley's architectural wonder with the stunning Corinthian columns. Tyler ducked into Penn Station from the south end of Eighth Avenue, after giving the grand old Post Office a quick glance and a smile. He dodged and weaved through the station, grabbed a first class Metroliner ticket to Washington, DC, and as the train pulled away through the bowels of New York, he settled back, Hermès attaché at his feet, with Chet Raymo's *Skeptics and True Believers*, a fascinating read about what really is, and isn't.

Tyler was unable to concentrate on his book. Imasu had crossed the line by endangering his family and it was making Tyler angry and paranoid—a bad combination that hampered his ability to think clearly. He'd check in with his mom in a few of days to make sure she was getting better, and see if he could get her to do one of her famed disappearing acts.

His mind was circling around his new problem, probing for a solution to how he might pull off this heist, and still remain among the living. This was the first time this many canvases, representing such diversity, had ever appeared together before. Tickets were selling out like a Springsteen concert. Beyond the security, Tyler's biggest concern was the time factor. It had been a while, but the last time he'd pulled off one of these jobs he was able to remove the painting from the frame in less than sixty seconds.

The problem was, he'd volunteered to pinch an even dozen. It's one thing to hang around for ninety seconds, and it's something else entirely when you're talking about ten to fifteen minutes in a room with cameras, motion sensors, and thermo detectors, monitoring any movement or temperature changes. He'd be up against the most modern and comprehensive security system money could buy. The other problem was assistance. Tyler would be a fool to attempt this solo, considering the magnitude of the project. But the only times he'd ever been caught, he'd used outside help. When outside help was involved there were too many factors you couldn't control, no matter how meticulous the planning. He had to figure out how to sideline Imasu's men without them realizing it. Concoct an entire plan, which he never intended to use. And then, the real plan.

While he was pondering all this, and watching the southern Jersey countryside zoom by, a wonderful dose of Chanel N°5 strolled by. It's funny how quickly you can lose your train of thought to something as simple as a woman's perfume. But then, isn't that the point? He got up and followed Chanel N°5 to the bar car.

By the time the train pulled into Union Station in Washington, DC, Tyler knew this: she was an editor at some glossy women's mag, named after the founder. She was in DC for a photo shoot and story about congressional wives. It all sounded quite boring to Tyler, but then being a congressional wife didn't sound like a day in the park. Who'd want to be married to some bulbous-nosed blowhard who said one thing, did another, and pocketed a lot of undisclosed "soft money" in the process? Arrogant predator was the term that came to Tyler's mind. He supposed it was a way for some women to get out of some godforsaken parts of America. Washington, as a city, had its moments. It wasn't New York or Paris, but then it wasn't Oklahoma City either.

Chanel N°5 gave Tyler her phone number and the name of the hotel where she was staying. He told her he was on his way to see relatives he hadn't seen for a while, and that if he could get away he'd love to meet her for a drink.

He walked to the Hotel George from Union Station. It was a pleasant five-minute stroll. The George was one of those newer "European style" hotels. Eddie, the bellhop, showed him to his room. The small suite had some nice touches, with a Warholesque print of a *George Washington Dollar Bill* over the couch. There was a fake Japanese screen as a divider between the sitting area and the king-size bed. After over-tipping Eddie, Tyler unpacked his camera gear, put fifty thousand from the Hermès attaché, along with two fake passports, in the safe in the bedroom closet. You never know when you may need fifty large in a hurry, plus he had some immediate expenses to deal with. Tyler threw on his tourist disguise: Dockers khakis and a simple white button down shirt with a navy blue crew neck sweater. A pair of Nikes, and a NY Yankees hat pulled down over his blond wig. And a pair of glasses he "found" at the Penn Station lost and found. He looked like Joe Tourist from Anywhere, USA.

It was early afternoon, one of those pleasant autumn days in Washington when the sun and the breeze conspire for bliss. Perfect strolling weather. It had been a while since he'd been to the National Gallery. Designed by John Russell Pope, built during the Great Depression, and donated by Andrew Mellon so he'd have some place to hang all his art. In his day, Mellon was almost as rich as Bill Gates. Tyler left the hotel and headed west on E Street, towards the museum.

Standing in front of the National Gallery a tingle went up his spine, and the hairs on his neck stood on end. The sensation of excitement mixed with a dash of danger. The museum's treasures always made his heart pump a little faster—and now that he was actually planning to heist something from the place, the feelings intensified.

Washington held a special place in Tyler's heart. His very first heist was from the Phillips Collection, a small museum/gallery in the Dupont Circle neighborhood. It was back before all the new-fangled, heat-sensitive, infrared video security technology. Ahh, the good old days, when capers were simple, and all thieves looked like Cary Grant in *To Catch a Thief*.

Tyler was kicking around Washington when he ran into an old school mate from his days at a New England prep school. His friend, a wannabe artist, was lamenting his impoverished life, and was telling Tyler about this rich guy who had told him how frustrating it was trying to buy decent art at a decent price. One thing (tequila) led to another (more shots) and suddenly Tyler's friend confessed that he'd all but agreed to heist a small piece of art for the rich guy. The friend was more talk than action, plus he was scared shitless.

Tyler thought his friend had lost his mind, but he also felt sorry for him. So in his margarita stupor, Tyler had foolishly agreed to help him. The next afternoon at the Phillips Gallery, Tyler, using his superior knowledge of art, told his friend that the best bang for the buck would be a delightful little Paul Klee called *Bird 6.*

Two days later, wearing a simple disguise that included black leather driving gloves, Tyler walked into the gallery carrying a briefcase about the size of the painting. They created a small diversion by pulling the fire alarm. Tyler switched the Klee with a painting by an unknown artist that he had picked up at a yard sale in Old Town Alexandria earlier that morning. The beauty of the unknown artist's work lay in the frame; it was the exact size as the Klee frame. Five minutes later Tyler was outside on the street moving briskly away from the museum. A half hour later, he was nervously downing a Guinness draft at Suzanne's Bar, just north of Dupont Circle. And that afternoon he was $50,000 richer. Big money for a twenty-one-year-old.

Tyler had jumped on the next flight to Jamaica and lay on the seven-mile white, sandy beach at Negril for the next two weeks. He couldn't believe what he had done. The ease of it all, and the inherent immorality. The Blue Mountain ganja helped lessen the guilt. While lying on the beach, after some of Captain Kirk's special mushroom tea, Tyler had a philosophical argument with himself about who really owns works of art. This was when things started to get blurry in his mind. Not all art comes to museums through honest channels. Just ask any holocaust survivor. Or the entire Hermitage collection, in Saint Petersburg, for that matter. And not all art in any one museum is, in fact, the real deal. More fakes abound than the casual observer could imagine.

Can you say *Mona Lisa?*

It was just after the Phillips job that Tyler saw his brother Alex and started to suspect that something might be seriously wrong. It was several months after Alex's return from the Middle East, and Tyler found the casual manner his brother assumed in telling some truly horrific stories of his time in Palestine to be startling. Alex's voice was chillingly flat, and devoid of the emotion that you would expect from a person describing a horror scene. At the time Tyler told himself it was probably just Alex's journalistic way of telling a story, or some kind of false bravado, but later he learned it was the beginning stages of his brother's mental collapse. Alex's downward spiral into the emotional abyss mirrored Tyler's success as a thief. The more successful Tyler became, the worse his brother got.

A diseased yin-yang.

Tyler was considering all of this as he strolled past the Canadian Embassy, which sat across the street from the East Building. He made a mental note to contact his brother sooner rather than later to make sure he was in fact okay, given Imasu's threats. He stopped, and was staring directly across the street at the back of the National Gallery. From any direction it was an imposing structure, large, windowless, and fortresslike. It consisted of two large, rectangular wings on each side, approximately seventy yards in length, connected by a substantial rotunda. There were entrances on all four sides: the one opposite the Pei building, the one around the "back," another side entrance that was exclusively for service, and of course the grand front steps, a prerequisite of most buildings in Washington, DC. In the summer the steps would be full of tourists, but today there were only a few folks sitting, drinking coffee, and enjoying the late-afternoon sun.

The front of the building faced the National Mall, which spanned from below the Capitol all the way to the Washington Monument. Trees surrounded the interior walkways of this landmark-studded national park. Extra-wide gravel footpaths ran in front of all the buildings. The institutions in the Smithsonian complex—the Air and Space Museum, The Hirshhorn, The Castle, Natural History Museum, American History Museum—lined the outer edges of the mall. The rest of this section of the park consisted of neatly trimmed grass with the occasional oak tree planted without pattern. The place had an almost collegial feel. Heading west along Constitution Avenue, Tyler arrived at a thirty-degree intersection where Constitution and Pennsylvania Avenues crossed. The Federal Trade Commission headquarters was the sole occupant of the wedge. Looking north, Tyler saw the ever-popular Capital Grille on the corner of Sixth Street NW and Pennsylvania Avenue. This was a favorite joint for lobbyists to ply their trade. The dark wood paneling was supposed to give it an air of seriousness, but between the lobbyists paying off congressional aides, or setting up new fresh-faced congressmen with stylish hookers, and the busboys selling nickel bags out back, the place was anything but serious. To its credit, The Capital Grille made a killer steak au poivre with a dry-aged seared sirloin and a dash of Courvoisier cream sauce. The restaurant sat on the ground floor of an old six-story building with offices attached to the original facade. This way they were able to preserve the facade, which wasn't a bad thing.

Tyler's plan was to rent a corner office on the top floor of the amalgamated building, as it had perfect views down to the Capitol and more importantly, looked down on the roof of the National Gallery.

The National Gallery had massive metal doors that were as rock solid and imposing as they looked. And a second, lead-lined door slid over the whole thing for added security. Tyler hated messing with bolted iron doors. It was looking as if this would have to be a roof job for him. Not a pleasant prospect. Roof work required endless sit-ups. He wandered around the far side and came to the front of the building. Most of the back and far side (the service entrance) had a tangle of large trees and shrubs that would provide decent cover. He made his way to the front of the building where the trees thinned, and the shrubs were immaculately trimmed. The flowers were making a last stand, but with the autumn breeze, they knew their days were numbered.

The steps and columns at the front reminded Tyler of the Supreme Court building, evoking in him a sense of supreme smallness. From the top of the steps you could see across the quad to the Air and Space Museum, the hippest museum at the Smithsonian. Tyler especially loved the Mercury 7 spacecraft, with the wax dummy that was supposed to be John Glenn. It made him appreciate the "spam in a can" concept. Plus, there was Orville and Wilbur's Kitty Hawk, and that wild man Lindbergh's Spirit of St. Louis.

To his right was the Hirshhorn with its modern sculpture garden (modern by 1970s' standards), and to the left the Botanic Gardens. In the distance were the roads leading to Interstate 395, the southwest freeway, running directly past the most-morbid building in DC. This was a four-story, square building whose solid granite walls did not have a single window. On top were more antennae than in Wan Chai, Suzy Wong's Hong Kong. This architectural wonder was the home of the NSA (National Security Agency), the domestic surveillance operations center for the US government. There was only one door, and an underground garage whose entrance had tighter security than the White House.

Tyler studied the view and snapped photos of the National Gallery where fifty-foot banners announcing the Millennium Show were flapping away. He took a deep breath and headed through the main entrance.

In front of him was the information desk manned by a female senior citizen—part of the national senior citizen volunteer brigade. Standing next to her was the obligatory guard leaning against a wall. To his left was the coat check. To the right was a large entryway that led to a set of stairs. There was nothing interesting beyond the guard, save for the Garden Café and the underground tunnel leading to the East Building, so Tyler decided to take the stairs. They were a beautiful light colored marble with streaks of tan running through them, like an LA sunset. The brass railing had the smell of fresh polish, indicating that building maintenance was constant. Tyler made a mental note to get his hands on a maintenance schedule, as well as the guards' schedule. At the top of the stairs was a large portrait of some otherworldly nobleman. As a rule, portraits bored Tyler although he understood their bread-and-butter potential to an artist trying to survive. Portraits had given many artists both the necessary patronage, and money to stay alive. Rembrandt, Manet, and Goya all honed their skills painting portraits. The only ones that had any real bite, as far as Tyler was concerned, were self-portraits. Van Gogh's *Self-Portrait with Bandaged Ear* immediately came to mind.

To Tyler's right was a marble wall with a small, locked doorway. The stairs forced a left turn, so through the entryway he headed. A guard leaned against the side of an open well that housed a two-story clock marking perpetual time. It hung from the ceiling by a series of cables that disappeared into the roof. The guard didn't even notice Tyler. Clearly they hadn't yet implemented the extra security they would need for the Millennium Show. Tyler guessed that each museum contributing a piece would have two of its own security people assigned, plus the

Smithsonian would hire additional security, probably from the Brinks art division. On top of that, the FBI would assign a detail, and of course Tyler's old friends from Interpol would be represented.

He passed the guard and stepped into the Rotunda, gazing up at a beautiful piece of cut glass, six feet in diameter. And below that was a wonderful airy space, thirty feet in diameter, with columns spaced every five feet or so. His eyes grazed a fountain with a sculpture of Mercury placed in the center. Between the columns were large pots filled with autumn flowers. All very graceful, the perfect place for the Mellons to hold their tea parties. He wandered slowly around the outside of the circle. A long corridor (fifty to seventy yards) filled with sculptures extended off both sides of the rotunda. The best news of all was the incredible amount of light that came in through the ceiling. There were large, continuous skylights all the way down both corridors. Tyler was thrilled to see this as it allowed much better natural lighting for the art. And more importantly, it allowed unparalleled access through the roofline.

Continuing around the rotunda, he checked the National Gallery brochure that the blue-haired volunteer had provided. It told him that the building was built in the 1940s, well before the advent of modern electronic security devices. He made note of the ceiling, and then headed down the long hallway. On his right were small rooms that interconnected, not unlike the maze that the ubiquitous mouse must navigate day in day out. Each of these rooms housed a different series of paintings, seventeenth-century Dutch, English portraits, French neoclassicism. Across the hallway was an identical maze of rooms, cordoned off by security partitions with posters promoting the Millennial Show. A mirror image of where he would perform the heist of the century.

Tyler approached the nearest guard, a black gentleman, about six feet even, easily over two hundred pounds. He looked good in his uniform, more bulk than fat, his longish face framed, by a pair of tortoise-shell glasses.

"So what's with all the rooms being closed off?" Tyler asked.

"It's for the big End of the Millennium Show," the guard said, pointing at the poster.

"Yeah? What kind of stuff?"

"One hundred paintings from all over the world encompassing all the greats," the guard said, adjusting his glasses.

"You mean like the Mona Lisa?" Tyler asked stupidly.

"To tell you the truth I'm not sure. I don't get invited to those meetings," the guard said with a wry smile.

"So who gets to pick?" Tyler wondered out loud.

"It's supposed to be a panel of experts from around the world, but my guess is it'll be the director and his poker buddies," he said with a chuckle.

Tyler had a hard time imagining J. Carter Brown playing poker or having "buddies" for that matter. On the other hand Tyler liked this guard's attitude.

"The only ones we're sure of are the ones on the poster," he said.

"Did they ask you for your picks?" Tyler asked jokingly.

He snorted when he laughed.

"Maybe next century," he said as he pushed his glasses up his nose.

"It sounds like you'll have your work cut out for you," Tyler said.

"Not hardly. They're bringing in a special security team just for the event."

"What's the matter, they don't trust you guys?"

"It's not that. It's more the politics involved in a show of this magnitude. Besides it's a huge load off me and the other regular guards," he said.

"Do you have any idea as to the monetary value of an exhibit such as this?" he asked with a knowing look on his face.

"I haven't a clue," Tyler responded. The truth was Tyler probably knew the answer within ten thousand dollars.

The guard's eyes widened as he whispered the answer to Tyler.

"More than One… Billion… Dollars," he said, quietly. He said it as though it was preposterous yet somehow true at the same time. He was shaking his head at the wonder of it all. Tyler pretended to bug his eyes out as his brain took in the information.

"WOW," Tyler said just loud enough.

The guard nodded his head in agreement. Tyler's mind was spinning from the guard's previous comment on the beefed-up security. He was expecting it, but standing only a few steps from where he'd be working was giving him the chills. The guard continued to explain why he and his guard pals didn't want to be responsible for that much art, worth billions of dollars. But Tyler was thinking of other things, and they were filling him with dread. He thanked the guard, pulled himself together, and wandered off.

What he needed was some air, but he still had work to do. He continued through the maze of rooms that were a mirror image on the other side of the long hall. He was beginning to realize that the only chance he'd have to see the room where the paintings would hang was after the show opened. And that would be a day late, and a dozen paintings short. He also realized this wasn't the most efficient way to case a job. It was always better to see the physical layout before all the changes had been made. And then go back a second time, to inventory guards and other security matters. At least that's what had always worked best for him in the past.

"Worked best" was a synonym for not getting caught. Tyler was having major misgivings about the job, about Imasu, and about his reckless lifestyle which had put not just his life, but possibly his brother's and mother's lives in jeopardy. It was Imasu's threats against his family that pushed Tyler to the edge and sent his mind into a fog.

Tyler had just finished mumbling, "God bless you sir," to no one in particular. Realizing he had just spaced out, way out. The prison doctor had assured him that his "fits" would disappear once he was back on the outside. Tyler took this as his exit cue, just as a guard started to amble towards him. Vermeer's *The Kitchen Maid* silently watched Tyler go.

He headed downstairs to the subterranean cafe and gift shop, which connected the East Building with the National Gallery. He noticed the slits over the doorways, in and out of the cafe. They could hold only one thing—stainless steel doors that dropped instantly at the sound of an alarm. The phrase "tighter than a drum" rolled through Tyler's brain. After studying the remaining downstairs area, he wandered out through the East Building so he could revisit the Calder that was the focal point of this part of the museum. As he exited onto the hand-laid stone drive that acted as a formal entryway, the cool autumn air hit him. The sky glowed with a slightly pinkish hue, as though layered with cotton candy. Twilight was moving in.

It felt good to be alive, at least for now.

ELEVEN

Tyler pulled the collar up on his suede coat. The late-afternoon breeze reminded him of his mother's constant warnings to button up. He headed for the Capitol Building, taking the long route back to his hotel, around the far side of the Capitol, past the Library of Congress and the Supreme Court. He needed to clear his head. The dark side of the job was creeping up his spine and infesting his medulla. He was a believer of the "do one thing a day that scares you" philosophy, but this was way more fear than he needed. Plus, the idea of being a thief wasn't something he was particularly proud of. For Tyler it was the moth to the flame syndrome. He couldn't help himself. He was addicted to the thrill, even though he knew the flame was deadly.

Viva Icarus!

After his brisk walk past the massive old federal buildings, with the sun clearly losing the battle to twilight, he decided to reward himself with a draft at the Dubliner, one of the great institutions of the federal city, just around the corner from his hotel. Cocktail hour was bleeding into dinnertime, and Guinness is considered an excellent source of vitamins and minerals. Meal in a pint.

Halfway through his second pint he reached in his pocket to grab some cash to pay the tab, and as he pulled out a fist of twenties he saw Chanel N°5's card with her cell number on the back. The bartender was kind enough to lend him the phone, and lo and behold she was in. They agreed to meet at Kinkeads, one of those hip new restaurants springing all over town. It was only a few blocks from the Four Seasons in Georgetown, where Chanel N°5 was staying. Tyler went back to his hotel, hopped in the shower, and threw on a cashmere V-neck sweater over his Missoni sport shirt, his suitable for all occasions suede jacket, and khakis—respectable dinner wear on any continent. He jumped on the underground Metro at Union Station, got off at Foggy Bottom, and walked the two blocks to the restaurant. As he exited the underground with its security cameras everywhere, he made a mental note not to use the subway as an exit strategy. Too many guards. Too many cameras.

Chanel N°5 was already at the bar with a cosmo martini in front of her. She had changed out of her work suit and looked even better than he remembered. Her dark hair was pulled back in a loose swirl and held there with a black-lacquered miniature chopstick. She was dressed all in black, in a slim miniskirt, opaque tights, a form-fitting cropped leather jacket and black Italian leather boots. Clearly she meant business.

As Tyler approached the bar she turned toward him and smiled. There can be something truly extraordinary about a woman's smile. So warm and inviting, yet so dangerous.

"You look great," he blurted out.

She smiled as though he was stating the obvious.

"Thanks."

"So did you get all you needed on congressional wives?" Tyler asked

"You remembered. Actually, I'm surprised you called."

"Why's that?"

"You seemed distracted when we talked on the train. Is everyone in your family okay?"

The only thing Tyler could remember about meeting her on the train was her perfume.

"Ah, yeah, all things considered, everyone's fine," he said, hoping to avoid any further discussion of his fictitious family.

"What can I get you?" asked the bartender. He had the perfect upscale bartender look. Waspy, crisp white cotton shirt, sleeves rolled up just once, a splashy tie loosened at the collar, with the top button undone. A starched white apron was folded in half around his waist, covering his dark slacks.

"How about a Tanqueray martini, dry, shaken. And another one here... ," Tyler looked at Chanel N°5 to make sure that was okay. She smiled and gave an imperceptible nod to the bartender, who tossed up two fresh bar naps and headed over to his spirits chem lab.

"So where were we?" Tyler asked her. She looked at him with a sweet smile and said, "I believe you were telling me how good I look?"

"Ah yes, and I love your perfume. What is it?" he asked.

"Chanel. Chanel N°5," she said.

"So, tell me about yourself," he said, "just the juicy parts. And leave out the husband or boyfriend."

This made her laugh.

"I grew up out on Long Island. Port Jefferson. Pretty typical. Was on the sailing team in high school, and a cheerleader."

Tyler grinned.

The bartender showed up with the drinks.

"You still have the pom-poms?"

"Yeah, that and the little, short, pleated skirt."

"Sweet."

Ignoring his comment, Chanel continued, "I went to one of those small New England colleges, where I studied international relations. Daddy only covered tuition so I had to work during most of college. I tended bar at the local college pub, and I was also a pretty fair pool player."

"Great. I'm having dinner with a hustler."

"When an obnoxious, drunken, college boy starts bragging with a pool stick in his hand, well, it's time to serve him up a little fresh humility."

"So after fleecing the local frat boys, then what?" he asked.

"After graduation, to please Daddy, I applied and was accepted at Harvard Law. To please myself I decided not to go."

Tyler shook his head.

"I went to Rhode Island School of Design instead. I loved the fashion industry, but was a terrible designer. So I ended up doing communications work for one of the big design houses. And from that I got my current job. What about you?"

Tyler thought for a long minute before answering.

"I work on the insurance side of large commodity deals. It's as boring as it sounds. But it pays the bills."

There was that "first date" awkward silence. Tyler tried not to stare. She was wearing an expensive-looking necklace in the shape of an ankh, which peeked through her jacket just short of her cleavage. Tyler was guessing she was somewhere in the neighborhood of thirty.

Chanel broke the silence. "And currently there's no one serious in my life. A few annoying pests but nothing worth bothering over," she said.

"OUCH," he said. "None up to the challenge?"

"Most men are scared of powerful women. If they can't control them they don't know what to do with them." She said this looking straight at him.

"Don't look so shocked… this is a common problem for most of my girlfriends. A gay friend once told me that what I really needed was a guy with a big brain, and," she mimicked a stage whisper, "a thick skin."

This made Tyler laugh.

"Well, I have a thick brain. Will that do?"

"At least you've got a sense of humor," she grinned. "That's a start."

The maître d' came up behind Tyler and announced that their table was ready. Tyler slid a fifty on the bar, and gently glided Chanel in the direction the maître d' was now heading.

The waiter recommended the fresh Wellfleet oysters from Washington Bay. Chanel winked, so they ordered up a dozen, and a half bottle of champagne to wash them down.

While they were studying their menus, Chanel asked Tyler, without looking up, "You were saying, about your sense of humor?"

"That it's gotten me into and out of trouble."

"At the same time?" she asked.

"Occasionally… when I was younger. Before I learned to keep my mouth shut."

She slid her menu down and glanced at him over the top. She didn't seem convinced. "And what occasion brought on such discipline?"

"It was usually when my hand was caught in the cookie jar. Humor always seemed to give me the edge with my mom. And I do recall an event in my younger adult days when an armed and angry husband was at the front door."

"So you told him a joke?" she asked.

"No. That time I hid in the kitchen, under the table, until he left."

"Coward," she said with a smile.

"Better a live coward than a dead fool. Besides, that time I was covering for a friend."

"They all say that."

The oysters and champagne appeared so they ceased their conversation with a nod and *"buon appetito,"* and dug in. She leaned forward and put a dab of fresh horseradish on a little bugger and slurped it down—clearly a pro. She finished sucking down number two.

"You've done this before, I see," said Tyler.

"Eating oysters allows for many things. First, true oyster eating involves no table manners and second, the myth about oysters... it's true."

Just watching her suck down an oyster straight from the shell was itself an erotic experience. It wasn't the oysters that were the aphrodisiac. It was the act of devouring them. When she finished she touched her mouth with her napkin ever so slightly, picked up her glass of champagne, tilted it toward him, and their glasses clinked.

Tyler noticed she had wonderful emerald-green eyes. Clear, like glass. He tried not to notice much else about her, at least not blatantly. He had learned long ago that women want you to talk to them, not to their breasts. Still, it was hard not to steal glimpses when she wasn't looking. She filled out her leather jacket perfectly.

She put down her wine glass.

"So why exactly did you call me? And don't give me some bullshit. Just tell me what you're thinking right now."

He was up against the ropes. Only two things came to mind so he opted for the more benign.

"I wanted to have dinner with a beautiful woman," he said, with total honesty.

Her green eyes lit up, so he continued.

"When we met on the train I was somewhat distracted, but later on when I found your card I thought of how easy it was talking with you and thought it'd be fun to see you again."

She raised her glass to him and sipped. He figured he'd reverse course.

"And you, how come you agreed to meet me for dinner?"

"Curiosity, and your boyish charm," she replied.

"Boyish charm?" he said smiling in disbelief.

She stared right at him and said, "Kiss me."

He leaned across the table. Her lips were soft and tasted sweet from the wine.

"Okay, now that that's out of the way, let's try again," Chanel N°5 said.

This time the kiss went miles beyond a "first" kiss. And she wasn't interested in letting go.

"Check!" Tyler barely managed.

TWELVE

The walk to the Four Seasons Hotel was only a few blocks, but with the chilly evening wind, it seemed longer. She put her arm through his as they walked. They went through the lobby, passed the giant ficus trees, and headed for the elevators. Once the doors closed, she turned to Tyler, grabbed his coat, and pulled him in. It was intoxicating, and his senses swirled.

Walking toward her room Tyler had a momentary flash of Lucy Phillips. What the hell was she doing in his brain? Who invited her? Here he was with a beautiful and willing accomplice when Lucy pops in for a visit. Lucy's image wouldn't retreat. When Chanel turned toward Tyler and unlocked her door, it was Lucy's face that he saw. This wasn't good. Of all the things his mom had tried to teach him, the one that stuck was to do the right thing when it came to dealing with women. He remembered mom clearly telling him as a mere ten-year-old to always respect women. Tyler had come home from school that day, pleased with himself and bragging to all who would listen that he had stolen a kiss from Marybeth, the cutest girl in class. His mom was getting dinner ready when he came into the kitchen to retell the story for the umpteenth time. She listened carefully as she stirred the spaghetti sauce. When he finished, she put down the wooden spoon.

Grabbing his shirt collar with both hands, Tyler's mother pulled him about two inches from her face and in a loud, stern voice she said, "You listen to me young man!" (Like he had a choice.) "You will respect girls. That means no kissing them or touching them in any way, unless they say so, and even then be ABSOLUTELY positive. Am I clear Tyler Sears?"

He got out a barely audible "Yes."

"WHAT did you say? I didn't hear you," she barked.

"Yes, I understand," he squeaked. And from that day forward his views on girls were forever changed. She'd kill him if she knew the line of work he was involved in. But at least she'd be happy with his standard of chivalry.

And that attitude was about to make him do—or not do, apparently—something he'd regret. They reached the door to her room and she stepped in. Tyler was about to say something when she looked right at him and gave him a wink that would have finished off any man. She put her arms around his neck, and her lips melted his. Life was full of choices, and right now he didn't feel like making any. But if he didn't say something now, the next words he spoke would be "Good morning beautiful."

"Uh, I'm not sure this is a good idea," he blurted. He couldn't believe he just said that.

She stepped back and looked at him with a half-cocked eyebrow.

"You got something you want to tell me?"

"No. I just don't want you to think I'm taking advantage of you or the situation."

"How about you let me worry about that?" she retorted.

"Look, maybe I'm an old-fashioned kind of guy, but believe it or not, I don't sleep with a woman on the first date," he stammered.

She started to laugh.

"What's so funny?" he asked.

"I don't know. It's sweet, that's all. And it makes me laugh."

The moment was broken.

"I'm glad you find it entertaining."

"Hey flyboy, it's your call," she said mockingly.

Tyler didn't blame her. "How about I give you a call when we're back in the city?" he said, trying to salvage the mess he was creating.

She laughed again. "I thought that was the line you were supposed to use tomorrow morning."

"I promise I'll call you when I'm back in the city."

"I won't hold my breath," she said, and with that the door was shut in his face.

Tyler walked away shaking his head. While he waited for the elevator he saw his reflection in the mirror opposite and mouthed, "Thanks Mom! I hope you're happy."

He cabbed it back to his hotel and spent the remainder of the evening with the mini-bar, watching bad late-night cable TV.

He made a mental note to call Lucy Phillips first thing in the morning.

After Tyler left, Chanel N°5 placed a call to her real boss, a grizzled Interpol director, who had been involved in Tyler's capture in Madrid. They had him fingered from the moment he stepped on the train back in New York.

The old man knew that Tyler would try something stupid. And for Tyler it'd be three strikes, and hello life, parole in twenty.

THIRTEEN

The next day, with a change of hair color (a black wig), a fake moustache, different glasses, and a beat up Mets cap, Tyler did round two at the National Gallery of Art. This go-round was much quicker and more efficient than the last time. He used a voice-activated microcassette to record information about the building and the surrounding security.

His last stop was DC City Hall, public records division. It took him less than an hour to get copies of the various architectural documents he requested. From there he made his way back to Union Station where he boarded the 11:55 Metroliner to New York City. Just before the Wilmington, Delaware stop he went into the changing room and emerged as his real self. He jumped off the train at Wilmington and tossed his disguise in the trash.

He walked the six blocks to the Brandywine Hotel, one of the last great old hotels in America. He was completely unaware of anyone watching him as he exited the train. He certainly didn't notice the elderly Asian couple sitting three rows behind him, who watched as he walked away from the train in Wilmington. Nor did he notice Chanel N°5 sitting in the first-class car, watching him as she spoke to her boss on the phone.

After checking in, Tyler headed straight to the bar for lunch. While he ate, he scanned the local paper, paying particular attention to the want ads, specifically autos for sale.

Back in his room, he made a few phone calls to local auto dealers, and arranged to have some funds wired through the three separate bank accounts he'd set up over the last decade (two offshore and one in Montreal). The money ended up at the Bank of Delaware, where earlier that afternoon he had opened an account. He fell asleep reading *Slowness* by Milan Kundera.

When he awoke, he threw on his sweats and went for a five-mile run. Back at the hotel and sufficiently sweated up, he peeled down to his shorts and did a half hour of yoga stretching. Afterwards he took a long hot soak in the claw-foot tub, sipping a Hopkowski from Iron Hill Brewery, and realizing just how much exercise was in store for him if he wanted any chance of pulling off this job.

He called room service and asked for the salmon entrée to be delivered at 7 p.m. He ate dinner watching Peter Jennings rambling on about the horrors of some Balkan nation.

Bad news.

The Dow was soaring.

Good news.

After dinner he studied museum blueprint plans in his room. He also studied roadmaps of the various route possibilities in and out of DC.

All in all, a productive yet dull evening.

FOURTEEN

Lucy Phillips was gnawing at his brain. He still couldn't quite figure it out. It was definitely her who had floated through his dreams in prison. He couldn't shake their whirlwind romance in Paris. It had hold of him in that way that things grab us sometimes. And don't let go. He stared at her card but decided not to risk it. It was better all around if no one knew where he was. The less traceability, the better.

In the morning he went for another light, easy jog in the early overcast that seemed to prevail ever since the du Pont family decided to settle in the Brandywine Valley over a hundred years ago. Afterwards he headed for the hotel gym and spent a half hour pushing weights. He had a hot shower, and then sixty seconds of cold water to invigorate him. He ordered the crab hash breakfast, and then checked out of the hotel. He caught a cab and headed south on Route 301, a typical non-descript highway like countless others that cut through the outskirts of every city in America, where fast-food heaven and every car dealer imaginable reside. As the cab dropped him at the Wilmington Porsche/Audi dealership, he noticed the cloud cover starting to break up. He entered the dealership and found a twentyish gum snapper flipping through a magazine. *Cosmo.* When he was right in front of her she finally looked up.

"Can I help you?" she asked.

"I'm looking for Tom Gardner."

"Jus' sec, I'll see if he's in," She had one of those accents specific to the Eastern Shore. Not quite a drawl, more like a hang. Definitely local. She paged Tom Gardner over the loud speaker so his name sounded like one long slur.

A moment later, Tom Gardner was standing in front of him. He was a tad shorter than Tyler. His hair was close cropped and slightly receding. Although the jowls were just starting to set in his face, he still appeared fit, and proud of his physique.

"Hi, Tom Gardner," he said, thrusting out his hand. He had a distinct accent, but Tyler couldn't quite place it.

Tyler shook his hand and smiled.

"Alex Hilton."

"We get a lot of du Ponts in these parts but I have to say, not a lot of Hiltons."

They both chuckled at the salesman's weak attempt at humor.

Gardner cleared his throat.

"So you're interested in the Audi S4?"

"You said you had one ready to go. Is that right?"

"Sure. You want to take it for a ride?" Gardner held out the keys. He had a pleasant calmness for a car sales guy.

"Actually I was wondering if you wouldn't mind driving," said Tyler. "You can explain the car and its speed parameters as we ride."

His grin told Tyler he'd have no problem obliging him. A few minutes later they were pulling out of the lot and heading south on 301.

As the car picked up speed, Gardner gave the basic pitch. "It's got a V-6, twin water-cooled turbos, 30-valve engine, which generates up to 250 hp. In a word, *fast*. This car comes with the six-speed manual transmission that's smooth as silk yet rock solid, ABS brakes, and of course Audi's full-time four-wheel-drive quattro system. This one's also equipped with a state of the art GPS system to make sure you never get lost. And of course, a built in radar detector in the front grill."

Gardner said all this in a smooth clipped fashion without overstating any one part or forgetting anything. Unlike most salesmen, he failed to mention the cup holders. Tyler took this to be a good sign. Gardner's driving style was different than most. Instead of slamming the car through its gears like most car salesmen, he shifted through the system like silk. The guy was no hack. They turned left onto Route 9 South and headed towards Delaware City. The traditional Americana-style houses vanished and were replaced by farmland Tom brought the vehicle up to the next level of performance, dropping it into fourth gear and adding power as the G-forces came into play. It wasn't so much being slammed into the seat as being pressed firmly by an 800-pound gorilla. They were traveling close to 100 mph in a very short span. Tyler noticed the car still hadn't crossed 3500 rpm. Plenty of giddyup left. The car looked like an overgrown VW, yet it was as quick and as fast as a Porsche 911, with four-wheel drive.

A getaway dream car come true.

Back at the dealership, Tyler filled out the required paperwork, using the fake IDs he'd commissioned from a Park Avenue counterfeiter he'd previously used, and it was then that he queried Tom on his accent. The accent was that strange mix that Americans get when they stay away, just long enough. No longer American but not quite Euro either.

"So Tom, where are you from? Your accent doesn't sound local."

"Actually just up the road, in the Lehigh Valley. But the accent is Euro pig Latin," Tom said with a laugh. Tyler looked at him quizzically.

"I worked in a rally garage in England the year between high school and college. I never made it to university. Got the rally bug and stayed for twenty some years as a mechanic and driver."

"And Wilmington?"

"The usual forty-year-old dilemma. My driving career was coming to an end. My parents weren't getting younger, and my beautiful French wife and I decided it was time for our two young kids to spend some time with their American grandparents."

"Do you still race?"

"Nah, just test drive for the Germans."

A mechanic put the temporary Delaware tags on the car and five minutes later, Tyler was heading north across the Delaware Bridge. He needed to get home. He had a lot of work in front of him. He decided to avoid 95 North and instead followed 295 northbound, blasting Mahler's *Fifth,* conducted by Bernstein. The clouds were beating a quick retreat in southern Jersey.

At Gloucester City, just south of Camden, Tyler turned south on the Atlantic City Expressway. He drove south past Cross Keys, Hammonton, and Penny Pot. He was amazed at how beautiful southern Jersey was. Really.

It was heavily forested with winding streams cutting through the landscape. Tyler was traveling on the deserted roads in excess of 100 mph past an endless flow of fields broken up by wooded maples. Most of the leaves were gone but some were still hanging on for dear life. The sun cut through the naked trees, creating an almost strobe-like effect. Canadian geese flew overhead, heading to their winter cornfield condos on the Eastern Shore. The landscape was alive in its own quiet way. The sort of pastoral scenery that Monet and van Gogh would have relished, Tyler imagined, as he approached Atlantic City. He turned right and headed north on the Garden State Parkway. The car was humming. The New York Philharmonic was crescendoing the magnificence of Mahler.

He wondered what Lucy Phillips was doing.

After cutting through the Barnegat Wildlife Refuge, Tyler returned to civilization near Toms River, just north of Loveladies. The towns started coming quicker and bigger, the closer he got to New York City. At Newark he finally pulled off and cut through the center of town till he found the appropriate nondescript parking garage. Tyler paid Homer, the attendant in charge, for two month's parking in advance, with cash. He walked the six blocks to the Newark Hyatt and grabbed a cab to the city. He had the cabbie drop him at the Empire Diner, on Tenth Avenue.

Tyler ordered the pork chops with applesauce. He watched the comings and goings of the diner as he ate in silence, and pondered the last several days. The museum research had gone well. He had forgotten how workmanlike he could be. But this time, serious pangs of doubt were creeping into his mind. This was the most-dangerous mission he'd ever agreed to. Hell, it was the most-dangerous theft ever considered in the history of the art world. This wasn't what he hoped for, and he was tired of work that required so much risk and returned so few tangible rewards. He worried about his brother. He'd need to do something about him. To make sure Alex was safe. *And don't forget to call Mom,* he thought.

His mind drifted over to Chanel N°5. He pulled out her card, wondered if he should call her. Instead, he had the blueberry pie à la mode.

He paid the tab at the register and as he turned to leave he tossed a double sawbuck on the table for a tip. He left Chanel's card behind as an added bonus.

FIFTEEN

The next morning an envelope was slid under his door. A welcome-home note from Imasu, complete with photos of him exiting the train in Wilmington. It was handwritten on Trans-Pacific stationary and read, "Hope you enjoyed the museum. Welcome home."

He had tried his best to be invisible. He'd have to try harder next time.

Suddenly worried about his mother's safety, he dialed her number. He was relieved when she picked up the phone.

"Hi Mom. How're things in the south of France? How's your arm?"

"We're fine, and my wrist is healing nicely. Your friend's doctor is keeping an eye on it. Meanwhile, Phillipe (she pronounced it phul-leep) just decided we're going sailing to Corsica for the next month. We leave day after tomorrow."

"That's great. I deposited some funds in your account."

"Sweetie, you didn't have to do that."

"I wanted to, and Mom, don't tell that doctor where you're headed."

"But I have an appointment to see him later today."

"Please Mom, skip the appointment, and do not call him again."

There was silence.

"Mom?"

"Alright sweetie, if you insist. Besides Phillipe didn't trust him for some reason."

"Phillipe sounds like a smart man. I look forward to meeting him someday."

"Really?"

"Sure. But I'm right in the middle of things, so I'm gonna jump. Safe sailing. I miss you," he said.

"I miss you too. *Au revoir*," which sounded like oh-rev-where.

Tyler hung up the phone, glad to have one concern lifted, at least for the moment. Imasu was a threat that wasn't going away. And Tyler couldn't have Imasu's goons shadowing his every move. He needed to be more careful. It was important to try and stay out in front of a guy like Imasu. Standing at his dining room table, Tyler spread out the National Gallery museum blueprints he'd picked up at the hall of records, as well as the photos he had taken and developed at a 1-Hour Photo booth at the Courthouse building in Washington, DC. He'd taken two rolls of exterior shots, plus a single roll of interiors that had turned out reasonably well, considering he'd had to hide the camera under his jacket. Studying the blueprints and the photos, he realized the outside of the building was a thief's dream. There was plenty of room to move around the exterior, lots of trees and shrubs. Plenty of running room for emergencies. Not many hiding places, but then a job like this required "grab and go" with no room for hiding.

Rule #4 in the Thieves Handbook: *Stay in motion.*

This job would require constant motion from the minute he started till he had turned over the paintings. No stopping, no resting. Just fucking pass GO, collect the money, and hope you don't get killed on either end of the deal.

Tyler had less than a month until the exhibition opened and he would need certain items for the job; but the most important thing would be to get into great physical shape. This job would mean being "on" for a full twenty-four hours, which would require large quantities of stamina. He laced up his running shoes and headed out the door. He ran towards the East River, headed uptown till he hit the Roosevelt Tram, then looped back and headed home. Back in his apartment he immediately started in with the sit-ups. Tyler remembered reading that Hershel Walker, the near-great running back, used to do a thousand sit-ups a day! He figured that should be his goal. Today, one hundred and fifty.

He stretched, showered, and studied the blueprints some more. He considered all possibilities for entry. After several hours of "mentally" getting in and out of the National Gallery, he was ready for a break. Tyler hunted in his wallet for Lucy Phillips's number. He hesitated but then dialed.

"She's not in right now, would you like her voicemail?" asked the woman who answered.

"Sure, that would be fine," he said. He left a brief message and his number.

Nothing ventured. Nothing gained.

He decided to get some fresh air and when he hit the streets, the electrical surge that New York can provide hit him full on. He loved that feeling. He dropped down to 14th Street to watch the sidewalk mob veering hither and yon. The never-ending hustle that only New York can perpetuate. Tyler stopped at the corner of Eighth Avenue and grabbed a slice from *THE* Famous Ray's. He headed south to Chelsea, the latest in New York's renovated and gentrified neighborhoods. Ten years ago it was filled with bodegas and fronts for betting parlors. Now it was all cleaned up with stylish designer boutiques and chic bistros, where the menus sat out in front on gilded pedestals for browsers to ooh and ahh over. And the streets off Ninth Avenue were loaded with spit-and-polish townhouses, now suddenly worth a cool couple mill or more. He zigzagged through the lower Village and SoHo, and made his way to the Art Bar.

It was midafternoon, and all but the true believers had gone back to work. When Tyler walked in, Tommy flashed him a quick smile from behind the bar. Maggie was also working, and gave him a quick kiss as she glided past with a tray full of empties. As Tyler sat at the bar, Tommy began to draw him a beer. Maggie asked if he wanted anything from the kitchen. Tyler mentioned a bowl of corn chowder, if there was any left, please.

Tommy placed the pint in front of him, on top of an Art Bar coaster, with a picture of the Mona Lisa on it. All class.

"Thanks Tommy. Max around?"

"Yeah. He's in the back counting his money."

Max, the owner, liked to come in almost every day just to see the fresh cash that rolled in daily.

"Tommy, you skim your 10% off the top before he got his hands on it?" Tyler joked.

"Of course. How else could I pay for my lavish lifestyle?"

They laughed.

"How's law school?" Tyler asked.

"You mean the Future Thieves Trade School? It's okay."

"Lot of work?"

"You know, the work after the first year isn't really that difficult. But the other students take themselves sooo seriously."

"So you see a difficult transition from comedic stand-up bartender to legal eagle?"

"Brutal. Worse than going from single to married."

"Ouch."

"How is your wife?" Tyler asked.

"Hasn't thrown me out."

"An angel sent to keep an eye on the devil."

Tommy laughed, and called Max back in his office, to let him know Tyler was here.

Maggie brought Tyler a bowl of corn chowder with some French bread, fresh from the oven.

"Where've you been?" she asked as she set the bowl on the bar.

"I had family stuff to deal with," he said. She raised an eyebrow, which was her way of asking whether or not he was telling the truth.

"Scout's honor." Tyler put his hand on his heart.

"I just want to make sure you're okay. My mothering instincts. How long are you here for? You working any shifts?"

"Not immediately. I just came by to see Max, and of course your beautiful smile," Tyler said.

Maggie chuckled.

"Talk like that will get you in trouble."

"One can dream," he said, as she went to check on customers at the Cézanne booth.

"Max said to go away and stop bothering the help." Tommy said.

"Ever the compassionate boss," Tyler said. "Anything else?"

"Yeah, he said to tell you that lunch isn't free," Tommy said. They both laughed at this.

"He must be going over last night's receipts. I love when he's in a good mood." Tommy was sloshing the glasses around under the bar as he pretended to clean them. Everyone figured the alcohol killed the germs anyway. He finished with the glasses and was wiping down the bar. "He said to go on back whenever you're done eating."

Tyler nodded, as he downed his beer. He slid off the barstool and caught a glimpse of Maggie in the mirror. He smiled. Tommy was waving a wine bottle at Tyler, which captured his attention again.

"Max asked me to give you this, to take back to him. It's a new Australian Shiraz the sales rep wants him to try," Tommy said.

"Lucky me." Tyler took the bottle from Tommy in an Olympic relay baton backhand handoff, and headed towards the back.

Max's office was about the size of two broom closets. There was no desk. Instead, it contained a small round table that six people could squeeze around for either wine tastings (when the reps showed up), or for Max's Tuesday night poker game. Tyler had been to both, and definitely preferred the tastings. There were two adding machines (why two, no one could figure out, nor would they dare ask, given Max's oddities), and a half dozen small pocket calculators that the staff used when things got hectic. A pile of white industrial aprons—some clean, some not. There was a metal file cabinet with the requisite TV sitting on top, and assorted magnets stuck to the side of it, which Max had collected in his world travels. He had a fetish for small magnets with thermometers. There was one from Norway featuring a reindeer and a troll, and of course the staff favorite, the one from Hawaii with the moving hula dancer. The walls were adorned with framed posters of different vineyards or wine festivals. Tyler's favorite was from Willi's Wine Bar in Paris, with a Picasso-like couple drinking wine from strangely shaped goblets.

And squeezed into the middle of this chaos was Max himself. He was of medium height and build, and his stomach was starting to paunch and veer south, having passed the half-century mark. He still had his hair, or most of it. It was turning more silver gray by the day, and was always neatly combed. A habit from his Wall Street days. Twice married, twice divorced. Number two had managed to fleece him, during both the marriage and the divorce.

At least she was consistent.

The result: Max had resigned as managing partner at a powerful Wall Street banking firm. Wife #2 had demanded a piece of his partnership, as well as future earnings. So rather than give in to her greed he simply walked away, closer to broke than he had been since college. He worked here and there, and then finally convinced a few friends to float him a loan to open the bar. A few years later, his parents died together in a freak accident. With the insurance money, Max paid off his partners in the bar and bought himself a forty-foot, forty-year-old wooden sailboat, on which he lived at the 79th Street boat basin.

Rule #17 in the Thieves Handbook: *KISS. Keep It Simple Stupid.*

Tyler stood in the doorway, observing the bar owner, his sometime employer and full-time friend, in his element. Max was on the phone listening, while picking at a half-eaten Italian sub from Anthony's deli as he counted last night's tally. He'd count it twice and if it all jibed, 80% would go to the bank in the canvas night deposit bag with the keylock. The other 20% would go into the floor safe that was under the table and the fake Persian rug. Those funds were strictly personal and off the books. It was used for vacations, emergencies, bail, employee parties (every couple of months Max would take everyone out for the night), and never-ending boat repairs.

Max tossed Tyler a corkscrew and motioned for him to open the bottle of wine. He abruptly hung up the phone.

"Problems?"

"Nothing that can't be solved by hanging up the phone," Max replied, in his staccato Brooklynese. "What's up? I haven't seen you for a few days. You alright?" Max motioned to the empty chair. "Sit."

"Yeah, I'm fine—" Tyler poured out two glasses of wine.

"You need money?"

Tyler handed a glass to Max. "No. I—"

"You in trouble?"

"Max, stop," Tyler implored with a smile. "I'm not in trouble, I don't need money and everything's good. Really. A job came up. Don't ask."

Max said nothing, and raised his glass. They clinked glasses.

Max took a slug of wine. He was definitely not a sipper. Tyler took a sip.

Max scrutinized Tyler, knowing he hadn't come clean, but also knowing he wouldn't. "And?"

"And nothing," Tyler shrugged. "I just need to take some time. I've got to sort a few things out, Max. I'll be away maybe a month, maybe more."

One of Max's eyebrows arched up as he guzzled more wine. "So what do you need from me?" He wondered out loud.

"Well there is one thing. Cover for me, if and when my parole officer calls."

"No sweat," he said. "You're making deliveries for me."

Tyler nodded as he finished his wine.

"Max, you know the deal with my brother, right?"

"Of course."

"I'm on my way out to see him and hopefully get him resettled in a better place, and I may need you to make sure the payments get made. I'll have some funds wired—"

"Ty, don't insult me. I'll cover it until I hear from you."

"But I can give—"

"Enough. I'll cover whatever is necessary. Do not worry about your brother. I'll make sure everything's covered."

Max had a strong fatherly nature and Tyler knew he could be trusted to cover for him. Max was of good stock. Tyler also knew the wheels were spinning in Max's brain.

"Here's some money." Max stuffed a thick roll of twenties from the pile headed into the floor safe, into Tyler's shirt pocket.

"Thanks, but I don't—"

But Max was Max, which meant he'd protect his young to a fault.

"Take it, and don't you tell a soul I gave you that. Otherwise they'll all be in here begging," he said, reverting back to the gruff Max they all knew and loved.

"You coming back?"

"I hope so," Tyler said. "I really hope so."

Max smiled and shook Tyler's hand.

As he exited by the back door and cruised down the alley, Tyler scanned for watchers. No Japanese gangsters in sight. He had a to-do list and people to see, but he figured a quick stop at The Guggenheim SoHo offices, a surprise visit to Lucy Phillips, was first on his list. There was something about Lucy that kept pulling on him, in a good way. The prison daydreams maybe? Or maybe it was simply the fact that she kept saying "No." The allure of the hunt? And then there was Paris. He couldn't shake those memories from his mind.

After stopping at the flower market on the corner to pick up something nice, he went straight to her office. He pushed through the front door and headed towards her office. He knocked. No answer. He tried again. Same silence. Finally her assistant came over and told him that Lucy was uptown at a meeting. She should be back after lunch. Did he want to wait? He realized he had too much to accomplish in too short a time. Waiting wasn't an option.

He left the flowers with a quote from Keats.

Beauty is truth,

Truth beauty.

SIXTEEN

Tyler was on the #6 subway train heading uptown to 135th Street, on the East Side. Spanish Harlem. He was on his way to see Ricardo Alvarez, weapons expert, professional hit man, and sometime Robin Hood.

To the Hispanic gang in the joint, Alvarez was godlike. One of the younger inmates Tyler had worked with at the prison library, a godson of Ricardo's, spoke of his legendary status. It was always helpful to have a prison referral, especially when you're going to see a professional killer.

Ricardo was older than Tyler and had survived far worse, by a factor of ten. He enlisted as a sixteen-year-old. The draft board told him he could get citizenship if he joined up. With the eyesight of an eagle he excelled at marksmanship, but he had little tolerance for chain of command. They sent him to Ranger school, then the Green Berets. By the time he was nineteen the US Army had created one of the most-ruthless professional killers the US government had ever known. He was shipped to Kuwait and reached legendary status on both sides in Desert Storm, not only for his ability as a sniper but also for his ability to slide in and out of areas totally undetected. The US government used him for the occasional hit requested by the CIA. Ricardo had kept copious notes and recordings of all these illicit activities—names, places, targets, everything. He had two sets of notes, one that he kept in a safe deposit box, the other he kept at his lawyer's office in case something "unexpected" happened to him. Once the US government realized this, they decided to cut him loose.

A natural outgrowth of his professional activities was an expertise in weaponry. Tyler changed subway lines four times and took two cabs in case he was being followed. Finally, he arrived at Park and 135th, a section of Park Avenue that was, shall we say, unique. After a pat-down just inside the bodega he was escorted to the inner sanctum, an office in the back of the store. Tyler recognized Ricardo immediately from the photo he'd seen in prison.

The first thing that caught his eye was the fact that Ricardo was no taller than five-seven. Powerfully built, with monster forearms and the close-cropped hair that is standard issue for lots of ex-military, he looked like an Hispanic Popeye. He was surrounded by a phalanx of associates who were eyeing Tyler with mistrust. But when Ricardo smiled and welcomed Tyler with a bear hug, the tension in the room eased.

"So you're the one that helped my Jorge." He said it more as a statement than a question.

"I got him a job in the joint library. No big deal."

"That, and you stopped him from getting eaten alive by the gangs."

"Jorge's a good kid who's a lot smarter than he thinks. He just needed encouragement," Tyler said. "And he never stopped talking about you."

"He's my favorite godson."

"He might have mentioned it," Tyler said as Ricardo beamed, thinking of his incarcerated godson.

"I was so angry at him for his stupidity at getting caught. There was no excuse."

"We all make mistakes. Especially when we're young."

"Did you not learn from your mistakes?" Ricardo asked Tyler.

This was not a crowd where a snappy retort would be appreciated so Tyler gave his response some thought. "My error was in trusting others," Tyler said.

"Always creates problems," Ricardo said.

"Be prepared," Tyler countered.

"Surely you didn't come here today to discuss Boy Scout philosophy, so how can I be of service?"

"I need two things. The first is a weapon."

Ricardo leaned forward. "I thought you art thieves never carried."

He had Tyler dead to rights. Except for the buffoons who did the Gardner Museum job in Boston, it was common knowledge both with crooks and cops that art thieves almost never used weapons.

Rule #62 in the Thieves Handbook: *If you get caught, don't be carrying.*

"I need a special kind of weapon. I'm not going to use it to shoot at someone."

Ricardo had a curious look on his face.

"I'm going to shoot a building."

This piqued everyone's attention as they gathered around the table, while Tyler unrolled the drawings he'd brought. What they saw were pieces of what looked like a crossbow. A crossbow on steroids. Numbers, and notes written down the edges of the pages. Draw weight, power stroke, titanium stock and shafts, velocity....

The final page had a drawing of what was supposed to be an arrow, but looked more like a mini-rocket with ceramic feathers.

Ricardo studied the different pages, made a few notes of his own and then looked up with an astonished look on his face.

"You planning on hitting Fort Knox with a bow and arrow?"

Tyler just smiled.

Fortunately, a man of Ricardo's background understood and appreciated silence. He looked at Tyler. "And the second thing?"

Tyler paused momentarily, as he realized the room had gone silent. "Well, I need to hire you."

Ricardo stared at him steadily, waiting for Tyler to finish.

"I need to hire you to *not* kill me, and to make sure no one else does," Tyler said quietly.

Ricardo just looked at him and laughed, as did everyone in the room. Even Tyler smiled, but more out of nervousness.

"Señor Sears you have nothing to fear from me."

"I just thought it wouldn't hurt to have an insurance policy against—"

Ricardo cut him off.

"You have proven your loyalty to my family as I will prove mine to you, and yours. I will ensure that you are safe. Do you have any other family members you feel could benefit from my services?"

Ricardo said something in Spanish and one of his cohorts tossed him a pad of paper and a pen. Tyler wrote down his brother's name and address, and then his mom's info. He figured Pepé Le Pew wasn't the brave and courageous type.

"I can't thank you enough."

"It would be insulting to do anything less."

Tyler felt enormous relief.

They worked out the details of his custom-made crossbow and Ricardo told him he'd call him within the week. As Tyler was leaving he noticed Warhol's *Muhammad Ali*. The gentle fury of Ali perfectly captured in Warhol's vibrant blend of colors.

"The real deal?" Tyler asked.

Ricardo just smiled.

Ricardo gave Tyler another hug and told him to stay safe. "Who am I keeping you safe from?"

Tyler whispered the name to Ricardo.

After Tyler left, Ricardo just shook his head and said, "*Dio mio.*"

SEVENTEEN

The next morning Tyler's phone rang. He was reading over the blueprints and factoring some time sequences. It kept ringing, finally he picked up.

"Tyler?" said the voice on the other end.

He was too distracted to recognize the voice.

"What?" he said distractedly.

"Tyler, it's me Lucy," she said.

"Lucy, sorry, I was reading something," he said as he turned away from the blueprints.

"The flowers are lovely."

He paused, not sure what to say next.

"The governor has commuted my sentence from death row to life imprisonment, but I'm allowed one final meal before I go to the slammer. And I was wondering if you'd have dinner with me."

There was silence from the other end, a good sign. It meant she was thinking.

"It sounds like the governor's a big softy," she finally said.

"How about tonight?" he asked.

"Hold on." He could hear her turning pages in a calendar book.

"Tonight works," she replied, "but as dinner didn't work out so well last time, how about something different?"

"Like what?"

"Surprise me."

Tyler put the phone against his leg and mouthed "YES!" while doing a fist pump with his free hand.

EIGHTEEN

He called Maggie to see if she had time for a coffee. Maggie was a lot of things to Tyler, but most important, she was one of his best friends. And he needed to talk to someone and Maggie was a great listener. They met at a small tea house near NYU. She knew from the minute she saw him walking down the street that something positive was up, and with Tyler that usually meant a woman.

Tyler told Maggie about Lucy and Paris, how it caught him off guard, and then seeing her again three years later at the art soiree. She asked a few questions. He blurted out his answers in his excitable state.

Finally, after listening to him blather on, she said, "Ty, it sounds like she could be the one, so don't screw it up."

"And how do I do that, or not do it?"

"All any woman really wants is honesty. Do NOT lie, under any circumstances. Almost all relationships head south as soon as Mr. Right starts telling lies. And turns into Mr. Wrong."

Tyler nodded.

Maggie stirred some honey in her tea, put the spoon on the edge of the saucer and said, "And the other thing is, don't come on too strong."

"What do you mean?"

"There's a fine line between being really interested, and being a stalker," she said.

Tyler laughed at this, pondering the difference.

"Make sure she knows you're interested, but give her the room to catch her breath," Maggie said.

Tyler was paying close attention to the teacher.

"And Ty, remember, we girls love romance." She pointed her spoon at him for emphasis.

Tyler smiled, savoring how lucky he was to have someone like Maggie in his life. Someone to set him straight. Light the path. The person to help keep his compass pointed to true north. She worried about him as she watched him in his adolescent enthusiasm. Maggie knew not to ask Tyler what he was up to, or where he was headed. She wanted to reach out and hold onto him. Not let him cross the line again.

"How's your brother doing?" she asked.

"He's okay, not great. I'm going out to see him soon. I'm moving him to a better place in the hills outside of Santa Fe. It's got views of the Sangre de Cristo range, and the Rio Grande. A place that will put him to work, not just leave him drooling out on the lawn," Tyler said.

"That'd be a great change for him," she said.

"It's much more integrated. More like a real community than a 'clinic,'" Tyler said, making quote marks with his fingers for emphasis.

"They do a lot of work with horses, gardening, and woodworking. It's time he actually learned a trade or at least something productive. I can't, and won't sit by and watch him turn into a middle-aged veggie. He's too valuable a human to just have life pass him by."

Maggie watched as Tyler's eyes welled up.

Telling Maggie made him realize how crucial it was to help his brother get on with his life. Telling her out loud crystallized it for him. It was the right thing to do. He'd leave as soon as he could, and get things right with his brother.

Maggie knew the situation with Tyler's brother all too well. She knew how devastating and consuming it had been for Tyler. There was a stillness between them. She reached across the table and squeezed his hand.

"You told me to be honest," Tyler said with a smile, trying to lighten the mood.

Maggie laughed lightly as she wiped a tear from her cheek with the back of her hand. As they stood up to part ways, Maggie gave him a hug. "God damn it Tyler Sears, be careful," she whispered.

"I will—" he started to say but she cut him off.

"Shush…. I love you Ty."

She held him tight and then finally broke the embrace.

"No worries." He kissed her on the forehead and walked away smiling.

It was the last time he would ever see her.

NINETEEN

Tyler punched in a number on his phone. It was Mikey G, his former cellmate at Camp Fed. Mikey G had been busted for computer crimes after breaking into the Pentagon's mainframe system. The Defense Department was less than thrilled. He was a certified math genius with a PhD from MIT. Tyler was hoping Mikey G would be able to help solve some of his technical problems with the heist. The problem was, he couldn't give Mikey G any real specifics. Nebulous at best.

"Hey, Mikey G. How goes it?"

"Aww, crazy, fucking crazy dude."

"I need your advice on a couple of things. Can we meet today or tomorrow?"

"Gotta be today dude, tomorrow may never come."

Tyler ignored the comment and wrote down his former cellmate's current address.

"Hey Ty, you know what Sir Isaac always said?"

"What?"

"The apple doesn't fall far from the tree," Mikey cackled in the background.

"Funny Mikey. I'll see you in a couple hours."

Tyler zipped open his pillowcase that was stuffed with hundred dollar bills, from the cash that Imasu had given him. Some people slept with a gun under their pillow, Tyler preferred to sleep resting his head on his money. Hundred dollar bills were almost as comfortable as goose down. And a lot more fun. He put the cash in a beat-up bike-messenger bag, repaired with copious amounts of duct tape, and headed out the door.

He took the subway up to Grand Central, hiked over to York Avenue, and at 60th Street he jumped in a cab and told the driver to take a zigzag route to the corner of Third Avenue and 86th Street. He told the driver to make sure no one was following them.

Handing the cabbie a hefty tip, Tyler walked across the street to Papaya King. He chowed down two dogs with mustard, and bought a papaya to go. He walked the rest of the way to 88th Street to Tony's TV Repair. The old guy in the front of the store took one look at Tyler and motioned towards the back.

Tyler walked through the doorway and entered what looked like Bill Gates's playroom. There were computers buzzing and giant screens showed everything from streaming data to women's mud wrestling in Bangkok. The place was totally dark. No outside light. The windows were covered with giant black trash bags.

"Hey, Mikey," Tyler said.

No response. Tyler tried again, amping up the volume.

A pair of headphones went flying and Mikey G jumped up like he'd been zapped by a taser. Mikey G was in his late twenties but looked closer to forty. Doughy skin, unwashed hair, and a belly that bragged Papa Gino's 2-for-1 special. The family-sized plastic bottles of half-drunk Diet Cherry Coke strewn around the place only added to the ambience.

"Hey Ty. Wow. How are you man?" Mikey said as he guzzled from one of the half-drunk cola bottles.

"I'm good. How 'bout you? What are you doing?" Tyler nodded at the screens.

"Oh, this," Mikey said pointing to a monitor. "Remember that mob guy at Lewisburg who got caught laundering money?"

"Yeah, kinda, not really," Tyler said.

"Well, I've created a program for him so he won't get caught next time."

Tyler was speechless, feeling sure that Mikey was probably on his way back to Club Fed, sooner than he expected.

"I need your help with some surveillance—" Tyler said but was cut off by Mikey.

"Internal? External?"

"Both. To monitor and override current system—"

"Weather conditions?"

"Current. Nighttime. For the next month—"

"Urban or rural?"

"Urban, but with open spaces—"

"Internal high security?"

"Not exactly. More cautious security."

Mikey G is furiously typing as Tyler answers his rapid-fire questions. "Main system on-site or off-site with third-party monitoring?"

Tyler thinks for a second. "Everything's on-site, but new system requires off-site—"

"Distance?"

"Couple hundred yards at most."

"We'll say quarter mile. Just video?"

"No. Thermo, weight, plus multiple hidden cams. And is it possible to get the two systems coordinated without the main system knowing the other one's there?"

Mikey looked at Tyler and just grinned.

"How soon?" Mikey asked.

Tyler thought about this for a moment. "Two weeks max."

Mikey G stopped typing and took another hit of cola. "Cash?"

"Why Mikey, you offering a cellmate discount?"

Mikey G snorted the cola through his nose. They both laughed.

"I'll have to create a special software program, and I'll provide you with all the hardware bits you'll need."

"How much?" Tyler asked.

"Fifty large. Half now, other half on delivery."

Tyler opened his messenger bag and took out $50,000 and laid it on the table next to Mikey. Mikey looked at it, looked up at Tyler, and smiled.

"Trusting."

"Always."

TWENTY

"Hey gorgeous," Tyler said into his phone.

Lucy smiled at the compliment.

"Busy day?" he asked

"No. The usual. Big egos bossing smaller egos around."

"Are you one of the big egos or one of the small ones?"

"Mmm, midsized ego. Besides women don't ever boss people. We just make friendly suggestions."

"Oh, that's what it is."

She laughed.

"Listen, I'd love to chat but I need to get back to work—"

"Wait, wait, wait," Tyler said quickly. "I wanted to ask how big a surprise?"

"Depends?"

"Well, it's a fun surprise," he said. "I'll pick you up at six. Your office."

"Don't be late."

"Very funny," Tyler said.

"Gotta run. The boss just walked in." And she hung up. Tyler couldn't stop smiling, even though his instincts were telling him to beware.

Rule #2 in the Thieves Handbook: *Never, ever fall in love in the middle of a job.*

TWENTY-ONE

Tyler decided a long, easy run along the East River would give him a chance to clear his head. And to sort through all the information he'd absorbed in the last week. The chilled air warmed quickly in his lungs as his legs pumped. The early beads of sweat at his temples told him his body was falling into its natural rhythms. The wind started to pick up the closer he got to the river. The aroma from the street vendors wafted along with the breeze. His breathing started to calm. Indian summer was putting up a good fight, but losing. Ten minutes in and his breathing became regulated, sliding into a slower, more natural rhythm. The edginess he was feeling faded as his heart pumped fresh oxygenated blood to his brain.

Each cycling of his legs brought more clarity of thought. By mile three he began to "see" the job exactly how it would happen, when, and how crucial the timing would be. As he left the United Nations Plaza behind him, everything was crystal clear. The pieces fell into place. He could see the job from start to finish. It would work. He would make it work. The alternative was not a possibility. Getting the job done was the easy part. Keeping Imasu and his men at arm's length would be the tricky part. He'd need to come up with two plans, the one he'd execute and then the one he'd sell to Imasu. A plan that would keep Imasu's boys busy long enough for Tyler to carry out the actual plan. Parallel plans, which hopefully never intersected. It was the only hope Tyler had of pulling off this insane heist, and getting out alive. Tyler's breath was calming even further as he visualized the actual heist. He was moving on automatic and at Stuyvesant Town he took the cut-through behind the Beth Israel Medical buildings. He didn't even notice the two runners on either side of him. His peripheral vision kicked in. He looked right then left. Imasu's men were running along beside him, one on each side. They didn't smile, neither did he. Tyler's brain zoomed back to reality. He did a reverse loop through the medical complex. His uninvited running companions kept pace. Tyler checked his heart rate monitor. Just ticking at 55%. Plenty of room. He picked up the pace. They matched his increase. Two blocks later he stepped it up another notch. He was now at 75% on his heart rate monitor. He stopped suddenly, turned and sprinted back towards Beth Israel Medical Complex. His running un-buddies were right behind him and catching up. He jammed on the brakes again, and then took off as fast as he could. A quick check of his heart rate monitor, he was nearing 85%. His legs were pumping hard. His brain, and all his nerve endings got a quick infusion of adrenaline. Fear will do that to the human body. He accelerated. They were no longer right next to him. One of them had stopped and was reaching for his cell phone. The other one was about ten yards behind and losing ground. Pure fear kicked in and Tyler accelerated faster than he thought possible. He kept up the pace for four more blocks, and took a sharp left at the next street and just bolted. His heart was pumping faster than Phar Lap's. At the next intersection he took a sharp right, ran halfway up the block, looked over his shoulder, saw no one in pursuit and ducked into an Irish tavern. He stood at the far end of the bar, trying to stay out of sight. He was breathing so heavily it seemed a heart attack was imminent. He was drenched in a combination of sweat and fear. Tyler checked his heart rate monitor. It was reading 145% of his target heart rate. He carefully bent over and tried to slow his breathing. The lone waitress left a pitcher of water and a glass next to him on the bar. His breathing was under control quicker than he imagined—a good thing. He had lost Imasu's men, this time, but they were still watching him—a bad thing.

Imasu was looming as menacing as ever.

TWENTY-TWO

Tyler's heart rate had finally slowed enough that his adrenaline was dissipating and he was feeling calmer. Calm was crucial, anything less made for a bad mental state when planning a heist. Nerves, and distractions like his new running buddies made him jumpy. And jumpy was how mistakes happened. He had to get Imasu to stand down. He decided a call to Imasu was needed.

"Hello, Tyler Sears for Imasu-san, please."

"So sorry. Imasu-san in meeting all day."

"Would you let him know it's Tyler Sears. I just need a quick word with him. Thanks."

"I check. You wait."

The wait was less than a minute.

"Imasu-san asked not be disturbed. He ask me to take message."

Tyler decided against slamming the phone down.

"A message? Sure I'll leave a message. Tell him to call off the dogs."

"So sorry, I don't understand."

"Tell. Him. To. Call. Off. The. DOGS! Please," Tyler said without sounding too angry.

"Okay. Bye, bye."

He realized he had to figure out a way to let Imasu know that his goons were only going to make things more difficult, for both of them. Tyler wasn't planning some B&E job, where a couple of trained thugs could power their way through the heist. This wasn't a redux of the Isabella Stewart Gardner amateur hour. This job required the deft touch of a Dr. George Jallo, not the raw power of a Mike Tyson. And he still hadn't concocted an alternative plan for the heist, the one he was going to sell to Imasu and his Yakuza pals.

He put the phone down and quickly unrolled the blueprints of the National Gallery. He flipped the pages to the systems' schematic drawing and looked at it carefully. There must be a simpler way that would make sense to Imasu, and seem plausible as well. He followed each of the internal systems with his finger trying to find a connection between the gallery the paintings would be hanging in and the rest of the museum. He turned the page over to the basement drawings and stared at them. He laid the pages on top of each other and pressed down so the two sets of drawings were lying on top of each other. As he pressed firmly it suddenly materialized. There it was, literally in black and white. It was so obvious he was surprised he hadn't seen it sooner. It was crude and primitive but to Imasu and his boys it would sound logical and most importantly doable. He was banking on the fact that neither Imasu nor his yes-men were professional art thieves. He would explain it so that it would make perfect sense. It would also give them things to do in preparation so they'd be preoccupied while he was performing the real heist. Tyler smiled as he rolled up the drawings and stuck them back in the tube, and put that in the back of his closet. He felt as if he had just moved the pieces on the chessboard without Imasu knowing. Check was still a few moves off, and a couple of weeks away, but for the first time he felt like it was his game now.

He hoped.

TWENTY-THREE

At two minutes to six Tyler was standing at Lucy's office door. The minute he saw her his thoughts of sprinting for his life, from Imasu, drifted away, and with it Tyler's survival radar. Instead he just stared at her.

Without turning around she said, "I'll just be a sec," as she shut down her computer. She was wearing a pair of leopard print pants and a soft black sweater. Her hair was hanging loose.

"Wow. You look great," said Tyler.

Lucy smiled. She walked up to him and gave him a kiss on the cheek. "Don't sound so surprised. Let's go."

"Any chance we might skip the surprise and head straight to dessert?" he asked with a hopeful laugh.

She raised an eyebrow.

"Later, if you're good."

"I promise to be on my best behavior."

"We'll see," she said as they headed out the door.

On the street, Tyler took a quick glance around, looking for any remnants of Imasu's hired goons. Nothing. He grabbed her hand and flagged down a cab. They got out at Eighth Avenue and 23rd Street, home of the Sky Rink, an indoor skating rink with views westward across the Hudson.

The lift was packed with preteen girls and their mothers on their way to an early-evening birthday party.

Lucy flashed Tyler a big grin.

"That was me twenty years ago."

"You've done this before?" Tyler asked.

"Once or twice."

Tyler rented two sets of skates and they hit the ice. He was confident on skates, thanks to his high school hockey days.

"You're pretty good," Lucy observed.

"Misspent youth," he said as he let go of her hand, turned, and skated backwards. She reached for his hand.

"It's just like riding a bike. Give it a try," he said as he let go of her hand.

She smiled and glided away from him, picking up speed. Lucy glided around the ice like she'd been skating all her life. After several go-arounds, she made a little leap in the air and didn't just land it, but managed to then skate backwards and forwards. Tyler caught up to her as she then did a near-perfect spread eagle 360-degree turn around him and fell into him.

"You have done this before! You played me."

Lucy gave him a wink.

"Now look what you've done?" he said pointing to the girls' party.

Lucy looked over to see the young girls glued to the railing staring at her. They applauded with their mittens on as Lucy did a slight curtsey.

"Come on, buy me a hot chocolate," Lucy puffed, out of breath.

Skates off and sitting at the cafe, they sipped hot cocoa with marshmallows.

"In Boise, my Mom used to take me to the neighborhood rink for lessons. I got good enough to compete in some local competitions."

"I forgot you told me about growing up in Boise when we were in Paris."

Lucy smirked and said, "Discussing one's family doesn't usually happen when naked."

Tyler grinned as his mind floated back to their whirlwind romance in Paris. She had a serious look.

"What?" he asked.

She waited before saying, "Well… what did happen in Paris? I know it was just supposed to be a fling, but what happened to you?"

Tyler flashed on Paris. Then he flashed on Maggie reminding him to be honest. He can't tell Lucy the truth. Not yet anyway.

"First of all it was more than just a fling, at least for me."

Lucy stopped drinking her cocoa and stared at him. A jolt of passion hit her. It was definitely more than a fling for her. Tyler had stopped talking.

"Really?" she asked.

"Well, yeah. I don't know about you, but I was falling pretty fast and hard for—"

Tyler suddenly noticed two of Imasu's men sitting down, four tables over. They were looking directly at him, taking pictures of him and Lucy. Lucy wanted him to finish his thought, the sentence….

"I'll be right back," Tyler said.

He grabbed their skates, and walked over to the balding, heavyset guy working the counter.

"Excuse me, is there security for this building?" Tyler asked as he handed the guy the two pairs of skates.

"Yeah, a couple of guys that roam the building, and one of the guy's sister is a cop. Why? Something wrong?"

"Those two guys over there," Tyler said, motioning with his head toward Imasu's men. "They've been taking pictures of those little girls at the birthday party. And they don't seem dressed for skating. I just thought someone should know.

The counter guy gave the two men a long look. He spotted the camera that one of them was holding. "Jesus, you're right. Fuckin' pervs, that's disgusting." He said as he grabbed the phone.

"Hey, it's me Larry.... Yeah, at the rink. I think I've got a couple of pervs watching little girls skate and taking pictures." He turned to Tyler.

"Thanks. You did a good thing."

Tyler smiled as he walked away.

"What were you and the skate guy going on about?" Lucy asked.

"He wanted to know if you were a former pro skater."

"Liar," she said.

"I told him you were the Luxemburg national junior champ but you gave it all up when you met me."

Lucy smiled.

"Now, Paris, you were saying?"

Tyler was about to say something when two cops entered with security guys. Larry, behind the counter, pointed at Imasu's men sitting near Tyler and Lucy.

"Hey, the police just walked in. They're not after you, are they?" Lucy asked jokingly.

Tyler turned to watch. "Not unless they found out about all my unpaid parking tickets. You hungry?"

"Famished."

"Let's go. I've got a great place in mind."

When they got up to leave, Imasu's men rose from their seats. The two uniformed cops were on them quickly. A scuffle ensued, some loud words, both English and Japanese, were exchanged. Quickly, handcuffs appeared and Imasu's men were taken away. Tyler noticed one of the uniformed cops pocketing the camera.

"I wonder what that was all about?" Lucy asked as the elevator door closed.

Outside they hailed a cab.

"Lex and 83rd, and through the park, please," he told the driver.

"Upper East Side?" said Lucy. "I'm not dressed for someplace swanky."

"Only the best," Tyler grinned. He looked out the back window to see Imasu's men, cuffed, being forced into the back of a patrol car.

Tyler and Lucy made small talk as the taxi headed up Sixth Avenue. Tyler admitted to the occasional opera, and she told him about her weakness for Steven Seagal movies. He told her Caravaggio was his favorite artist. Lucy talked about wandering the ruins of Pompeii and Tarquinia.

As the cab bounded into Central Park, and past Wollman Rink, Lucy reached over and casually took Tyler's hand and interlaced her fingers with his. He could feel the tension slip away as they rode through the park. Lucy told him about the time she'd been in Central Park during a blizzard and how extraordinary it had been, not only the serene beauty of whiteness, but also the deathly quiet that fell over the park. No cars anywhere and only a handful of souls willing to brave the blizzard. The snow-covered trees, statues, and benches. He hoped he'd live long enough to see his next blizzard.

The cabbie dropped them off at Park Avenue and 83rd Street.

They walked the remaining block to Lexington Avenue. Tyler opened the door to a very old and weary-looking luncheonette/diner. An equally old and weary-looking gent stood behind the counter.

"Is this swanky enough for you?" Tyler asked.

"Perfect," said Lucy.

They sat at the counter. There were old photos hanging behind the counter, framing customers from years long past. The same gentleman who was standing behind the counter was in each photo, with a much more rakish look.

"What can I get you two?" the proprietor asked.

Tyler looked at Lucy to see if she knew what she wanted.

"I'd like a ham and cheese, toasted, on wheat,' she replied.

"Lettuce and tomato?"

"No, but some mustard on the side would be great," she said.

The counter man pointed his finger at Tyler, as if to say, "You're up."

"Tuna melt on wheat," said Tyler.

"You love birds want fries with that?" asked the counterman.

They both blushed and then Lucy said, "Sure, why not."

"Whaddya want to drink with those?"

"I'd like a black-and-white soda," said Tyler.

"And I'd like a Broadway soda please."

The counterman turned to prep their orders.

"Wow, Broadway soda, that's a throwback to the thirties. Chocolate ice cream and coffee syrup, right?" asked Tyler.

"No, it's coffee ice cream and chocolate syrup, Mr. Know-It-All," Lucy replied. "This is a great place. I didn't even know it was here."

"My brother and I used to come here when we'd sneak into the city. We'd tell our parents we were going over to a friend's house, and then we'd hop the train to Grand Central and wander around New York. This was the only place where we could afford to eat so we came here a lot. Plus, they've got the best ice cream sodas in town."

"Was the guy behind the counter here when you were a kid?" she chuckled.

"Yeah, same guy. He's older, and it looks like he's put on a few pounds," Tyler said.

Lucy rested her elbows on the counter as she looked around.

"I'd put on a few pounds too if I owned a soda shop."

"He used to scare the bejesus out of me and my brother. But he never threw us out. And sometimes he didn't charge us."

"Think he remembers you?" Lucy asked quietly.

"I doubt it," Tyler said. "I haven't been in here in over twenty years."

"Hey kid, you staying out of trouble?" the old guy asked.

Tyler's eyes widened in amazement.

"Yes sir, I am."

"And how's your brother doing?"

"He's okay," said Tyler.

"Good. Tell him I said hi," said the counterman.

"How've you been?" asked Tyler.

"Same old, except I'm not so fast anymore," he said as he placed the sodas in front of Tyler and Lucy.

"Enjoy."

Tyler and Lucy both nodded.

"Where's your family now?" she asked.

"After Dad died Mom kinda lost her bearings. She got remarried and then divorced all within a year."

"She still live around here?"

"After the husband #2 debacle, she headed to the south of France to do Lord knows what. She's currently on a sailing cruise with Pepé Le Pew."

"She sounds like quite a character."

Tyler nodded.

"She's trying to outrun her expiration date."

"What about your brother? He still in the area?" asked Lucy.

Tyler decided to tell Lucy the complete unvarnished story of his brother Alex. He had to trust her, and hope that his brother's life wouldn't scare her away. He took a breath.

"Alex was the perfect older brother. Star athlete, great grades, easy smile. Every college wanted him, and every girl. I was really envious of him when I was younger. He ended up at Columbia in journalism. After graduation he landed a job at the *New York Times* and was assigned to the Middle East desk. He was the *Times'* youngest-ever Pulitzer winner. He stayed in Palestine and Israel for close to two years, and by the time he returned he was a total basket case. Hospitals full one day, then bombed the next. Young kids limbless due to landmines. Incoming and outgoing missiles were part of daily life. The horrors he witnessed on both sides turned him into a human head-on collision."

"By the time he returned to the States he was heavily medicated and drinking. It broke my dad's heart. Literally. The *Times* cut him loose eventually, and from there he spiraled down with pills and drink."

After a long silence Lucy finally asked, "Where is he now?"

"He's in a clinic out West that has him so medicated all he can do is drool and slur," Tyler said with a bitter taste in his voice.

"Tyler, I'm so sorry," Lucy said as she reached for his hand.

"Thanks, but the days of feeling sorry for him are over. I've decided to get him out of there and get him someplace that'll put him back on his feet. And not just keep him medicated." Tyler's voice was quivering slightly.

Lucy sat quietly, trying to take it all in. She leaned forward and kissed him, and then hugged him, and didn't let go for a while.

"So, naked dessert, my place?" she whispered, trying to break the gloomy mood they had shifted into.

Tyler threw a hundred dollar bill on the counter and they were gone.

As they walked up the stairs to her apartment, Tyler remembered Maggie's second rule: be romantic.

It all fell apart when the door shut and Lucy grabbed him and started unbuttoning his shirt, and then in a moment of frustration just ripped the buttons away. It was then that Tyler picked her up in his arms and carried her down the hallway to her bedroom. Everything after that was a blur of lips, hands and limbs.

They lay next to each other exhausted, trying to gain some sense of consciousness, Tyler stared at the ceiling.

"I thought women liked romance."

"So, romance me," Lucy said, smiling.

TWENTY-FOUR

He awoke to the smell of coffee. Lucy was up, and walking around wearing only Tyler's shirt with a single button done. She brought toast, coffee, and the *New York Times* into the bedroom. He rubbed his eyes, and focused on her.

"Don't take this the wrong way but you look even better without makeup," he said as he sipped his coffee.

"I'll take that as a compliment," she said.

He put out his hand and she took it. He pulled her close.

"You're a great woman Lucy Phillips, with or without makeup, but preferably without clothes," he said as he wrestled her to the bed next to him. He leaned on one elbow and stared at her.

"Remind me, how did you get interested in art?" he asked.

"My first finger-painting masterpiece when I was four. Never looked back."

"You miss Boise?"

"Boise, not really. My family, lots. I'm going out for Thanksgiving." She decided to roll the dice.

"Feel like a trip to Boise? Great food, lotta laughs," she said with a hopeful smile.

Tyler felt like he'd been punched. He'd like nothing more than to spend a holiday surrounded by the warmth of Lucy and her family. A fading wish at best with what his immediate future held.

"What's the matter? You look so serious," she said.

"I need to talk to you."

She said nothing. The worried look on her face said it all.

"Nothing bad. Just some things I have to do." He smiled awkwardly.

"My brother. I'm going out this week to move him from the drool factory to a place that will actually get him back on his feet... I hope." Tyler's eyes started to well up as he talked about Alex out loud. Lucy waited. Tyler took a breath.

"And then I've got this job that will keep me tied up for a while."

"Like a week?"

"No, longer. Maybe a month. Not sure."

"Are you *not* coming back?"

"No. No, just the opposite. I want to come back... for you... I just... I hope you'll wait."

Her smile returned.

"Less than three years right?"

Tyler smiled as he nodded. Lucy swung up and straddled him. She unbuttoned the lone button on her shirt and pulled it open.

"The girls are gonna miss you," she said nodding at her breasts.

Tyler grinned, sat up, grabbed her, and they fell backwards laughing. Life was good... for now.

TWENTY-FIVE

"Sears-san, you have greatly disappointed me."

"Humblest apologies Imasu-san, but it is I who am disappointed." Tyler decided to let that sink in.

Silence.

"You have my money. Surely you don't expect me not to keep tabs on where my money is? I was quite clear, my men were to be involved. And now I'm afraid you owe me for their bail money. That was a foolish stunt you pulled at the rink. You may incur a penalty."

Tyler was seething. He wanted to reach through the phone and throttle the son of a bitch.

"And I was quite clear. I plan the job, your men merely aid in the execution. Besides, those two "gentlemen" were taking pictures of little girls. Most inappropriate behavior. As for a penalty, if you prefer I will happily return your funds and we can go our separate ways." Tyler said, as close to a FUCK YOU as he would dare.

"Sears-san I don't think reneging on our deal is in yours, or your family's best interest." Boom! A sharp left jab. A direct hit.

Tyler absorbed the blow, took a breath and regrouped.

"You threaten my family, well, that will have a most unfortunate outcome for all of you. You stay away from them. Simple? Simple."

Silence, and then some.

Tyler refused to say another word. Imasu was livid at Tyler's threats.

"Sears-san are you headed out of town?" Imasu asked completely avoiding Tyler's threat. Tyler waited before he spoke.

"Yes. For some research."

"And when will you return?"

"In a few days, at which time I will come by your office to discuss the plan I've devised. And yes, your goons are welcome to lend a hand. However, they get caught, they're on their own. I get caught and you come with me. Is that simple enough?"

"Sears-san there's no reason for any hostility. I'm sure we can all work toward a mutually beneficial outcome."

"Swell. I'll see you next week."

Tyler slammed his phone shut, as the taxi he sat in crossed over the Triboro Bridge. He turned and looked back at the looming cityscape.

He jumped on the next available flight to Phoenix. If he was headed for a suicide mission he wanted to make sure his brother was safe, for good. Tyler was mentally exhausted. He shouldn't be getting into pissing matches with someone like Imasu. He should have run like hell after Imasu's first offer. His shoulders sagged at the weight of it all. He made a pledge to himself: this would be the last job. He was thirty-three-years-old and feeling older. As strong as he was becoming physically, he knew he was weakening to the life he'd been leading.

And now there was the Lucy factor. Their time in Paris had been fun, but this time was different. He'd been bit. The virus called love had taken hold of him. Terrible timing, but then maybe his mom was right, love happens when you least expect it. It was time to create a totally new life. Move away, move on, and get Lucy to go with him.

TWENTY-SIX

Continental flight 343 began its descent into Phoenix and the captain's voice pulled Tyler from an unsettling dream. Tyler stared out the window as the plane glided past distant desert hilltops. He realized how mentally exhausted he was.

He walked through the Phoenix airport, taking a moment to appreciate the preponderance of old people, cowboyed up, with big hats and shiny boots, like an old folks' rodeo. He made his way to the car rental desk where he encountered a woman with bigger hair than he'd seen in quite some time. She was so insistent he upgrade to the convertible—her sales pitch so bad it was funny—he couldn't say no. He walked out into the Phoenix sunshine knowing he'd just helped her get that much closer to winning the monthly sales contest. He was thinking how important certain things are to some, and totally irrelevant to others.

With the top down on the Mustang, he headed north out of Phoenix and watched as the landscape shifted from faux green lawns and suburban tracts to what could only be described as a moonscape. A moonscape sprinkled with cacti. When Tyler had last seen his brother, Alex had been a drooling sloth, incapable of complete sentences. Tyler didn't know if it was the drugs, the horrors that invaded his dreams or some combination. It sickened him to remember his brother that way. More important than staying alive was making things right with his brother. If he was headed to an OK Corral shootout with Imasu he was going to make damn sure Alex was safe and in a better place than the drool factory.

An hour later he pulled into the clinic parking lot. Even though he had called the day before to make sure everything was in order they insisted on an exit debrief with Tyler. The man sitting across from Tyler in the Spartan office was Alex's lead "therapist," Dr. Mitchell. The doctor was lightly pockmarked beneath a deep tan. Tyler noticed that his left hand was whiter than his right. A direct result of too much time out on the links.

"Mr. Sears—"

"Please, call me Tyler."

"Tyler, you understand the dangers of taking your brother outside of professional care?"

"As you know I'm planning to take him to the clinic near Santa Fe. I was under the impression you had spoken to the doctor there?"

"Yes. We had a lengthy discussion of your brother's situation."

"But you don't approve of me moving him?"

"I have no problem with that. It's the time in between I'm concerned about."

"You've got him so heavily medicated—" Tyler was about to lash out at the doctor and then pulled back.

"Tyler, you and I live in a world that your brother is no longer familiar with. What you and I accept as daily life—getting up, making breakfast, going to work, the grocery store, basic interactions within normal societal structures—these are all foreign to Alex. You have no idea how he will react once he's exposed to the normalcies of everyday life."

"Doc, I'll have him there in two days' time, tops. I'll be watching him every second."

The doctor leaned forward, opened a folder, and pulled out a series of sheets of paper covered in writing. It was Alex's handwriting, although it looked as if it had been written with his left hand. He handed them to Tyler. Tyler read through what he could. His expression turned ashen.

"These are the notes, letters, scribblings from your brother. I know you think we've done nothing but drug him into a stupor, but the reality is we believe we've saved his life. We shut down the horrible nightmares and we eliminated his constant thoughts of suicide."

Tyler sat and read some of the notes Alex had written. It broke his heart. His eyes welled up. His stomach churned. Alex was screaming for an end to it all.

"Please understand, the medication was used as a tool to pacify your brother. I know you think we turned him into a zombie, but he already was one when he walked through our doors. Our concern all along has been to keep him from harming himself, and as I said to eliminate the horrible nightmares."

"I just want my brother back."

"I know. He will come back, but not as you remember him. He will be a different person. Please be mindful of that when you are with him."

"Doctor, I'm sorry for any anger I've expressed towards you and the clinic, it's just that—"

"No need to apologize. Just take good care of him," the doctor said as he stood up.

They shook hands and Tyler headed back toward the reception area. One of the nurses approached Tyler.

"Mr. Sears, we've put Alex's belongings in your car. He's sitting right over there," she said pointing towards a bench just outside. "Please take care of him. We'll miss him."

He wandered over towards his brother. Alex was staring at the Mustang, and the world beyond. A dog-eared copy of *The Adventures of Tom Sawyer* sat next to Alex. Tyler sat down next to his brother.

"Hey Alex, whaddya say we go for a drive?" Tyler asked him.

"Really... ?"

"Yeah. A road trip. Just the two of us."

"Wow... I donknow... whabout... dinner?"

"Dinner's my treat. Anything you want."

"Really... ?"

After Alex got hugs from the nurses they were in the Mustang convertible driving down the main drive. The doctor that Tyler had just met with was on the phone, watching as they drove away.

"Yes, Mr. Imasu they are just pulling away now."

TWENTY-SEVEN

They drove along a deserted state highway when Alex suddenly stood up in his seat gripping the top of the windshield, taking the wind full on.

Tyler smiled, watching his brother enjoy his freedom.

After his initial burst of energy Alex fell asleep, slumped sideways in his seat and snoring loudly. Tyler managed to angle Alex's seat back, as he drove, so his brother could stretch out. Tyler's phone rang.

Tyler drove for a couple of hours until they reached the entrance to the Grand Canyon. It was late autumn; the park wasn't crowded so Tyler had reserved one of the small cabins on the south rim, just down the path from the main lodge.

He parked and then woke his brother.

"Where... are... we?" asked Alex.

Tyler let his hand rest on his brother's shoulder. "We're at the Grand Canyon."

"Wow...." Alex stood on the car seat and stared out into the Canyon's abyss.

They sat at the small circular table on the cabin's porch, looking out over the vastness. A couple of sandwiches unwrapped on the table, along with two bottles of root beer.

"You feeling better?" Tyler asked, taking a bite out his sandwich.

"Ah... kinda... sleepy, but... okay," Alex said grabbing for a root beer.

Tyler just wanted to enjoy his brother's company, so he kept things simple. He had serious doubts that Alex would ever be back to "normal." He hoped a new Alex would emerge. Not quite as intense, not as "on the edge," but happy. He wanted him to appreciate life again. They ate their sandwiches in silence, enjoying the spectacular landscape in front of them.

"Pretty great view, huh?" Tyler asked.

Alex looked up, dropped his sandwich and just stared out at the reddish hues of the afternoon sunset on the canyon walls.

"You... gotta... girlfriend?" Alex asked.

"Yeah, I met someone. I think she's pretty special. How 'bout you?" Tyler asked.

"Nahh... everyonethere... is... too... fucked up.... I... donlike... gurlz that... drool."

Tyler was both startled and amused at his brother's honesty.

"So... who's... the... lucky girl?"

Tyler proceeded to tell his brother about Lucy. "She's funny, smart, and has an easy way about her."

"Is... she... pretty?"

"Yeah, very pretty," said Tyler.

Alex raised his eyebrows. "You... always... get... theprettyones."

They both laughed at this.

After they finished their sandwiches Tyler decided a walk on one of the hidden paths along the canyon rim might be a good idea. The desert air and light were magical.

"Hey... Ty...."

"Yeah Alex."

"Pretty neat... the... flowers... don't step... on them."

Tyler had never seen such delicate plant life surviving in such a harsh environment. If the most delicate flowers could survive the harsh desert environment, then surely his brother could survive too.

Alex was lying in bed reading *Tom Sawyer*.

"Ty...."

"Yeah?"

"You... remember... Tom and Huck... of Tarrytown?'

A huge emotional wave rolled over Tyler. "Yeah, of course."

"Good... me too," said Alex.

Tyler fell asleep with a smile on his face.

He dreamed of his childhood. Young Alex, already a daredevil, swung out on a rope over the Hudson River, and let go, his last words being, "C'mon Ty, don't be chicken!"

When the rope swung back, young Tyler reached out to grab it. He stood on the edge of the slight embankment, unable to jump, but unable to let go of the rope. Finally, he jumped off the ledge and swung out over the river, which now looked ominous compared to the safety of the embankment. As he swung back he let go only to discover the river was gone, replaced by a dark abyss. The ultimate black hole. The darkness took over his sleep.

TWENTY-EIGHT

The next morning after they packed up the car they headed east toward Flagstaff. Alex fiddled with the radio and poked around in the glove box. Tyler watched as Alex's natural curiosity began to stage a comeback. Alex even looked at the map once or twice after they passed a road sign. The lack of medication was making him slightly edgy but also curious. The landscape went from desert to high alpine.

They stopped in Flagstaff, with its mix of college kids, ex-hippies, outdoor enthusiasts, and the occasional cowpoke. They stopped at La Bellavia, the local breakfast hangout. Alex ordered the koala pancakes with chocolate chips, off the kids menu. Tyler had the chorizo scramble.

"Hey Ty… where we headed?"

"I thought some fly-fishing on the Rio Grande might be nice," Tyler said.

Alex's eyes lit up.

"Really?"

"Gotta try everything once, right? But first, let's get you some new clothes." Alex looked down at his hideous clinic-issue outfit.

"Yeah… good idea," he said.

That afternoon they stood knee deep in their waders in the Rio Grande, the legendary river, which acted as a border between Texas and Mexico. It also made for some killer fly-fishing in the northern stretches in New Mexico. Tyler and Alex were on a less-daunting stretch, about twenty miles north of Santa Fe, with the Sangre de Cristo Mountains visible to the west. The sun was warm, the water was cool, and a few puffy clouds floated by.

A perfect day.

Tyler hired a guide, an older gent who loved fishing, talking, and just being out in nature. Tyler made it clear he needed the guide to hang with Alex, to keep an eye on him as well as to help him catch a fish. It was late in the season so they were using "dry" flies. This meant that the fly actually floated on the surface, and you could watch the trout break the surface and lunge at the fly. After a few casts, Tyler had seen a few trout show interest, but nothing definite. And then, suddenly, he heard his brother let out a whoop from downstream. Tyler almost dropped his rod thinking something bad had happened. Then he saw the guide standing right next to Alex, almost like a shadow, whispering in his ear. Alex's rod was bent at what looked to be a ridiculous angle, and a good ten feet from that was a fighting-mad rainbow trout. The fish was slashing this way and that, doing everything it could to rid itself of the faux fly it was now sorry it had ever bothered with.

Tyler slowly backed onto the embankment, lay down his rod, and pulled out the small digital camera he'd bought. He quietly made his way up the river to where his brother and the guide were moving slowly backwards. The closer the fish got, the angrier it seemed to be. Tyler could just hear the guide whispering.

"That's right... gently... slowly bring in the line... keep the rod pointed high... perfect."

Alex was all focus. He wanted this fish.

"Okay, let her run a little bit, rod tip up," whispered the guide.

Tyler could hear the whizzing of the line running out as the trout made a last ditch run and hide effort.

Suddenly, all was quiet.

"Stripthelinestripthelinestriptheline," the guide said quickly.

Alex followed the commands perfectly as he ripped the now slack line past his hip, keeping perfect tension on the line. Suddenly the trout exploded directly up out of the water, and appeared to be diving straight at Alex.

Alex was locked in on the trout.

The guide, in a smooth motion, reached over his shoulder for the net attached to the back of his vest and quickly brought it around.

Alex was in his own world, playing the fish perfectly, a look of total determination on his face. The guide stopped talking. Alex was in command. The fish swung wildly upstream and then jerked back down in a last valiant attempt at freedom. In the blink of an eye, the guide submerged the net and came up with a beautiful seventeen-inch rainbow trout.

With his rod under his arm and a now-docile trout in his hands, Alex was standing in the Rio Grande with a huge grin plastered on his face.

"Smile" was all Tyler said as he snapped Alex beaming, gently holding the trout. Alex carefully released the fish back into its wet home. With a flip of his fin the trout disappeared into the cool water, wondering what the hell had just happened. Alex grinned as the trout swam away.

He looked at Tyler.

"Thanks Huck" was all he said.

For dinner that night, they had the house special at a local Santa Fe spot, and of course it was trout. They talked about simple things. The fish figured prominently.

"Thatwas... really great today... thanks," Alex said.

This would be a slice of memory to hang onto till Tyler could get back to him, if he made it back. For a second, Tyler felt a chill run down his spine as he considered his near future.

After dinner they wandered around the main square of Santa Fe. It was nearly empty, save for the odd worker heading home. The moon was halfway somewhere, and the night was blissfully still. The air, desert chilled. They walked in silence, simply enjoying being with each other. Tyler was feeling remarkably peaceful.

Alex stopped, motionless, and stared at the landscape beyond. Without turning towards Tyler, he spoke.

"Ty... you gonna be okay?"

Tyler was so startled by his brother's question, both for its insight and for its straightforwardness, that he wasn't sure what to say.

Alex continued to stare out into the void of the night.

"Yeah, Alex, I'm gonna be fine. No worries."

Alex turned, a small tear streaking down his left cheek. He put his arm around his brother's shoulder and they walked on. "Just don't... get into trouble, okay?"

"Back 'atcha," Tyler said.

Somehow, Alex knew.

TWENTY-NINE

The next morning, Tyler and Alex drove north on the back roads, heading out of Santa Fe towards Kit Carson National Forest. Civilization seemed to disappear altogether as they wound through high alpine forests. They spotted a herd of elk making their way down through the forest, heading to the desert floor, to their winter digs. The New Mexican sun shone brightly. It had already worked its magic on Tyler and Alex the day before. They drove on.

Cat Stevens's "Peace Train" came on the radio. Alex turned it up. Then he turned it up louder, louder. Finally he and Tyler were singing at the top of their lungs amidst the quiet of the surrounding forest. Tom and Huck were back, if only for a moment. The bond of brotherhood was unbreakable.

A half hour later, they approached the south end of Kit Carson Forest. The air was faint with the smell of pine. Off to the right Tyler spotted a sign that said Double H Ranch. He turned onto a dusty road lined with aspens and followed it for several miles. Finally they came to a clearing where a large ranch house stood, with Double H fashioned in wrought iron over the front door. There were several outbuildings, as well as a corral where a dozen horses roamed and nibbled at the earth. Everyone seemed to be moving with purpose, carrying hay to the horses, moving equipment around, carrying baskets of vegetables. There was a makeshift parking area with a few dented pickups and a couple of dusty Jeeps. Tyler pulled up next to one of the Jeeps.

"Where are we?" asked Alex.

"At a ranch," said Tyler. "Give me a minute to talk to the owner. I'll be right back. Okay?"

"Yeah, I'm gonna… go watch the horses," Alex said.

Tyler headed towards the main building, an old western ranch house with a few people milling about inside. There was a large foyer, two stories high, with a lounge area downstairs. The place was all serenity, with Mission-style furniture and Native American rugs on the floor. The art on the walls was an eclectic mix of almost primitive folk art, and some of the most daring modern stuff Tyler had ever seen. And of course there was the ubiquitous wooden howling coyote in the corner, painted in crazy colors.

Off to the side was a rolltop desk where a woman sat reading *Cowboy Magazine*. She looked the part.

"Hi, I'm here to see Dr. Baldwin," Tyler said.

Less than a minute later Tyler heard his name.

"Mr. Sears?" said a voice from behind.

Tyler turned, and nodded.

"Dr. Baldwin. A pleasure."

Tyler had expected someone in a white coat with an air of academic and practical experience, based on their phone conversations. Instead he found himself facing Calamity Jane. She was in her late forties, with a broad, sun-weathered face and intense brown eyes. A warm smile softened her face with dimples, and a gangly mess of brown hair flowing out from under a battered straw Stetson. She had on a simple blue-jean work shirt with the Double H brand on the pocket, a pair of Wrangler jeans (the ones real cowboys wear), and chaps. This was all finished off with a pair of brown cowboy boots that were as worn as the hat.

The doctor pulled off her leather work gloves and extended her hand. Tyler shook it. Her grip was as solid as her outfit.

"I'm sorry for staring but... well, you don't look like the typical shrink," Tyler said by way of explanation.

"As I told you on the phone, this place has two functions. The first is healing, but the second is that this is a real working ranch. Let's go back to my office and we can chat privately," she said as she ushered him down the hallway. The small office was furnished with simple pine furniture, a computer, some photos on the wall, and a well-weathered saddle sitting on a stool. Out the side window Tyler could see Alex standing by the corral as several people were saddling up horses.

"So, where is your brother?" she asked, as they settled into chairs in her office.

"Outside, watching the horses," Tyler said, as he pointed out the window.

Alex was leaned up against the corral, a horse stood close by. Dr. Baldwin looked out the window and smiled.

"Perfect," said the doctor. "I read your brother's file."

"So how's it work? What's your secret?" asked Tyler.

"The secret's out that window," said Doctor Baldwin, nodding at the view.

Tyler stared, not sure what he was supposed to be looking at.

"The horses, Mr. Sears. It's all in the horses," said the doctor.

"Really," said Tyler with a hint of amazement.

"You know all that talk about horse whisperers, and how they can help heal an injured horse?"

"I saw the movie," said Tyler.

Dr. Baldwin raised her eyebrows. "Well, horses can have the same effect on humans. We only use horses with sweet dispositions. Docile horses. Each patient is assigned their own horse to look after. They feed it, clean it, shovel its shit, and completely connect with the horse. They are responsible for that horse the whole time they're here. They learn to ride, and how to care for their horse. No two horses are alike, just like people. And we've found that this responsibility pays huge dividends in other ways."

"Exactly how?" asked Tyler.

"It's the simple things, really. First, it gets the patient away from thinking only about themselves. Too much of this business is self-pitying, alcoholism, drug addiction, food addiction. It's all about the self. I'm not opposed to a little navel gazing, but not at the expense of crippling someone's true potential. The horses bring them out of that shell, and literally force them to be responsible for something, someone, besides themselves.

"Don't get me wrong. We still believe in one-on-one sessions, as well as a weekly group chat time, but our goal is to get a patient on his or her feet as quickly as possible, and to start believing in themselves again, first by believing in, and caring for, someone other than themselves. Everyone on our staff is a trained therapist, and trained in horsemanship, as well as wilderness first aid. They are the true believers. They see the results, not in the reports that I file with the *Journal of American Psychiatry,* but in the small, daily achievements that happen for people like your brother. The first time they shoe a horse, the first time the horse jumps over the low branch, or they make it back from an overnight trail ride. These are the small victories. And we build on those victories." Dr. Baldwin paused, letting Tyler absorb what she said.

"And you really think you can help Alex?" Tyler asked.

"What happened to your brother Alex, what he witnessed, was horrific; but keeping him medicated for the rest of his life, that's not the answer. At least not if we want him back as a functioning member of society. He needs to regain his footing, his voice, and it will be a different voice from who he was, and it's crucial *he* find it, and our job is to help facilitate that."

Tyler stood up and extended his hand. "Doctor, you're the first person I've met that's made any sense. Please take good care of him."

"It's between him and the horse, you'll see," she said.

"I may be away for a while. I've instructed my bank to send you monthly payments until they hear otherwise."

"Hopefully sooner rather than later you'll be hearing from us," said Dr. Baldwin. "And try to visit whenever you can. It'll be as important for him as it will be for you. In the meantime thanks for entrusting your brother's care to us," she said as she released his hand.

Just as Tyler was about to leave he turned back towards the doctor. "Hey Doc, can he go fishing?"

She nodded as though she expected the question. "Lots of fishing," she said with a wide smile.

Tyler left the doctor in her office and went out to see his brother.

Alex was still leaning up against the fence of the corral. "Hey… Ty, these horses… they seem really… friendly. One of them came right up to me, and licked my hand," he said.

They both leaned on the fence to watch as the horses moseyed about.

"This is my new home, isn't it," Alex said, not as a question.

Tyler was startled by his prescience.

Skip the crap. Get to it. Tell the truth.

"Yeah, this is your new home. What do you think?" Tyler asked.

"Can I go… riding?"

"Lots."

"How 'bout… fishin'… can I go fishin'?" Alex asked.

"Lots of fishing," Tyler said.

Alex turned toward Tyler with a smile on his face. "Seems pretty good to me. You gonna… stick around?" Alex asked with a hopeful tone.

"I've got a project I have to complete, and then I'll be back. Okay?"

Alex looked at his younger brother for a long time and then said, "Promise?"

"Promise," Tyler said, and he meant it.

"Is Mom coming to visit?"

"Of course. She'll give you a call next week. Okay?"

Alex smiled and gave his brother a hug.

They walked to the car and got Alex's things. Doctor Baldwin came out the door of the main building with an assistant.

"You must be Alex?" the Doctor said.

"Alex… Alex Sears," he said as he extended his hand.

"Welcome to the Double H Ranch. I'm Dr. Baldwin and this is Robert. He'll show you to your cabin." Everyone shook hands. Alex stood and stared at Tyler.

"Don't forget, you promised," Alex said as he hugged his brother good-bye.

Tyler watched his brother amble off to his quarters, more hopeful about Alex than he'd been in over a decade.

Tyler smiled as he headed out the dusty road, back to his own personal purgatory. Like Dante, he'd have to go through hell to get to heaven.

THIRTY

After following the dirt road back to the highway, Tyler turned south and paralleled the Rio Grande River, enjoying the dramatic view of the Sangre de Cristo Mountains floating on the western horizon.

At the Albuquerque airport he hopped on a flight to Dallas that had a late connection to Newark. He arrived back at his apartment late, dog tired, and crashed without even changing out of his clothes.

The next morning he was too mentally exhausted to silence the alarm. He had arrived home after midnight from his emotionally exhausting journey to visit his brother. He was supposed to meet Ricardo that afternoon. His order was ready, was the message he received from Ricardo, while waiting for his return flight from Dallas. He lay there with the pillow pulled over his head, he just wanted to return the money to Imasu and make a run for it. How far would he really get, and how long would it take for Imasu to track him down? A day, a week, if he were lucky. No, this nightmare was really happening.

He forced himself out of bed and decided a run was the best medicine. He went for a ten-mile run, which he did in spurts, a slow easy half mile followed by a brisk quarter mile and so on. He sprinted the last mile. He couldn't let his nerves and heart rate get the best of him on a job like this. His worst fear, besides being caught, was panic. He was the fittest he'd ever been. After showering he noticed the answering machine was flashing. He hit the play button and heard his mom's cheery voice, giving him a number at La Signoria hotel in Corsica where she and Pepé Le Pew were taking a short break from their sailing adventure.

He dialed his phone.

"Hi Mom. It's me, Ty."

"What? You think I'd forget my own son's voice?"

"How're you guys doing?"

"We're staying at a fabulous hotel. Phillipe knows the owners."

"That's great. And how're you feeling?"

"Much, much better. I think the sea air is good for me."

Tyler smiled trying to imagine his mom out on the high seas.

"Mom, I moved Alex to that ranch I told you about."

"Oh sweetie, how is Alex?"

"Drooling when I picked him up, and smiling when I dropped him off. I think he's finally at the right place."

"I'm so glad. And I'm sorry I couldn't be there."

"Mom, it's okay. He asked when you'd be visiting."

"What'd you say?"

"I told him you'd give him a call sometime next week."

"Really? He's okay to talk to?"

"Call him. You'll see."

"He asked when we'd be visiting… as a family. I said possibly at Christmas. Hopefully by then he'll be back to some sense of normalcy."

"Tyler, you'll be there too? A family Christmas would be really nice."

"Mom, I wouldn't miss it."

"Sweetie is everything okay for you?"

"All good, Mom. Not to worry." Tyler said, lying to his own mother.

"Is there someone special?"

"Mom, hold off on the grandchildren questions until Christmas. I'll fill you in then."

"I wasn't trying to—"

"Gotta go, Mom. But let's talk in early December about getting together for the holidays."

"Tyler. I want you to know that you've been a great brother to Alex. I know it's been difficult for all of us, but you've been great looking after him the way you do."

"Thanks Mom. I'll see you in a month. I love you."

And then he hung up. Tyler stared out the window not knowing if he'd ever see his mother or his brother again. It was exactly ten days before Thanksgiving.

He knew it was now or never. Game on.

THIRTY-ONE

Next stop was Ricardo's. Tyler filled his crapped up messenger bag with the necessary cash for Ricardo. He then left his apartment, trying not to notice the large black SUV parked a block or so back. He moved swiftly through Gramercy Park and jumped in a
cab, a subway, then another cab, and hopped out near The Guggenheim. He entered Central Park at 90th and Fifth, across from the Cooper-Hewitt. He hustled up to the jogging track and moved quickly clockwise around Jackie O's reservoir, exiting at Central Park West in front of the El Dorado building. He crisscrossed his way uptown and entered the bodega on 124th Street. He went through the tiny shop and stopped at a thick door with a sliding peephole slot. Tyler knocked. The slot opened momentarily, then closed. The door opened and Tyler went in.

Ricardo sat at a table in the middle of the room with three other men, playing dominoes. They were arguing intently in Spanish, and barely acknowledged Tyler. The man to Ricardo's left started waving his arms frantically and shouting. Ricardo said something and everyone started to laugh, except for the arm waver. He pushed his chair away and stood. The laughter halted. Ricardo stood and put his arm around the angry one's neck and whispered to him in Spanish. A begrudging smile emerged and then they hugged. The game was over and the others went by the disgruntled one and they all shook his hand with a slight hug included.

Crowd control, Amsterdam Avenue style.

Ricardo turned to Tyler and smiled.

"*¿Mi amigo, cómo estás?*"

"Good. Things are good," Tyler said. "You called?"

Ricardo nodded.

"The items you requested are ready for your inspection."

Tyler tossed his messenger bag to Ricardo, who glanced inside and then tossed it to one of the men at the table.

Ricardo motioned for Tyler to join him at the dominoes table. Dominoes were swept up and a black velvet cloth was draped over the table.

"I believe this is what you are looking for?" Ricardo slid a custom-made case over to Tyler. It was slightly larger than a violin case.

Tyler snapped open the brass buckles on the simple black leather case. Inside was an array of carbon fiber and titanium pieces, glimmering against the dark velvet lining.

Ricardo very carefully pulled the pieces out, one at a time, assembling the weapon. Tyler stared at the space-age version of a crossbow. Ricardo detailed the weapons specifics. "The arms are thinner than a normal crossbow, and made of titanium, making them exceptionally light and strong."

Tyler took the weapon from Ricardo and weighed it in his hands. He couldn't believe how light the thing was.

"The power stroke, the distance between the resting point and when it's fully cocked is in excess of sixteen inches, which means the lighter, titanium shafts you requested will be propelled at over a thousand feet per second," Ricardo stated. "Basically, the arrow will explode out, and reach its target before the target has even heard the sound."

Tyler let out a low whistle as he handled the weapon. He studied it carefully and then popped up the sighting mechanism. Tyler stared through the mechanism.

"That's a digital range-adjustment sight, with night-vision capabilities, as per your request," Ricardo explained.

"It's got a Zeiss magnifier sighting system so you can see a fly's ass at a hundred yards."

Tyler pulled on the inside tab of the case. It popped open to expose four shafts. They were thinner than normal arrows. They looked more like small rockets than anything Tonto would have used.

"Titanium shafts," said Ricardo.

"How do I practice with this thing?" Tyler asked.

"You can use my private outdoor range. It's north of the Meadowlands. It's an old quarry I bought and reconfigured as a shooting range."

Tyler knew that no matter how much he practiced, he'd only get one shot, two if he was unlucky. Under Ricardo's tutelage, Tyler disassembled and reassembled the crossbow a dozen times. Eventually he was able to do it smoothly and without mistakes. Ricardo showed Tyler how to wipe the weapon down, leaving no prints.

"Your other requests are being handled, discreetly. I'm having your apartment swept for bugs twice a week. Phone too," Ricardo said holding up a bug that was found in Tyler's phone, and the one that was in the clock-radio on his bedside table.

"You have a car?"

Tyler nodded.

"Let me have the address of the garage and the plate number, we'll give that a sweep as well." Tyler wrote down the information on a pad Ricardo handed him.

"Thanks, but is that really necessary?" Tyler asked.

Ricardo waved the two bugs he'd already found as his answer.

Tyler smiled in agreement.

"And your brother, he's safe, but he seems kind of out of it. Is he okay?"

Tyler shook his head.

"I just moved him to a new, hopefully better place," he said as he handed Ricardo Alex's new address.

Ricardo knew better than to press. He handed Tyler a card with his private number.

"I will answer no matter the time."

Ricardo embraced him and wished him luck. He was beginning to realize just how valuable Ricardo really was.

The ultimate wingman.

THIRTY-TWO

Tyler spent the next couple of days practicing at Ricardo's shooting range. His aim was getting better. It would have to be close to perfect. His body was ready, he had gone over the details again and again, and still he was scared shitless.

He had also met with Bart to give him details of what he'd need. Bart didn't even flinch, especially when Tyler wired a quick mill into one of Bart's Bahamian accounts. He merely smiled and said, "No problem."

Tyler packed the essentials—including the tech devices he'd picked up from Mikey G, his custom-made space-age crossbow, some clothes, an emergency medical kit, a couple of harnesses, a climbers backpack, and a couple of Mini Maglites—into a large, black hockey duffel and headed out.

When Ricardo showed Tyler the various bugs and tracking devices he'd found it made Tyler aware of how mistrustful Imasu really was. It made him extremely paranoid of Imasu. And that was a good thing. He decided the double con was the only way to survive.

He dialed Imasu.

"Imasu-san, I was hoping you might have some time for me tomorrow, after five p.m.?"

"How good to hear your voice Sears-san. Six p.m. is better. Shall I send a car?"

Tyler looked out his window at the black SUV down the block.

"Sure, why not. See you at six p.m. And I need your boys to get maintenance uniforms identical to the one's used by the National Gallery."

"It will be taken care of tomorrow before you arrive."

"Great. And I'll have the plans with me. Your boys speak English, correct?"

"Of course."

"Tomorrow then," Tyler said, and hung up.

As Imasu hung up he motioned to the two thugs standing near his desk.

"I want you to get over to Sears's place immediately. I want to make sure he doesn't forget our meeting tomorrow."

They both nodded without saying a word and turned to leave.

"Try not to lose him this time," Imasu said

Tyler went down a flight to his neighbor's apartment. When the door opened Richie, the young kid who had moved in about three months before, stood there in his boxers and a Rangers jersey.

"You're the guy from upstairs, right?"

"Yeah. I need a favor."

"Keep talking," Richie said over the hockey announcer yelling from the TV.

"I was wondering if you wouldn't mind taking this bag over to Pete's Tavern across the street," Tyler said lifting up a large duffel bag with the CCM logo splashed across the side.

"It ain't drugs is it? I don't want to get in trouble."

"No, it's not drugs. I got this angry ex-girlfriend who keeps threatening to come over and trash my place. It's just a few things I need to get out of the apartment for safe keeping."

Richie eyed the bag. Tyler bent down and unzipped the bag.

"See, no drugs, just personal stuff."

Richie was staring at what looked like a musical instrument case, clothes, a bunch of Clif bars, and some techie looking things. He was staring at everything you'd need to pull off the greatest art heist in history.

"Cool. So what do you want me to do?"

"I need you to take this bag over to Pete's, across the street, and then have a long lunch with your friends."

"Dude, you gonna buy lunch for me and my friends?"

Tyler smiled, reached in his pocket and handed Richie five fresh hundred dollar bills.

"Steak sauce!" Richie said as he pocketed the five Franklins.

"Steak sauce?" Tyler asked.

"A-1, you know the steak sauce."

Tyler nodded, clueless what Richie was talking about.

"Right now?"

"Maybe head over there in about twenty minutes. Right around lunchtime."

"You got it."

"Make sure you give the bag to the bartender. And tell him it's from me. And here's an extra two hundred for you."

Richie pocketed the loot, grabbed the hockey duffel bag, and gave Tyler a thumbs-up.

Tyler wondered just how stoned Richie was, standing there holding a beer at ten a.m. Oh well, gotta work with what you've got.

Tyler went back to his apartment and called Pete's Tavern and told Otto, the bartender, that Richie would be dropping a bag off around noon, and would he mind leaving it near the back door of the tavern.

He did a quick check, then a recheck of his list. And then he did a thorough search of his apartment to make sure he wasn't leaving any clues behind. He dressed in his running clothes and headed out the door at exactly 11:30. He slowly jogged north toward Gramercy Park, completely ignoring the black SUV that was a block behind him, sitting parked. On the flip side of the park he picked up the pace. He then did a zigzag heading uptown, up an avenue, along a street, down the next avenue, across to the next street, up an avenue, etc. Twenty minutes of this and he was running along First Avenue. He checked his watch. He realized he wasn't even breaking a sweat as he motored along. He took a shortcut through NYU Medical Center and ducked into one of the buildings. The clock on the wall read noon. He ran down the stairs to the basement and followed the tunnel along to the south end of the building.

If Imasu's boys were following he'd know in the next minute. He waited. Nothing. No beefy Japanese boys in brand new track suits to be found. Tyler left the complex at the far south end exit.

Imasu's two goons were still sitting in the black SUV a block south of Tyler's apartment.

"How poetic, the idiot is out getting in shape and he'll be dead in a month," said the driver.

"And it won't be pretty," said the one riding shotgun. He smiled.

They were laughing at how they might kill Tyler when Richie and his friends walked out of the building, chatting, carrying a large hockey duffel bag. They crossed the street and walked into

Pete's Tavern. Imasu's hired guns didn't even notice the group of twenty-somethings walking into a bar with a duffel bag.

One minute later Tyler jumped in a cab at Bellevue Hospital and headed downtown. At 19th Street he told the cabbie to take a right, and then had him turn down an alley that ran parallel to Irving Place. He told the cabbie to pull up to a beat-up old fire door, laden with DO NOT OPEN signs. Tyler pulled open the door and there was his duffel bag. He pulled out an envelope which contained five hundred dollars, and taped it to the inside of the door. It had Otto written on it. He jumped back in the taxi and instructed the driver to head Port Authority, and make sure they weren't being followed.

Tyler unzipped the duffel bag, and everything was just as he left it, including the hidden false bottom compartment that contained the rest of the cash Imasu had given him. When the cab reached Port Authority Tyler jumped out and moved quickly into the building, jumping on the escalator and then heading to the far end of the second floor. He pushed open the fire stairs door and dashed down the stairs. He then exited at the near corner, opposite of where he entered. He hailed a cab and told the driver to head to Newark, and quickly.

Imasu and his Yakuza goons be damned!

THIRTY-THREE

His alternate plan that he was going to sell to Imasu consisted of flooding the entire National Gallery and sending Imasu's goons in as maintenance workers. Simple, yes. Workable, unlikely. And Bart had sent up enough warning signals that Tyler worried he'd be dead before he even left the Trans-Pacific building, so in the interest of expediency (and self-preservation) he decided a quick, stealth exit was in order. And best of all, he'd have a day's head start on Imasu.

He retrieved his car from the garage in Newark and jumped on the Garden State, heading southbound to Cherry Hill. From there he went south on Interstate 95 to Wilmington, ending up on Maryland 301 southbound, an old roadway that cut a swath through the Eastern Shore of Maryland. Tyler would be able to spot a tail if one still existed, due to the dearth of traffic. Halfway along he turned onto State Road 213 and headed to Chestertown, an historic colonial town perched on the banks of the Chester River. He pulled into the White Swan Tavern, an original colonial mansion that had been converted into a typical charming inn. For Tyler it was perfect, far enough off the beaten path, and small enough that he'd know if anyone was snooping around. He stayed in the top floor room with a balcony that looked out over the tranquil Chester River.

After a dinner of local crab cakes with a silver queen corn relish, he spent the rest of the evening memorizing blue prints, and was asleep by ten. While he slept the entire heist happened in his dreams. Dreams were the easy part.

The next morning he went for an easy run along the edge of the Chester River. There was so little development in this area, after Baltimore won the title of major port, that Tyler sensed not much had changed along the river in two hundred years. After a Southern breakfast of grits, loaded with fresh butter and cinnamon, he drove south along Route 213, a meandering road that cut through Churchill and Queenstown, sleepy Eastern Shore villages. He pulled off the road on the far side of Queenstown, drove down a deserted road a few hundred yards, and then walked back to the main road. He waited thirty minutes, to see if he was being followed. *Nada.* Still the knot in his stomach was starting to tighten as he jumped back in his car and drove towards his destiny.

Driving across the Chesapeake Bay Bridge he marveled at the beauty of the bay. He saw the small port of Annapolis off in the distance, and then crossed over the Severn River Bridge, which gave him a glimpse of the Naval Academy. The road widened as the edges of civilization started cropping up, with modern housing developments and shopping malls appearing on both sides of him.

He wished this were a road trip with Lucy. He really wanted to call her, just to hear her voice. Would she still want to be with him after he confessed everything? He had to maintain his silence, his isolation. The job was on. No distractions. No interference. Watch your back, and hope to come out alive.

That was all he had to do.

Simple.

THIRTY-FOUR

The closer he got to DC the tighter he gripped the steering wheel. As he came up over a slight rise there it was, the Capitol Dome. His pulse was quickening, his jaw tightened, and he would have crushed the steering wheel if it wasn't made of some newfangled space-age material. He tried calming his nerves when he pulled off the road to get some basic supplies for his extended stay in his new digs. He tried convincing himself this was just another job.

Bullshit!

As he drove on he thought of Lucy in an effort to stay calm. It worked right up until the moment he stopped at an intersection, and directly in front of him was the Smithsonian. He turned right onto Indiana Avenue, and pulled into the parking garage near 6th Street NW.

It was late afternoon when he grabbed the huge duffel bag from the trunk, locked the car, and headed to his new temporary home, the top floor of the small office building at the corner of Pennsylvania and 6th Street. He had persuaded the building's owner to let him rent the top-floor office even though they weren't done with the renovations. He had rented the entire floor so the place was empty and cavernous. Claiming he was representing an international lobbying group and would pay cash, the owner was more than willing.

Tyler wore thick horn-rimmed glasses, a badly fitting brown suit, nondescript dark-brown shoes, a pork pie hat, and a basic London Fog overcoat. He rode the elevator up to the top floor, unlocked the door at the end of the hall, and dropped his bags. Out of the large hockey duffel he pulled a bed pad, sleeping bag, and camp stove. The only thing the builders had completed was a small bath with shower. Otherwise, the place was a gaggle of wires and exposed plywood flooring. He wouldn't even let them put in the carpet. He did not want carpet fibers with his name all over them.

He stood at the window and looked down the street at the Capitol, looked up the street toward the FBI building on Pennsylvania Avenue, and then stared directly across the street at his target—the National Gallery of Art. The solid granite fortress-like side he was facing seemed to dare him to try. He didn't blink, mesmerized.

THIRTY-FIVE

The area of Imasu's office where Tyler had sipped tea, and enjoyed fresh sushi, was now covered by several tatami mats. Several of Imasu's yes-men stood nearby silently. The driver of the SUV and his cohort stood dressed in martial arts robes, called *gi*. They each had a worried look on their face.

Across from them on the other edge of the mat stood Imasu, also in his *gi*, a black belt tied around his waist. His face showed nothing but anger.

"Keep an eye on Sears. A simple job, yes?"

Both men were too nervous to speak.

"So where is Tyler Sears?"

Again, nothing from either man. Imasu's anger rising, he pointed at the driver of the SUV to step forward. He did. Imasu stepped into the ring on the mat, and bowed. The other man nervously bowed. They circled each other and quickly Imasu stepped into his sparring partner, reaching for his *gi,* and pulling him off balance. As the driver tried to defend himself, Imasu grabbed his hand and leveraged the man onto the mat. The driver was in pain as Imasu squeezed his opponent's hand, holding him down on the mat.

Imasu looked up at the other man who was also responsible for watching Tyler.

"This will be your fate if you are unable to locate Tyler Sears in the next twenty-four hours."

In a blink Imasu had turned his opponent's arm and applied so much force that everyone heard a snap as the arm twisted out of its socket and faced the wrong direction. The victim let out an almost animal-like scream before he passed out from the pain. As the others carried the limp body out of Imasu's office, Imasu motioned for his two most-trusted men to stay behind.

"I want eyes on Sears's mother and brother in the next twenty-four hours."

The older of the two men nodded silently. Imasu then turned to the younger one, with the bald head and gold hoop earring. Imasu handed him a small case, which held several hypodermic needles and two small vials.

"As soon as Sears has the paintings I want you to kill him."

A vile grin spread across the younger man's face.

THIRTY-SIX

Crouched by the window Tyler stared through the high-powered binoculars, which were locked onto a small tripod. They had a matte black coating so there'd be no reflective glare when he observed during daylight hours. The field glasses were fitted with night vision filters, so he could monitor nighttime activity as well. He was recording the security guards' movements in and around the National Gallery in the late afternoon. Next to Tyler was the notebook he used to record times, number of guards, and length of time it took each guard to complete his rounds.

While he studied the guards' movements, his brain was also contemplating the heist based on details from the architectural blueprints, which sat nearby. When the National Gallery's East Building was constructed they conjoined the security systems for both buildings in the lower level, by the concourse. Although the systems were still separate, everything was located downstairs, between the two buildings. This was done for efficiency, as well as for centralizing the main internal systems. The systems for the National Gallery had been put together in a patchwork fashion over the years. It ended up as a hodgepodge of systems, similar in efficiency to the Italian postal service. This would make Tyler's work easier. There was an outside chance that updates were made that never made it into the hall of records system. Clerical errors were a fact of life, especially with local governments. He could only hope the system Mikey G had designed was "smart" enough to overcome any recent internal building security upgrades.

Lucy sat in her office, bored, wondering if and when Tyler would call. She had that tingling sensation you get when you feel like you've known someone your whole life, but you just met. She was nervous about admitting to these feelings, especially over someone who'd walked out on her in Paris. He hadn't actually walked out, more like disappeared. A rap on her office door caused her to swing around and she was greeted with a huge bouquet of flowers, passed to her by the receptionist who would have stayed to grill her about them if the phones weren't ringing off the hook.

The card read:

> Brother is good, and getting better.
> You're great. Hope to see you before these die.
>
> Miss you,
> xo Tyler

Lucy was thrilled. She tried calling him but got no answer.

That morning after the usual weekly meeting, her boss had taken her aside to congratulate her for doing such a great job on the motorcycle exhibition that had opened to skeptical, and then critical success. Tickets sold faster than any recent exhibit in memory. The director of the museum sent a personal note of thanks to Lucy, and her boss, Mr. Collier, handed her an envelope with two VIP passes, and an all-expenses-paid trip to Washington, DC, for the biggest art exhibit of the century. An amazing art exhibit combined with a long weekend at the Four Seasons Hotel. Lucy was ecstatic. She really wanted Tyler to be with her in DC, but where was he? The flowers were from a Union Square florist, so clearly he had returned from dealing with his brother. She wanted to meet him someplace romantic for a leisurely lunch, and more. She couldn't get him out of her head. She was happily desperate to talk to him.

Tyler's longings for Lucy kept interfering with his work as he stared through the lenses of his Nikon 1200 super optical binoculars, recording the comings and goings of the various guards on duty at the National Gallery. He knew what he was headed for was 99% boredom and 1% sheer terror. The boredom was starting to get to him. He drifted off.

Sheer terror would arrive in a few days.

THIRTY-SEVEN

Tyler awoke early the next day and headed to the museum. He entered the building at the 4th Street entrance on the ground floor. He paused to gaze once more at the large iron doors that closed shut every evening. His destination was downstairs to the maintenance room behind the cafe.

Lunch hour was in full swing and by 12:30 the place was packed with customers. Tyler slung his large overcoat over his arm and headed towards the back of the cafe. He leaned against the Staff Only door and, to his surprise it easily fell open.

He slipped into the maintenance area and slid the phony badge, which he had had made by his Park Avenue counterfeiter, onto the pocket of his tweed sport coat. With his tweed jacket and glasses he looked like any other academic who could occasionally be seen wandering through the bowels of the building. To anyone watching on the monitors he looked non-descript, and as though he knew where he was headed. But because the glasses he was wearing had a small reflective line along the inside bottom of the frames he was able to see *up* without actually looking up. This allowed him to look ahead while actually being able to see the security cameras overhead.

He could see the red light at the corners to tell if that particular camera was the one being followed by the monitors in the central security office. There was a doorway to a stairwell just ahead and to the left. The camera at the far end of the hallway was dead on him. The minimum-wage-earning guard who sat in the security control room watching the monitors paid him no attention.

When the camera started turning down the adjacent hallway, Tyler dashed for the door and slipped through. As a general rule, museums did not have surveillance on internal stairways. It was deemed cost prohibitive and somewhat redundant, as whoever was in the stairway would eventually have to reemerge into the main areas of the building.

The guard watching the monitors didn't even notice Tyler's disappearance as the hall camera swung back across the now-empty hallway. The guard was thinking about Isbett, the sexy new hire who was working in the west garden court that day. These were the kinds of unknown variables that Tyler always hoped for but never knew when, and where, they might arise. There was also the chance that a variable could work against you. There was no way to predict how they might affect your outcome.

He headed down to the lower level where the guts of the internal systems were located. He delicately opened the door less than an inch and peered around using a small dental mirror. No cameras. It was absolutely silent down there, except for the droning hum of electrical generators. He pulled out the small hand-drawn rendering he had made from the larger blueprints. Tyler was amazed at just how much public information was available. Every inch of every federal building, with the exception of the NSA, CIA, the Pentagon, and the White House, was available to anyone who asked at the local office of records and deeds.

According to his sketch, the room he wanted was straight ahead, and then left, down the second corridor. His only real concern was running into someone, anyone, who questioned what he was doing here. He swapped name tags and was now wearing one from Allied Security Systems with his photo on it. Allied was well known in the security community. They were worldwide, and covered everything from home alarms to setting up systems for some of the most secretive of Swiss banks. Tyler was about to turn left when two guys from maintenance turned the corner. Tyler's heart skipped a beat but his stride didn't change. He walked past them with utter confidence in his step, and total fear in his heart. They passed each other with nary a glance.

"Excuse me" came the voice.

"Sir, excuse me," came the second voice.

Tyler froze, took a breath, and turned to face the two workers with as much nonchalance as he could muster.

The first one, who was stockier with curly long hair and a serious forehead said, "Are you lost?"

The second one just stood and stared at Tyler for a moment.

Tyler looked at the shorter one and finally said, "I'm with Allied Security. I'm just double-checking the work for the new exhibit." He pointed to the fake security badge he was wearing.

The taller one who was going bald and had a large paunch said, "Man, they just had a guy in here this morning. Any problems?" he asked with real concern.

"No. We just like to double- and triple-check our work," said Tyler, feeling more confident.

The shorter of the two shrugged his shoulders and said, "Okay, good luck."

The taller one looked at his watch and said, "Come on man, I'm hungry, let's go eat." He tugged on the shorter man's arm.

The three of them nodded to each other and turned and walked in different directions.

Tyler's heart rate fell back to a normal pace as he headed down the hallway. He couldn't waste time now that he had been seen. He had to move quickly.

He pushed down on the handle and slid past the door marked: ELECTRICAL-HAZARDOUS. The only information he had was that the electrical systems were located in this room. As Tyler made his way to the center of the room, what lay before him looked more convoluted than the Los Angeles highway system. There were more than two dozen large electrical boxes with heavy-duty, industrial-strength coated and wrapped cables coming and going from them. The morass in front of him was even more complex then he'd imagined. He knew that his time was limited after the two maintenance guys saw him. If they even casually mentioned seeing him, it was over, so he had to work quickly to figure things out.

The boxes themselves were all locked but easy to open with a key stick, a kind of second-story man's utility tool. The insides of the boxes were pretty straightforward, if you were an industrial electrician, which Tyler was not. Fortunately the insides of the boxes were labeled either Main Gallery or East Building. Tyler pulled out a device no bigger than a credit card, but about double the width, with a tiny antenna that popped up from the back. It had four flexible tiny "legs" that stuck out the bottom of the device. This was a "toy" called a squirrel that he had acquired from Mikey G. The squirrel acted like a small transceiver, capable of sending and receiving signals, able to glide along a coated cable filled with wires. It could "jump" from one cable to another using the flexible legs, hence the name squirrel. The device drew its power directly from any cable that was functioning, so it worked on a low-power system.

It would be able to transmit and receive signals, at least that's what Tyler was banking on. Mikey G had showed Tyler how to attach the squirrel and get it up and running. Watching Mikey work the device in the comfort of his workshop was one thing, but Tyler remembering exactly how to attach it, and then get it running, and finally, trying to control it from a couple of hundred yards away, well that was a whole other thing.

Knowing that he'd be unable to get a direct connect from the squirrel to his computer, because of the distance and number of impediments (walls, windows, roads, etc.), Tyler had come equipped with SONS—Self-Organizing NetworkS. These were cheap, very small nodes, which sent and received signals between each other.

They were used by the military as locators, and also by farmers on large farms, to collect data about soil content, moisture levels, and other pieces of information. The SONS "talked" to each other and when connected to a mainframe they acted as a daisy chain, providing information from far distances to one central location. SONS were so small they could be disguised as tiny rocks, the military's method of choice, or as kids' marbles, which was the format of choice for farmers.

Tyler had come equipped with both.

He attached the squirrel to one of the cables in the panel marked Main Gallery. Which cable didn't matter. He placed it so as to be almost unnoticeable.

Never before had he relied so heavily on technology. Even though he wasn't using a human partner, the squirrel, the SONS, and his laptop were technological partners he was depending on. This made him nervous, as Tyler tended toward low tech. Too many "what ifs" for his taste, but he'd had no choice. Within seconds of attaching the squirrel the tiny light on the backside began flashing green, signaling that the device was operational.

So far so good.

He felt in his overcoat pockets for his bag of SONS marbles and small pebbles. The trick with the SONS was to make sure that more than enough were used. Some would never turn on, some might be batted around by a cat, or some other creature, and some could be swept up by the cleaning crew, completely unawares.

Tyler began tossing the marbles around the room. He checked his watch. It had been three minutes and thirteen seconds since his encounter with the maintenance guys. It was time to get out.

He took out one of the tiny SONS, camouflaged as a small stone, and placed it above the doorframe. He exited quickly, discreetly tossing marbles in various spots as he headed back towards the elevator.

Next to the elevator was a fire extinguisher in a large metal case with the word EMERGENCY in block letters diagonally across the glass cover. He placed one of the tiny stones on top of the metal case, out of view. He walked past the elevator and entered the stairwell, discreetly dropping marbles along his route, and placing the miniscule rocks in strategic spots.

Before he left the stairwell he replaced the security badge he was wearing with the visiting scholar badge he had originally worn into the building. He stepped back into the concourse level, the hubbub of lunchtime activity still in full swing. He walked to the far side of the cafe and ordered a cup of coffee. While the woman behind the bar was getting his drink, he dropped several marbles behind the cafe counter.

Next he headed to the gift shop area against the north wall, which ran all the way to the glass opening above. Tyler surreptitiously placed more of the marbles throughout the gift shop area. He exited the gift shop and headed back towards the cafe, stopping to tie his shoes and roll a few of the marbles over by the baseboards. As he got up and headed towards the East Building he felt a bit like Hansel and Gretel spreading bread crumbs along his path.

He made his way up to the ground level of the East Building with its enormous Calder dangling from the ceiling. He exited the building, crossed 4th Street, and continued across the central courtyard between the two buildings. He continued seeding his path with marbles and pebble-like fragments as he walked. He cut across the courtyard and headed for Constitution Avenue, depositing marbles about every ten yards. He cut close to the corner of his target, the National Gallery, and tossed a slew of marbles as he neared the corner of the building. He was hoping that since it was late in November, the landscape crew would have no need to mow the lawn, thereby leaving his SONS undisturbed. With every swing of his arms he managed to throw out a few more marbles or stones. And like Johnny Appleseed, he hoped what he was planting would bear fruit. A bounty of a dozen art masterpieces.

THIRTY-EIGHT

Tyler was sitting in his sweats and black ski cap. He unlocked a case that looked like it was designed to hold a trumpet. He pulled out the stock and half barrel and snapped the pieces together. Next, he attached a metal flap and gave it a final twist. He pushed a small button on the side of the stock, and the nifty contraption instantly flared open to reveal a tiny satellite dish. It was a directional antenna. Once the signal was aimed at a target, it would provide pinpoint accuracy to send and receive information. It was the mother ship for all the marbles and tiny stones (SONS) that Tyler had strewn between the National Gallery and his temporary digs.

As Tyler fired up his computer, he took the cable that Mikey G had made especially for this project, attached it to the butt end of the rifle stock Sat-dish, and plugged it directly into the computer. The computer was specially loaded with software designed by Mikey G, and should be able to carry out all the necessary functions Tyler had requested, hopefully. If it worked it would allow Tyler to view the various systems of the National Gallery through a series of schematics—courtesy of the squirrel he had attached. It would also provide real time video feeds of the rooms inside the museum, identical to those being seen in the main security control room. And, in theory, he'd be able to watch the watchers.

He aimed the satellite dish out the window realizing he wasn't quite sure what he was aiming at. The computer was up and running, the software was preinstalled so everything should be ready to go.

Tyler thought back to his meeting with Mikey G, who said the system was pretty straightforward, and self-explanatory. The military uses them all the time, how complicated can it be. The problem was twofold. First, Mikey G was Nobel Prize smart. So simple for him was Fermat's theorem. Second, Tyler was on his own if any "problems" arose. He couldn't exactly call the Mikey G tech support line.

Tyler was staring at the blank screen. He typed in "National Gallery" and waited. A black screen stared back at him. He tried again. Nothing.

Shit, thought Tyler. He'd taken on a partner, the computer, which was completely obedient, but if he didn't know how to give it the proper commands, he was fucked. He tried to remember Mikey's exact wording.

"How hard can it be? The military uses it."

Tyler tried to remember exactly the keys on the computer Mikey G had hit, but Mikey was one of those geeks who treated a keyboard in the same way Lang Lang did. With an intensity that a normal human could never comprehend.

He'd done everything as Mikey had instructed. Nothing. Not sure he decided to resort to a Luddite maneuver: he hit the restart button.

Everything on the screen went dark. Tyler's expression became gloomy. Just as he was about to punch the screen, he heard the familiar musical sound of the computer starting up. His gloom transitioned to hopeful optimism.

When the screen came alive, so did Tyler. The computer asked him for his password, which he quickly supplied.

The screen went blank again. He waited. The computer made a low humming sound. He waited some more. A series of flashes flew across the screen. Tyler positioned the rifle sat-dish on its tripod. He aimed it in the general direction of the corner of the building.

Suddenly a picture of Mikey G's face came on the screen.

"Congratulations! You are up and running on MGXT 2000 security program. Have fun and good luck." And just as suddenly, the head exploded. Tyler laughed. It was amazing to him the extent geeks would go to for any sense of notoriety. If this really worked, it'd be worth every penny he'd paid Mikey.

Tyler activated the rifle-sat dish. It moved ever so slightly, looking for the strongest signal. It stopped and the blinking red light on the left side of the rifle stock turned to solid green. It had locked on to a signal. Tyler hit the return button on his computer and a series of scrambled numbers and letters flew across the page. He hit the return button again, and this time pages of schematics popped up horizontally.

He hit the button again. "Third time's the charm," he said to himself.

The screen went dark. No noise. No nothing. He wanted to shoot the damn thing. Suddenly, the screen came to life and he was looking at an exact architectural rendering of the National Gallery. The SONS and the squirrel were working perfectly.

He scrolled through until he was looking at the blueprints for the electrical systems. Suddenly a tiny, animated squirrel came to life, and started flying around the screen. The words "Squirrel is active" popped up on the screen. Mikey had planted a microscopic camera inside the squirrel so it was able to recognize which cable it was sitting on, similar to the system doctors use for scoping.

The wire the squirrel was sitting on was for the air conditioning ventilation system. With a couple of keystrokes he got the squirrel to slide over to the next cable. The squirrel was now sitting on the cable for the lighting system. He moved the squirrel again and it was now sitting atop the cable for the video security camera system. He hit the return button and suddenly he was watching the various video feeds in real time, exactly as they were being seen at the command security station of the National Gallery.

He popped over to the various video screens now available to him. And suddenly there they were, the twelve paintings. Twelve truly extraordinary pieces of art, all in one room. He stayed on this screen as the cameras cut between different angles of the same room. His jaw dropped.

Mikey G had assured him he'd be able to download the actual video feed and be able to reuse it as a video loop. He pressed the command buttons for "record." A small light flashed in the upper corner of his screen and a timer split into 1/100s of a second began ticking away.

As he watched and recorded, several people came and went from the room, pointing at some of the paintings, and occasionally pointing up at the cameras, which were hidden in the wall of the gallery. Tyler knew these had to be either gallery employees, or security personnel, because that entire end of the museum was shut down in preparation for the show. After recording for 5:05:87 minutes/seconds/hundredths he decided to check his work. He hit the rewind button and then watched. It was exactly what he had just seen, minus the flashing light and time code.

He went back to the squirrel. He had it slide to another cable. As it glided up and down the encased wire looking for an optimal contact point, Tyler realized he was tapping into the cable that monitored the weight-sensitive security system. This allowed the floors in all the galleries to sound a silent alarm if the weight on the floor, at any spot, was above a certain level. Most systems used a standard ten-pound weight as this would allow for mice to roam freely, but not a man. Mice seldom stole art, but man, well, that was a different story.

From the computer screen readout, Tyler judged that the weight security system was on an automatic timer, which came on seven minutes after the doors were locked and stayed on until seven minutes after the doors were unlocked. This would allow the guards enough time to get from the furthest places in the museum back to the central command spot. The problem for Tyler was that seven minutes wasn't enough time for him to get in, do the job, and then get out. This meant he would have to do the entire job hanging from a wire. He had planned for this, but was hoping to avoid it.

Work from a wire was both physically exhausting and extremely stressful. He wished he'd done more sit-ups as his stomach was starting to ache just considering the task ahead.

He moved the squirrel again, and this time it was sitting on the temperature alarm system. Each room was equipped with a highly sensitive special thermometer that was activated by any small temperature changes within the room. After closing, each room was set at 68°F. Once the temperature in the room rose above 68°F, a silent alarm automatically sounded in the security control room. A human at 98.6°F would set the alarm off almost instantly. Tyler recorded this system for five minutes and would loop the temperature control along with the video feed later that night, as a first practice.

He carefully slid the squirrel back to the video cable. The signal was incredibly strong and the pictures were as good as if he were sitting in the security command station. He'd been watching the blank rooms for thirty minutes and began to grow weary. He opened his eyes wide to try and stay focused, and wondered how the hell the guards managed to stay awake. He got drowsier and suddenly he was out, dreaming of van Gogh.

Tyler woke two hours later. It was dark outside. He had that disoriented feeling you get when you wake up in the dark, yet it's still relatively early. He splashed cold water on his face. The computer was still on, and shots of various rooms at the National Gallery flashed across the screen.

Tyler decided to try the video feed that Mikey G had assured him would work like a charm. He slid the squirrel into location and when it was centered on gallery 80 he watched a continuous feed of the very room he'd be entering in less than twenty-four hours. He hit a few keystrokes and the REC signal appeared on the upper corner of his screen. The digital timer started simultaneously. He waited exactly five minutes then stopped the recording and hit rewind.

The moment of truth was at hand.

He slid the squirrel over to the master video security cable. After an agonizing minute he was able to locate the slot for gallery room 80. He then fed his previously recorded five-minute digital video onto the real-time feed that was being seen in the central security control room. He waited. A small drop of sweat was beginning to run down his chest, and his palms were sweating.

He hit the return key and his prerecorded loop kicked in. The break between the real time and his recorded feed was less than

1/100 of a second—so quick that the human eye could not catch it.

With no one in the museum, except the occasional guards who were never allowed in the actual gallery rooms (except in emergencies), the view was exactly as it would normally appear in the security control room, except there was a five-minute delay. Tyler watched the timer in the corner of his computer as it counted down the five minutes. They were the longest minutes he had ever witnessed. His grandmother had always told him that a watched clock never moves. Grandma was onto something. 1:26… 1:25… 1:24. To Tyler it was crawling. :54… :53… :52.

It was under twenty seconds. Tyler had no idea what to expect as the museum security video transitioned from his video feed back to real time. :04… :03… :02… :01…. In a moment, a thousand times faster than an eye blink, the screen had changed from his video feed back to real time.

"Holy shit," Tyler said out loud. "It works." He had factored in exactly nine minutes and forty-nine seconds in the room procuring the paintings, another minute and fifty-three seconds to actually get into the room, and forty seconds to exit. All told he figured on no more than thirteen minutes total, so factoring in the unknown X-factor for unseen complications, he allotted a total of fifteen minutes video recording time. He reset the squirrel directly on the gallery 80 video feed line and then hit the record button and decided to just let it run for a while.

While the computer was recording, he unrolled the National Gallery blueprints he'd acquired from the District Hall of Records.

In the background a local radio station was announcing the upcoming weather report: clear and brisk for the next few days. Weather was an unknown variable that often could hamper a job, but never cause a cancellation. The job was always based on time factors, never weather. It'd be great if it was clear skies and moonless, and Tyler didn't favor working in the rain, but ultimately it didn't matter.

He checked his watch. It was later than he'd thought and his stomach was beginning to growl again. The thought of yet another Chinese dinner was more than he could handle as he looked around at the multiple takeout boxes with chopsticks sticking out of them. He decided to walk to Georgetown for some exercise, and to eat at one of the many bistros scattered throughout the neighborhood.

THIRTY-NINE

Lucy sat on a plane, thirty thousand feet above Lake Michigan, headed to Washington, DC. She had promised her parents she'd make it home for Thanksgiving. The last time she saw them, she'd discovered that her father, a man who'd always had endless energy, had started taking naps every afternoon, and her mother was making early dinners. It was a sober reminder about mortality.

When she'd promised to spend Thanksgiving with them in Boise, she hadn't known she'd be involved with a guy she really liked, a man she couldn't stop thinking about. Nor did she know that her boss would get her VIP tickets and a weekend at the Four Seasons Hotel in DC. She had to tell her parents she'd be leaving the day before Thanksgiving. Her dad had that sad smile on his face, the same one he had when she headed off to college, and then when she went off to Paris on her own. Her mom just fussed.

While changing planes in Chicago she made a quick call to the office and picked up her messages. There was nothing crucial as it was preholiday time—more importantly, no word from Tyler. She had already left him enough messages, from the very concerned to the slightly pissed, "Where are you?" She saw no reason to compound things. But she tried him one more time, and when she heard his voicemail she closed her cell phone and wandered to her gate at O'Hare, wondering if Tyler was okay.

Tyler was walking along Pennsylvania Avenue headed for Georgetown. It was a long walk, but stretching his legs would do him good, and would help clear his head.

It was Thanksgiving eve. Almost everyone had left work early, and they were flooding the neighborhood bars. At the FBI building he cut across 9th Street and went around to the back of the building. Across the street was Ford's Theatre, famous for the death of Abraham Lincoln. In anybody's book, presidential assassination beats regular theater any day. Just to the right of the theater was a pay phone that was partially obscured by a small alley that ran between the theater and the adjoining store. He got out his roll of quarters and started dialing.

The first message was from Bart, checking to see how he was, and to let him know things were progressing nicely on Tyler's work order. Very unlike Bart. The next was from Lucy thanking him for the flowers, telling him how sweet he was, and asking him to please call her as soon as possible as she had some news.

The next one was from his brother. That in itself was amazing, as he had never called Tyler before, at least not since his clinic stays.

"Hey Ty, it's me Alex. I just wanted to call and check in. Things here are really great. I've got this great horse called Heaven. Wait till you meet her. She's really easy going, calm but fearless. We've been on a couple of great rides together. I'm also building a desk out of local wood for my room. Nothing fancy…. Hey Ty… I just wanted to say happy Thanksgiving."

Tyler hit replay so he could hear it again. It was so great to hear his brother back to being productive, sounding almost normal. It seemed like the horse as a healing agent was really working. Tyler was thrilled by the enthusiasm in his brother's voice. This was the clearest his brother had sounded in over a decade. He thought about that last fishing trip. On the river, calmness, and a jumping rainbow trout. Tom and Huck.

The next call was from Lucy, again.

"Tyler, it's me. I am on my way to Boise for Thanksgiving. Where are you? It's not good to make a girl worry. I have, well had, a surprise for you... for us. I got a free weekend at the Four Seasons in DC, plus two VIP passes for the Millennium exhibition at the National Gallery. I hope you can join me at the hotel. I promise to wear something sexy... like nothing. I miss you, and Tyler, wherever you are happy Thanksgiving."

He played the message again.

And again.

He couldn't believe it. The chance for a romantic weekend with the girl of his dreams, all while he was planning to heist the same show at which he was supposed to be a VIP.

The next message was from his mom.

"Hi sweetie, it's me, your mom. We're on Corsica, and we ran into the nicest man. He says he knows you from the city. Apparently you two have the same boss. He's invited us to go out on his boat tomorrow. Happy Thanksgiving. Hope to see you soon."

Tyler held the phone stunned. He quickly dialed a number. When the phone was answered all Tyler heard was, "Yes?"

"I've got a problem" is all Tyler said.

FORTY

Imasu was at a breaking point. Beyond anger. Apoplectic.

Tyler never showed when the limo sent by Imasu sat in front of Tyler's building. When his two Yakuza agents broke into Tyler's apartment they found no trace of him, and no clues as to where he might have gone. Last week, unbeknownst to Imasu, Ricardo's man had found the GPS tracking device under Tyler's car. He'd simply removed it from Tyler's car and attached it to a late-model station wagon with Pennsylvania tags, parked next to Tyler's. For several days the station wagon just sat there. But yesterday, the owner of that car, a periodontist from Wilkes-Barre, PA, who had driven to a conference in Newark, on digital dental imaging and gums, returned home to Wilkes-Barre. The periodontist, newly educated to the wonders of ultra-sound imaging in the evaluation of periapical lesions and dental abscesses, was oblivious to the black SUV Suburban with heavily tinted windows following him. That black SUV Suburban contained two Japanese Yakuza, and enough light artillery to take on the Pennsylvania National Guard. Nor did the periodontist find it unusual that he suddenly had two new Japanese patients, for which to try out his newly acquired knowledge.

Imasu had no idea where his fifty million, might be. Imasu knew Tyler was on the move, which meant the heist would be sooner rather than later—assuming that Tyler was still planning to go through with it. As insurance, Imasu had sent a couple of young men from inside his organization to keep an eye on Tyler's brother, and another of his thugs to keep watch on Tyler's mother. If the deal went sour, or if Tyler decided to try and back out at the last minute, Imasu intended to use Tyler's family as leverage. What Imasu hadn't counted on was Ricardo Alvarez and his pledge to keep Tyler and his family safe.

To Imasu, the fifty million he'd paid Tyler was peanuts compared to his fortune, estimated at fifteen billion, and to the amazing art collection he would control once Tyler handed over the paintings. He had already planned Tyler's horrible demise as soon as the art was in Imasu's hands. Imasu felt a minor tinge of remorse for the trusted lieutenant that would inject the viruses into Tyler, as the young man himself would definitely become infected. How many lives had already been sacrificed throughout history for the paintings he was soon to acquire? The tinge faded quickly. Imasu wanted to know where Tyler Sears was, and he wanted an answer NOW!

FORTY-ONE

Tyler continued walking towards Georgetown. At the Treasury building he cut across Lafayette Park, towards St. John's Church, the oldest Episcopal church in Washington, DC. The sign in front read:

ST. JOHN'S PARISH
ESTABLISHED 1815

ALL THOSE IN NEED, WELCOME

Even though it was late, the door was open for those in need of sanctuary, in dire straits. A storm was brewing in Tyler's head and he was desperate for a safe port. He wasn't religious, but jail had certainly made him spiritual. The one thing prison provided was solace. Solace in spades. Time to think, and then time to think some more.

Tyler walked halfway to the altar, bowed slightly, and sat. He folded his hands and rested his head against his knuckles. He sat silently for a long time. He needed help. He was in WAY over his head.

He silently ran everything through his head.

The job.

Lucy.

His brother.

Mom.

Imasu.

Fifty million.

Return to jail.

Death.

He sat in silence, breathing quietly, trying to clear his mind. He looked up at the altar hoping for some kind of sign, some guidance, anything. All he heard was his breathing. He looked up at Jesus, who was stuck in a stained-glass dinner with a group far more menacing than Imasu. He stared up at Jesus, eternalized at that dinner, Tyler whispered, "Lord, I'm not one of your followers, but then you're probably not one of mine either. I don't blame you, but this time I need your help. I'm in way over my head.... I guess you'd understand that.... I've got this job I really don't want to do.... It's okay if I don't survive, but... but I need you to keep an eye on my mom, she's really sweet and means well, so just make sure she's not in any danger... and my brother Alex... he's going to need you pretty much full time... just keep them sa—"

The door creaked behind him. Was it opening or closing? Did someone just walk in, or did they just leave?

Silence prevailed. There were no footsteps, at least none he could hear. He focused on his breathing. Fear started to creep back in on him but he pushed it away mentally. The hardest part was how to come out alive. No mean feat. He heard a noise to his right. His eyes blinked open. No sudden moves. If someone was in the church it might just be another lost soul. And if it wasn't, if it was someone following him, he knew it was crucial to act as normally as possible.

He waited another minute but no more sounds came. He rose from his pew, touched his forehead, and pulled his two fingers lightly across his chest. He stood quietly for a long moment, and with head bowed, eyes closed, he listened. It was amazing what you could hear in a silent room. Tyler was listening for a pin to drop, or a shoe to shuffle, or a breath other than his own.

Dead silence.

He turned and walked down the aisle toward the exit. At the end he turned and faced the altar one last time. *Please Lord deliver me from this fucking mess I'm in,* he pleaded. He left St. Johns church without the answer he had hoped for, but calmer nonetheless.

He walked quickly in the cold evening air to Georgetown, and sat by himself at the bar in the French bistro. All around him everyone was in a festive pre-Thanksgiving mood. The bar, and the streets outside were all jam-packed with festive seekers. Tyler sat at the far end of the bar, in disguise, a bowl of *soupe de poisson* with *pomme frites* in front of him. He'd wanted to enjoy his last meal before the 1% of terror showed up. He ignored the revelers and they him. He didn't even notice the woman coming out of the ladies room. As she turned to put her coat on he sensed the movement and momentarily looked up—*it was Lucy!* He gazed back down at his soup. When he looked back up to catch a glimpse, she was staring at him.

BUSTED!

"Tyler?"

Tyler stared down into his soup.

"Tyler? Is that you?" She asked, perplexed and annoyed all at once. He took a breath and looked up at her.

"And why are you wearing that— What are you doing here?"

"The fish soup?" is all he said.

Her voice rose in tandem with her frustration.

"I don't mean this place. I mean Washington! Why are you...
? I thought you had some job?"

Tyler put his hand up to stop her.

"Can we go somewhere else and discuss this?" he pleaded.

"No I want to know—"

"PLEASE. I'll tell you, just not here. Okay?"

Tyler stood, Lucy was already heading for the door. He
followed her out, but as he got to the door some of the revelers
forced him to step sideways as they pushed through.

In the back of the bistro sat a couple on a date. The noisy
entrants caused the woman to look up at the door. As Tyler
approached the exit, she noticed him.

It's HIM.

Chanel N°5 grabbed her phone and hit speed dial as she
deserted her date and headed for the door. Her job, and all her
training at Interpol, was about noticing people. It took her a
moment to realize it was really Tyler, due to the disguise he was
wearing. It was his gait that gave him away. It was definitely him.
She was certain. Rosenwater, her boss, was convinced Tyler Sears
was planning something, another heist, and here he was in
Washington, DC just before the opening of the biggest art exhibit
ever, at the National Gallery. Chanel's boss didn't believe in
coincidences. And he wasn't going to rest until he caught Tyler in
the act. Putting Tyler Sears away for good was going to be his
retirement gift to himself. And all Tyler had wanted was a decent
meal before all the madness that loomed in the near horizon.

Chanel's boss barked at her to not let Tyler out of her sight.
Barking was his only form of communication, which Chanel

figured explained his multiple failed marriages. Rosenwater was as shocked as Chanel N°5 that Tyler Sears had just walked back into their lives.

FORTY-TWO

Thanksgiving morning in New York City began with a bright blue sky but the high winds made for bracing temperatures close to freezing. It seemed as if everyone was lining Central Park West and Broadway in anticipation of the annual Macy's Day Parade. This was the granddaddy of parades, as far as Americans were concerned. Tens of thousands of people from all across the country came to watch, and millions more watched at home on TV.

Komate Imasu was not one of them. He was sitting in his office waiting, impatiently, to hear of Tyler's whereabouts.

Thanksgiving morning in Washington, DC was clear and bright, with winds swirling the leaves of the Mall in every direction. Few cars were about, as the city itself was all but abandoned. The Smithsonian and all the galleries were closed for the holiday. Only the occasional jogger moved along the inside perimeter of the Mall, looping the wide inside area of the Smithsonian Mall, heading directly for The Castle, which was the centerpiece of the Smithsonian. It was the original building, funded by James Smithson, a Brit, in the middle of the nineteenth century.

Beyond The Castle and the Agriculture building you crossed behind the Bureau of Engraving and Printing—the home of the money. And beyond that, and across the 14th Street Bridge, you'd end up at the Jefferson Memorial.

Standing immediately in front of T.J., Tyler imagined the stone president wondering about all he had witnessed through the years, with his ever-vigilant view of the White House. He had watched over Ike, and the short-lived, youthful Kennedys, he'd watched as Johnson, and then Nixon sent tens of thousands of American youths to their deaths. He'd seen Nixon pushed out in disgrace as a valiant Ford tried to band-aid an ailing country. He'd watched as Carter came undone by his own righteousness and Reagan had brought glitz and glam to the revered house. He watched as Bush stewarded, and then Clinton moved in with spirit and energy, only to be undone by his own demons. T.J. was witness to all of this. He watched stoically. His expression never wavered.

Tyler stood on the edge of the Tidal Basin and sucked in the crisp Thanksgiving air as a calm came over him. He was more ready than ever. His brain was clear, and his body fit. Most important, he had devised a plan for how to deal with Imasu—how to stay alive, and keep his family, and Lucy safe. He had admitted to the depth of his feelings last night when he confessed all to Lucy. He'd come clean, on everything. It was the first time he had ever told anyone everything. Lucy's immediate reaction was one of comedic disbelief.

"You expect me to believe you're some kind of international art thief?" Is what Tyler remembered her saying, and then laughed, and laughed. He couldn't help but laugh along, it did sound pretty incredible as he heard himself confessing all. Tyler's life had, for him, become as matter of fact as it does for, say an X-ray technician, or a plumber. Tyler had spent so much time with so many lies that it all swirled together to be the life he led. And like so many others it wasn't the life he had dreamed of. It was merely *his* life. And like so many of us his chance to hit the reset button was ever elusive.

Until now.

Last night as Lucy laughed at his "ridiculous" fantasy of an explanation, he realized here was that one moment, the do-over, we often fantasize about but never quite have the nerve to make the proverbial leap of faith, that moment that Hollywood uses at the beginning of every Act III, which for everyday mortals doesn't exist, but for Tyler that moment reared up and dared him.

"Come on, I want to show you something" was all he said, as they walked on, and approached his temporary digs above The Capital Grille saloon.

As Tyler was about to open the door to his "headquarters" he knew there was no turning back. He wasn't sure what Lucy would say, or do once proof was staring back at her. She could end his mission from the devil in a matter of minutes, or she could try to understand the hows and whys of what he had to do. And it was at that moment that the clarity Tyler had sought from the solace of St. John's, was sitting on the front of his brain as he swung the door open and led Lucy into his world.

FORTY-THREE

Thanksgiving Day, Noon

Imasu was climbed aboard his Bell 430 Jet-Helicopter, which sat at the ready, rotors warming up, atop the Trans-Pacific building. He was headed to his manse in Greenwich to spend the afternoon with his family. As the rotors roared to life and the chopper became airborne, Imasu pulled out the latest copy of Christie's auction book on impressionist and postimpressionist artists. The artists and paintings he was about to possess would command staggering sums, in the hundreds of millions, but it was never about the money. By possessing a dozen of the greatest paintings, he would effectively control the impressionist market. Imasu knew that all other impressionist paintings would skyrocket in value, once it was established what had been stolen, and that they were not soon to be recovered. He already planned to sell his other, lesser, impressionist paintings once he took possession of the collection. He would be the single most important person the art world ever knew. He would be beyond legendary, he'd be immortal!

And, he had arranged Tyler's imminent demise. He had instructed his Yakuza associate to inject Tyler with a serum that took three days to paralyze its victim. The toxin would work its way through Tyler's nervous system, causing a slow and painful shutdown of all his other systems. It would impair Tyler's ability to speak, swelling his tongue, and make him seem wildly incoherent if he tried to go to the police. He would then lose all use of his motor skills and finally his lungs would stop working and then his brain would run out of oxygen and he'd suffocate.

Normally, Imasu would have killed him with a quick, 9 mm, double shot to the back of the head. But after Tyler had rejected Imasu's request of using his men to help with the job, and had shown the audacity to threaten him, something more was called for. Sears had brought about his own horrific death. Arrogance was unacceptable to Komate Imasu, and it would be a necessary pleasure to make an example of this arrogant thief. One man's hideous death is usually a good lesson to others.

Imasu's immediate concern remained, where was Tyler Sears? It had been a full twenty-four hours and still no word from any of his men. Two of them were tracking Tyler's New York City haunts and movements, and the other two were in Washington, DC keeping an eye on the National Gallery. Imasu had no intention of paying him the final fifty million. He should be grateful for the extra three days of life he'd get, painful as they would be. Imasu closed the Christie's catalog as his helicopter headed up the East River. He looked out the window as a sickening smile slid across his face.

FORTY-FOUR

Tyler returned from his run, and quiet time with Thomas Jefferson. Lucy was awake but just staring up, lying in the sleeping bag. She looked shell-shocked. She was. He was carrying a bag with bagels and coffee. She shook her head. Not meaning no, but rather, how can you eat with what, with what you are about to do. So far Tyler was grateful she hadn't called the cops, or anyone for that matter. After Tyler had led Lucy into his world last night she was in disbelief at what she was looking at—computer screens watching the museum security cameras, the odd-looking contraption that looked like some Star Wars rifle with a satellite dish, and the crossbow that looked too weird even for Hollywood. And of course, blueprints strewn around.

"I'm sorry I drew you into this craziness, but you said you wanted the truth, and I thought—"

"Who are you?"

Tyler stood quietly, allowing all that had happened to sink in.

"Just remind me, you're going to steal the paintings, and then return them?" Lucy asked with a look of confusion.

Tyler nodded. He waited. Lucy reached for one of the coffees.

"I'll understand if you want to leave, but for my family's sake—"

Lucy put her hands up to silence him as she sipped her coffee.

"Do they know?"

Tyler shook his head.

"Does anyone?" she asks.

"Just you."

Lucy took a deep breath. As she exhaled she reached for him.

After they had made love in that sweet end-of-the-world kind of way, they then moved to the devour-each-other phase. Where you are trying to satisfy desire only to have it explode into something ever more volatile. And finally, they fell into a deep sleep. No dreams, just darkness.

Tyler woke up and went over his checklist yet again. He had everything factored down to seconds. The squirrel and the SONS were working perfectly. He had done a final record of video footage he'd need for the actual job.

He re-oiled the custom-made crossbow and checked each of the shafts for potential flaws.

He coordinated his watch with the computer timer. Tyler knew which roofline window he would slide through, and the exact dimensions of gallery 80, where the booty was hanging. He visualized his moves inside gallery 80.

He practiced flipping a frame, extracting the canvas in less than seventeen seconds, and stowing them in the expandable quiver he'd had made for the occasion.

In order to remove the twelve paintings in under ten minutes, each second was crucial.

Lucy began to stir. She leaned on her elbow trying to wake up. To what, was the question spinning in her head. She pulled her hair back, blinked a few times, and then looked at Tyler. Tyler looked at her and realized he was the luckiest guy alive, at least for that moment.

"Now I know how Alice felt when she tumbled down the rabbit hole," Lucy said.

Tyler gave a half smile.

"I need to make a phone call, and I need to do it from a phone booth. I should be back in ten minutes.... You okay?"

"I have no idea," Lucy said as Tyler threw on his coat.

"Hi, it's Tyler Sears for my brother Alex."

"Please hold on...."

The air was getting colder by the minute.

"Hello?"

"Alex? Hey, it's me Ty."

"Wow. Ty, how are you?"

"I'm fine," he lied. "How are you?"

"I've got this great horse, Heaven. She's kinda shy but we go for rides almost every day."

"She hasn't thrown you or anything?" Tyler asked.

"Nah. She's really sweet. We went for a long evening ride yesterday and something weird in the woods spooked her. And then we heard this high-pitch scream, which sounded like a person, but then Wiley, one of the horse trainers said it was probably just a coyote."

Tyler couldn't believe how coherent Alex sounded. No slurring, no verbal stumbles. He started to smile.

"That sounds pretty great Alex."

"Wait'll you see the desk I'm making for my room. I'm gonna make matching bookcases. Nothing fancy, but practical."

Nothing fancy, but practical. That's exactly the life Alex needed.

"Hey Alex, how about you, me, and Mom spend Christmas together?"

"Really?"

"Yeah. Mom says she really misses us and wants to have a family Christmas. And we'll come stay with you. I already checked with the folks at Double H."

Tyler could almost hear Alex smiling through the phone.

"Happy Thanksgiving Tom Sawyer. You better have some adventures ready for us," Tyler said.

"I've found a great fishing spot…. Happy Thanksgiving Ty. I gotta run. We're all about to have dinner."

"Take it easy," Tyler said and then the line went dead.

FORTY-FIVE

Thanksgiving, 9 p.m.

It was pitch black outside, the window slightly cracked, and a chilled breeze flew in. Tyler looked up and down Pennsylvania Avenue. Thanksgiving night. The place was deserted. Not a soul in sight, save for the errant taxi, but otherwise the city was dead. He looked across the street at the National Gallery, half the lights around the Mall had been dimmed, for reasons of economy.

Everything was set. It was now or never.

Lucy watched silently as he dressed. He pulled on a black Dri-FIT turtleneck, black climbing pants that tapered at the ankles, and a black ski mask, which he rolled up on his head like a watch cap. The ski mask had two purposes: first, it would hide his face if he happened to be seen. And second, it would keep sweat from dripping down his brow. He carried with him several pairs of surgical gloves. No prints, no suspect. He was ready.

Lucy looked at him in his thief's outfit.

"Not exactly Cary Grant."

He gave her a look, realizing he needed to get her to safety.

"Thanks. This would be a good time for you to head back to the hote—"

"Not a chance," she says.

"Lucy, I mean it. You need to get to safe—"

"Last time I didn't see you for three years. This time I'm not letting you out of my sight. We have a deal right?"

Tyler nods.

"You're returning the paintings. I trust you, you trust me. Right?"

Tyler smiled. Nodded. Lucy raised an eyebrow. Damn she looked good.

"Fine. Then make yourself useful." He said as he grabbed the SureFire LED military-grade flashlight and handed it to her.

"If you see anyone while I'm on my way back here, give me two flashes."

"You mean like this?" she said as she pulled her top up quickly twice.

Tyler had a serious look.

"Sorry."

"I should be back in twenty minutes. If you don't see me in twenty minutes, get out of here. DO NOT WAIT. Clear?"

Lucy nodded. Tyler handed her the car keys.

"Remember where the car is?"

"Yes," she said saluting him.

FORTY-SIX

Earlier that day, and half a world away in an island off the coast of France, Tyler's mother was having dinner. Corsica is one of those places people have sort of heard of but probably couldn't locate on a nameless map. It's a hybrid island—part French, part Italian. Needless to say it's impossible to get a bad meal anywhere on the island. And the views from anywhere, are, well, pretty sweet.

Tyler's mom sat at a table at an outside balcony of the Kalliste hotel, which sat perched on a cliff's edge. The dark of the water still visible through the partially moon lit sky. She and her companion, Phillipe, were enjoying a lovely local pinot noir from Domaine de Saline. She had ordered the daily catch—a grilled red mullet freshly caught. He, the local lamb, on skewers. They were having a wonderfully relaxed evening and all of it was being watched from above by Imasu's man, Rusutsu, who was two floors above on a small balcony, just off his room. Earlier that day he had "run into them" at a local market and after a few pleasantries he explained that he in fact was friend's with her son back in New York. How amazing, said she. He passed on their invitation to join them for dinner, and instead had persuaded them to come along on a sail the next day. A polite form of kidnapping.

As Tyler's mom and Phillipe pondered dessert, there was a knock on the door of Rusutsu's room. He ignored it, except it didn't go away. Realizing that his target wasn't going anywhere as he observed them being served a limoncello, he left his post to deal with the knocking.

"Yes?" is all he said through the unopened door.

"Room service" came a female voice with a hint of a Spanish accent.

"Wrong room," Rusutsu replied.

"It's a gift from your boss in New York," replied the sultry voice.

Rusutsu knew that NO one at the hotel knew his connection to Imasu, so it had to be legit. Erring on the side of caution he pulled out his Walther P99, the handgun of choice for 007, and opened the door with the handgun pointed through the door at the threat—if that's what it was.

Standing in the hallway was Sonia, a sizzling-hot Spanish beauty. She wore a trench coat, hands in pockets. Rusutsu was not smiling. Sonia slowly pulled her hands out of the trench coat and held them up, at which point the coat partially fell open, revealing, well, next to nothing. Sonia wore a racy red lingerie outfit. Rusutsu motioned for her to open the coat all the way. Sonia pulled the coat open revealing no weapons, unless you're a male with a pulse. Rusutsu smiled and opened the door all the way.

As he closed the door behind her he took the Walther, with the safety still off, and slid the barrel down her neck to her cleavage. She just smiled.

"I'm a gift from Imasu," Sonia said as she let the coat slide to the floor.

Rusutsu's blood flow rushed upside down. She opened a small box with two small blue pills.

"Imasu said you'll need these if you expect to keep up... with me," she whispered in his ear.

Rusutsu's blood flow now forced that betrayal that afflicts most men in his position. They had a glass of champagne in anticipation as he downed the pills, smiling.

"You get ready, I'll just be a minute," Sonia growled as she tossed her red brassiere at Rusutsu.

Two minutes later Sonia opened the door to the bathroom. Rusutsu was at the epicenter of a massive heart attack. She casually walked past him, his body writhing with wild spasms. She headed out onto his balcony and looked down to see Tyler's mother laughing, finishing her after-dinner drink. By the time she moved back into the room two things had happened. First, Rusutsu was dead. Second, an enormous erection had created a tent-pole effect under the sheets.

Sonia dialed emergency services. Thirty minutes later she was standing in her trench coat, the Walther P99 in her coat pocket, the local EMT guy asking her what happened. Behind them the other EMT is calling the time of death.

Sonia told the medic that he swallowed a little blue pill. He was fine one minute, and then suddenly... she looks quite distraught. As she completed her Academy Award acting job as the concerned hooker, the body is zipped into a body bag. The erection saluting through the body bag, as the dead, bagged, Rusutsu is wheeled out of the room. The medic raised an eyebrow as it rolled by. Sonia agreed to stop by the local gendarme office to file a report. As Sonia exited the hotel, through a back exit, she jumped into her Mini Cooper. She dialed a number.

"Ricardo, all set.... Very," is all she said as she headed off along the twisty D81 road on her way to Porto, where she hopped a private yacht back to Spain.

FORTY-SEVEN

No more hesitation.

Tyler set up the tripod for the crossbow, at the window with the crossbow locked in place. He checked the computer and the video feed. He hit the "send" button, and in less than thirty seconds, all visuals in the museum's security system would be coming from Tyler's computer for the next half hour. The Thanksgiving guards on duty, usually the newest hires, and those with the least seniority, wouldn't even notice the 1/100 of a second blip that would cross their screens as the information from Tyler's laptop (via the squirrel) overrode their systems. Tyler and Lucy would be able to watch on the computer screen if there was any reaction from the guards, as the feed overrode real time.

He had set several small incendiary devices he'd been given by Ricardo, which were timed to ignite forty-five minutes after he left. The computer, the sat-dish, the tripod, all of it would be blown up and burned beyond recognition. He splashed lighter fluid on anything that might have his, or Lucy's fingerprints, so the small explosions and the lighter fluid would burn off any prints left behind.

He opened the window all the way. The cold air hit his exposed face. The sky was closing in. Not a star in sight. His backpack was already loaded with the NASA gyro-belt he'd need inside the gallery, and the rest of the specialty tools he'd need.

He crouched down and looked through the Zeiss Conquest 12x56, 30 mm nightscope attached to the crossbow. The National Gallery glowed green in the viewfinder. Tyler made some minor adjustments to get the aim exactly where he thought it should be. The titanium arrows would be able to travel farther and faster than normal shafts. A standard shaft could travel at speeds up to 300 feet per second. Tyler's were designed to travel up to 1000 feet per second. He needed the arrow to hit eight inches below the top of the wall. Too high and it would crack the wall and fall away. Too low and he'd have difficulty pulling himself up onto the roofline. The drop down to the ground would probably break his legs, or worse.

He could feel the beads of sweat forming above his brow, the adrenaline starting to pump through his veins. He needed to stay steely calm for the next twenty minutes.

Factoring in height, speed, distance, and wind, he made a final microadjustment. He pulled back on the wire string and locked the crossbow in launch mode. He took one of the specialty shafts and clipped it in place. A final look through the scope, his finger on the trigger.

"Deep breath," he inhales, "and… squeeze the trigger slo—"

His finger doesn't move. He rolls back for a moment as his breath quickens.

"What? You've got performance anxiety, now?" Lucy says.

He gives her a look. His breathing calms. He looks back through the nightscope. The roofline comes into focus through the crosshairs. As he exhales he squeezes the trigger. Tyler watched through the scope as the arrow exploded away. It sounded like a small rocket taking off. There was no whoosh like in the old days with a bow and arrow. It sounded more like jet propulsion as it whirred towards the intended target. A quarter-inch diameter titanium line attached to the back end of the shaft unraveled as the arrow sped towards the museum. Lucy was startled by the sound. She stared through the binoculars.

"Wow. That's a hell of an arrow."

Tyler just watched through the night-vision scope as the arrow zoomed across Pennsylvania and Constitution Avenues. The velocity was so great that the gravity drop factor was a non-issue. In that second he realized the arrow was going to miss, high.

"Damn it!"

He watched as the arrow sailed over the roofline.

"Nice shot Robin Hood."

He instantly hit the rewind button. Time was Tyler's biggest obstacle. He prayed for the second time in two days, as he watched and listened to the line zipping back into the crossbow casing. With a snap, it came flying back in through the open window, knocking over the tripod and crossbow. He checked his watch.

Ninety seconds wasted. And one ceramic shaft wasted.

He quickly set the tripod back in place and looked through the scope. This time he lowered the sight pins six inches farther below his original estimate. He pulled back on the bowstring and locked it down. He clipped a second arrow in position. He peered through the scope, had the target in sight, and squeezed the trigger. The shaft exploded with a jolt and rocketed away towards the target. He watched. Lucy watched. They both held their breaths. The arrow struck the granite wall at over 600 feet per second, almost exactly where Tyler had aimed it. The instant it made contact it started spinning faster than a propeller, driving itself into the wall. When it had drilled in six inches, the tip of the arrow slowly flared open, making the hole slightly larger until finally the drilling stopped and the tip flared completely open, then reversed itself for a second, creating an anchor inside the granite wall.

"Good God, it works," Tyler said as he stared through the scope.

Lucy is equally stunned.

"Wow. You really are a thief."

Tyler looked up at her.

"Can we not call me that anymore?"

Lucy shrugged.

Tyler unclipped the wire from the crossbow and attached it to the climber's block he had imbedded into the floor below the window. He began to tighten the wire until taut.

He took a deep breath and then gave a tug on the wire. It held. He pulled harder. It held. A titanium wire was now strung seventy feet above street level from Tyler's perch to the roofline of the National Gallery of Art. It crossed Pennsylvania and Constitution Avenues, two of the busiest streets in Washington, DC.

He broke down the crossbow, wiped it clean. It saddened him to leave behind such a beautiful piece of machinery. Tyler pulled on his backpack, stepped into his climbing harness and put the quiver across his chest.

Lucy watched all this stupefied. She was witnessing things she couldn't even imagine. Tyler clipped onto the zip-line assembly. There would be a three-degree down slope to the point on the wall at the National Gallery where the arrow was embedded.

"Charges are set for forty-five minutes from now. If things get ugly, get out of here. I'll find you."

Lucy looked uneasy.

"I promise."

He stepped onto the window ledge, looked down, and was about to launch himself. He wasn't big on heights, and standing seventy feet above Pennsylvania Avenue suddenly gave him a rush of vertigo. He opened his eyes and looked at Lucy.

"How about a good luck kiss?"

"On the return... have a good day at the office honey," she said trying to lighten the mood. Tyler winked at her. And then he was gone....

FORTY-EIGHT

RUSH!

Tyler zipped along on a quarter-inch wire, seventy feet in the air, headed for a granite wall. He was more than halfway there. The rushing cold air was numbing his lips. Below, a homeless guy, trying to stay warm up against the Federal Trade Commission building, looked up from the covers of his heavy-duty corrugated box home, and thought he saw someone swinging across the avenues above his head. It was too dark and he was too bleary to believe what he saw. He shook his head and crawled back under the scratchy covers of his big refrigerator box home.

The National Gallery wall came screaming towards him. Tyler swung his legs up to act as a buffer when he hit the building. He was still gaining speed. Too much speed. The wind whooshing by as he zipped along. It was freezing cold. His feet were poised and ready for impact. His knees slightly bent. He tilted his chin forward bracing for the impending contact.

Lucy watched all this through the night-vision binoculars.

BANG!

When his feet hit the wall, he relaxed his body as best he could. The impact was so great, his chin smashed into his knees.

He dropped his feet, and quietly hit the wall on a rebound with the full weight of his body.

"Ouch. That's gotta hurt," Lucy said as she watched him crash into the wall. Tyler reached up and felt the top of the wall and the roofline. In one acrobatic move he swung up and out from the wall, so that his leg and foot found purchase. He pulled himself up onto the roof. Wheezing, he looked at his watch. It had taken him nine seconds less than he had anticipated. Lucy checked the computer screen to see if the guards noticed anything. Nothing. The two guards were chatting, barely glancing at the screens.

Tyler put his hands on his knees to steady himself and took a deep breath. Directly in front of him was the dome—the centerpiece of the entire building. He stared at it for a moment, taking in the architectural beauty of the roofline, and then moved cat-like across the roof to the northeast corner and pulled his backpack off.

This section of the roof was directly over gallery 80, the room that contained the coveted paintings. The roof consisted of large glass panes that were set at about a fifteen-degree angle, meeting at a peak in the middle. This provided sunlight (ideal for viewing) but angled ever so slightly, so as not to scorch the paintings which were further protected by a muslin cloth hung just inside the window area to diffuse the sunlight. Tyler knew that the cloth covering was rolled up in the evening, and unfurled during daylight hours.

He also knew that there would be no direct alarm system on the roof, or any of the glass panes as any bird, mouse, or hard rain that landed on the roof might set off the alarm.

He felt a few snowflakes land on his cheek. It was getting colder by the minute. He didn't give another thought to the cold, or the snowflakes, as he pulled out a tiny drill and made a small hole in the base of the roof about two feet back from the overhead windows. He carefully hammered a climber's expansion bolt in the hole, tugging on it to secure it. Then he hooked a carabiner to the bolt. Lucy watched all this through the binoculars. She checked, and rechecked the computer screen to see if there were any sudden changes, or movement from the guards.

He stared down through the large glass pane that was directly over gallery 80. Looking into the darkened space and seeing the frames in darkened silhouette gave him pause. He pulled out an odd-looking, four-legged device from his backpack that looked like a mechanical spider with a solid center core. He extended the legs until each was snug against a corner of the glass pane. He turned the small dial at the center of the core and watched as the legs stiffened into each of the corners until there was just a touch of tension. He then attached a bungee cord from the center of the core to the carabiner. This provided constant tension and would ensure (hopefully) that the glass didn't fall inward and crash on the floor below.

He pulled a small penlight from a velcro pocket on his right hip. It was a laser pointer, but this one was a hundred times more powerful than a normal laser pointer. Tyler clicked on the laser, and a small intense beam shot through the cold night sky. He aimed the beam at the edges of the windowpane, where the tar molding seal held the pane in place. The laser light seared through the seal. Tyler's mind was solely focused on the task at hand. He was following the procedure manual he had prepared, and it consumed his focus. He had cut the time factors so close that he knew from one task to the next there was not a moment to spare.

Around him, the snowflakes were starting to get bigger but Tyler was oblivious. He'd be inside the gallery in less than ninety seconds.

The seal was finally broken but the glass didn't budge. He grabbed the handle at the top of the spider core and pulled gently. Nothing. Tyler's brain flooded with possibilities. He mentally scanned the blueprints he'd studied. The pages flew by. Suddenly his brain stopped. He could see the page, and in the corner of the page was the date: 1937.

He realized at that moment that a vacuum had been created from the years of the window being sealed in place. He didn't want to risk using the laser light on the glass for fear the shards might fall inward. Quickly he pulled out a tiny drill. He put two pieces of duct tape in an X on one side of the pane and drilled very slowly at the center of the X. He silently prayed the duct tape X would contain any cracking that might occur. Hurrying wasn't an option. "Be quick but don't hurry," the Wizard of Westwood use to tell his charges before each game.

Tyler was so consumed with the drilling he had forgotten to release some of the tension on the bungee cord. As the drill sank through the glass, and the vacuum seal broke, the entire pane snapped back under the tension of the bungee cord and smacked Tyler in the chin and chest, knocking him onto his back. The pane of glass thudded against the granite roof but did not break.

"I hope that wasn't part of the plan," Lucy said, looking through the binoculars.

Tyler was stunned, and it took him several moments to regain his breath. He could see from his reflection that he had a minor cut on his chin. Nothing to worry about, and certainly no blood would drop on the floor.

He clipped off the mechanical spider, folded it up, and stashed it back in the backpack. He placed thin titanium rods on the edges where the window used to sit. These would be his safety net if everything went to shit. He hoped.

He double-checked the contact points on his climbing harness, and then put on a vest with a large circular device in a pouch on the front. It was the NASA gyroscope that would allow him to move dangling in midair inside the gallery.

He attached a small disk, like a fishing reel, to his climbing harness and then double-wrapped that to the military belt around his waist. He then clipped this to the carabiner he had locked into the roof. He pulled on the cam with all his weight. It didn't give. Pray to God it didn't, was Tyler's last thought as he leaned into the window ledge. He swung the expandable quiver over his shoulder so that the strap crossed his chest.

He pulled the ski cap down over his face, so that only his eyes, nose, and mouth were visible, and disappeared headfirst down through the opening.

The snow kept falling.

FORTY-NINE

Tyler slid through the opening while Lucy stared intently at the computer screen. Still no change in the guards' behavior. The worsening snowstorm was the only thing she noticed. As she looked out the window her eye saw something. She swung the binoculars up and looked down at the street. A vehicle. It looked like a large, dark SUV. The kind you'd see in the president's motorcade. It turned up the street next to her and disappeared.

Tyler released the tension on the line with a small thumb-controlled button as he entered the room headfirst like a deep-sea diver going straight down. He could feel the blood rushing to his head as he released more and more wire. He was now suspended inside the room, upside down. When he was two feet off the floor he scissor-kicked his legs, and the momentum swung him around, upright and facing forward.

He paused to get his bearings. Checked his watch. He had burned up less time than expected on the entry. He steadied himself as he came face to face with Vincent van Gogh. *Self-Portrait with Bandaged Ear* stared grimly back at him. A shiver went up Tyler's spine. The faint reddish glow from the dimly lit room gave the image a sinister feel.

"I'll come back to you in a minute," Tyler whispered to Vincent.

Inside the command center the two guards were bored and getting tired. They both saw the storm on an outside monitor.

"That's a helluva storm out there."

"Fucking weather idiots never get it right."

"You got that. Listen, I'm kinda sleepy after that big dinner, and listening to my mother-in-law jammer on about fuck all. Okay if I take a quick nap in the employee lounge?"

The older guard shrugged.

"Sure, why not. Only thing's gonna happen here is us getting snowed in."

They bumped fists and the younger guard got up to leave.

Lucy watched this on the computer screen not sure what was going on. When the guard got up, she panicked but didn't know what to do. She looked closely. The guard took his time leaving. She relaxed.

The small gyroscopic device Tyler wore allowed for forward, reverse, and sideways movement. He had procured it from a disgruntled NASA employee, with Mikey G's assistance. It was a smaller prototype version of the device astronauts used when walking in space. Tyler was amazed at its simplicity and efficiency. Basically you leaned in one direction, and off you went in the other. Tyler leaned left and slid to the right, and was now hovering in front of Manet's *A Bar at the Folies-Bergère*. He stared at the ill-fated woman bartender for a second and then moved closer to the painting, now within easy reach. He unsnapped a velcro hip pocket, and pulled out a custom-made knife with a magnetized blade that was dull on the edges, but had a sharp point. The knife was the one constant from job to job. Reaching out for the canvas he flipped the frame over, and began removing the staples with the knife. The staples clung to the magnetized blade. In less than fifteen seconds Tyler had the canvas free of its frame. He carefully scraped the staples off the blade into a lower pants pocket and then put the knife back in his hip pocket. Tyler rolled the painting inside itself to protect it. He pulled the quiver around and slid the painting inside.

He moved a few feet to his right and began the whole procedure again, only this time with Cézanne's *Still Life with Apples and Oranges*. He flipped the canvas, and in rapid-fire motion pried the industrial-strength staples free of the wood frame. Again, he rolled the canvas inside itself and slid it into the quiver with the other painting. He moved two feet to the right and was facing Degas's *Prima Ballerina*. Tyler stopped for a brief second and realized that even in the reddish glow of the after-hours lighting, the vibrancy of Degas shined through. His brain alerted him to why he was here face to face with an original Degas. He allowed himself a brief moment to admire the beauty, then returned to the job at hand: flip the frame, pry the staples, roll the canvas, slide the canvas into the quiver, slide sideways to the right, REPEAT.

Tyler was just sliding canvas number five, Monet's *Water Lilies* inside the quiver and moving to the next painting, van Gogh's *Self-Portrait*, when the first of the SONS became completely covered by the snowstorm outside, now at full-throttle blizzard.

Lucy continued to monitor the guards watching. She could barely see the National Gallery through the storm.

The blizzard continued to cover the SONS with snow, Tyler had no idea of the effect this would have on the network connection between the museum's mainframe, where the squirrel sat in quiet warmth, and his mini-sat dish that was sitting across the street, and up six stories, quickly absorbing the frigid air.

So far, no change in the central command security monitors. The guard sat watching darkened empty rooms where nothing was a good thing. Without him realizing it, monitor four went fuzzy for the briefest of seconds. He looked up. Nothing. The outside monitor showed the storm worsening by the minute. The guard shook his head. Lucy watched. The guard went back to his magazine.

Tyler was directly in front of van Gogh's *Self-Portrait with Bandaged Ear*. He was mesmerized. So was Vincent. Certainly not van Gogh's best work, but probably one of his boldest and most revealing. Vincent, dressed to go out, without regret in his face, even with the bandaged ear clearly visible. Where *was* he going? His final departure? That, was mere months later? Was the single button on his jacket the only thing holding him together? A single button. This one painting told us more about van Gogh than any book, or any of his other paintings. He knew his exit was at hand.

The first of the cursed.

As Tyler contemplated all this he reached for the painting. He held it less than arm's length away and stared at Vincent who stared back, beguiling.

As he began to flip the frame over....

Monitors two and four in the security room turned "snowy" and now the guard couldn't help but notice. He leaned forward to get a closer look at the fuzzy screens. Suddenly an image appeared on the monitors.

The snow outside continued to fall.

Lucy watched the guard staring at the object.

The SONS sensed an interruption in the connection to each other.

Tyler flipped the frame and pried Vincent's staples loose.

The guard watched as the monitor flipped from snowy fuzz to the silhouette of a person who appeared to be floating in midair in gallery 80, and then the screen blipped, and the monitor showed a normally quiet room. Perplexed, the guard continued to stare at the screen. Did he really see what he thought he saw? Impossible. All the other security monitors showed no sign of any change in any of the other rooms. He called the napping guard on his walkie-talkie.

Lucy was paralyzed in her panicked state. The storm had moved to white-out conditions.

Tyler freed Vincent from his years in a taut frame. Instead of just rolling up the canvas, Tyler took a moment to view it up close. As he gently held the canvas it seemed as though Vincent was stretching his neck and shoulder muscles after years of maintaining a single pose.

The snow outside was getting deeper.

The two guards watched as the monitors in the security room flashed from blank rooms to horizontal designs, to a distorted picture of a person, or what appeared to be a person, floating in gallery 80, then back to an empty gallery, then snowy, then blank.

Neither guard could make hide nor hair of what they saw. Clearly something was amiss.

They knew if they rang the silent alarm, all hell would break loose. The entire building would be sealed up and they wouldn't be done answering questions, or allowed to leave, until well into

Friday morning. If anything went wrong, they'd be the first to catch blame.

Outside, the snow continued to fall. Most of the SONS were now completely covered by snow. The connection was deteriorating quickly.

In the dim glow of the reddish light in the gallery, Vincent's serious demeanor took on an almost impish look. Tyler smiled beneath the ski mask as Vincent slyly stared back at him. Tyler heard a strange humming noise. He jerked his head in the direction of the sound, but his movement was too severe for the directional gyro attached at his waist, and he swung wildly out of control to his left. He barely managed to hang on to Vincent. The canvas slipped in his hand. He could hardly believe what he saw. The lead doors to the gallery were sliding shut. He instantly looked up and realized the windows had begun to close over him with their lead curtain.

Outside, the weather had turned from worse to not-fit-for-man-nor-beast. The connection between the squirrel, which sat warm and comfortable on the cables of the mainframe in the basement of the East Building, and the SONS, had completely disconnected. The signal was broken. Lucy stared at a blank computer screen.

The guards in the security command room were dumbstruck as they stared at the monitors for gallery 80 which clearly showed a dark figure suspended in midair. It had been seventeen seconds since they pushed the silent alarm. The other guards in the building rushed to the security command center. They arrived sixty seconds later. It was the night supervisor's responsibility to double-check the monitors, to confirm what the other two guards already knew—that security had been breached. Their first call would be to Helmut Strell, the head of security, brought in specifically for this exhibit. He, in turn, would immediately call his counterpart at Interpol. This would all take less than five minutes.

Tyler had steadied himself and hastily slid Vincent's portrait into the quiver with the others. Leaving behind the remaining paintings, he immediately began zipping skyward up the titanium wire using the automatic recoil system. He could see the lead curtain as it closed over the skylight windows. He prayed that the eighteen-inch-long titanium rods he had placed at the window would hold the quarter-ton lead curtain that was threatening to seal him in. Lucy saw something moving on the roof, but the storm made focusing a problem. She grabbed the binoculars. She watched as the lead curtain enclosures were sealing Tyler's fate.

"Oh my God," she said as she dropped the binoculars.

Tyler was moving too fast towards the ceiling and was unaware that the internal reel on the directional gyro had come unhinged when he had jerked severely to his left moments before. Instead of spooling up cleanly, the internal workings struggled against each other, the internal wire was off track and filled the chamber helter-skelter. The pressure inside the small chamber on the harness around Tyler's waist continued to build.

Tyler zoomed skyward, planning his next move, the entire contraption exploded, the chamber shattered, the pulley fell to the floor and the wire fell freely. And suddenly Newton's theory of gravity took hold as Tyler fell at sixty feet per second.

FIFTY

Tyler hit the floor hard, landing on his hip. He shook his head and took a couple of deep breaths. His body ached everywhere. He looked up. The hole in the skylight was still there, which meant the titanium rods were holding the lead enclosure at bay, but the opening looked a lot farther away from where he now sat. He checked his watch. He had burned up almost two minutes. He knew the security guards would be stationed outside the sealed gallery door.

DO NOT GO TO JAIL! flashed through his brain. He immediately grabbed the wire that hung free, down through the skylight to the floor. He wrapped his right hand around the wire, and pulled himself up as far as possible, and then, bending his knees tight, he wrapped the hanging wire around his left foot. He then stepped up as high as possible, grabbing the wire with his left hand, and then quickly wrapped it around his free hand. He repeated the procedure, opposite hand to foot as he slowly, and painfully, pulled himself skyward. He could feel his face sweating profusely under the ski mask.

Slowly, the opening above came into focus.

He was so preoccupied trying to escape he had no time to consider what had gone wrong or why the alarms had gone off. His sole focus was to make it back to the rooftop... alive. He knew if he could make it back up to the rooftop he'd have half a chance. His muscles worked overtime, his body aching from the fall, exhausted from the task of trying to climb up a thin wire.

The tension on the wire was so great that it was tearing through the surgical gloves he wore, cutting into his skin. Both hands were bleeding, cut through with wire marks.

Tyler didn't have the time or the energy to consider the fact that he was leaving a potential DNA trail behind. He could hear the muffled sounds on the other side of the door. Stay focused, his brain commanded.

The rookie desk clerk at Precinct 16 of the District of Columbia, had received a call eighty-eight seconds ago from the security command room at the National Gallery. His boss, the evening desk sergeant on duty, had stepped away for a "minute" approximately forty-five minutes ago with instructions that the rookie page him if anything "major" happened. So, being a rookie he did as he was told, and no more. He paged the desk sergeant who was momentarily indisposed with a woman he'd met while working vice half a dozen years before. He was currently out of uniform, save for his birthday uniform, *in flagrante delicto,* as a Thanksgiving treat to himself, for having to work the Thanksgiving shift, when his pager went off. He wasn't about to be interrupted. He would wait another two and a half minutes before calling back the rookie desk clerk whom he had left in charge.

Tyler continued his struggle up the thin wire. He could hear shouting on the other side of the lead doors. And then the same hum he'd heard when the doors closed him in suddenly started up again and he realized the doors were opening. He pulled himself up with renewed motivation.

DO NOT GET CAUGHT.

Tyler's sole focus, the eighteen-inch-wide opening directly above him. The guards now stood in gallery 80 but saw no one in the darkened room. They heard a noise from above.

A final step up and Tyler grabbed the edge of the opening with his right hand and pushed off with what strength he had left in his legs. He grabbed the other side of the opening with his free hand and pulled himself up only to realize that he wouldn't fit through cleanly.

"HEY YOU! STOP!" shouted the older guard.

As Tyler twisted and turned to get through the opening, he looked remarkably like a newborn, appearing into the world for the first time.

"I said STOP!" the guard yelled.

Tyler kept moving through the tight space.

"Maybe he's deaf?" said the younger guard.

The older guard just shook his head as they watched Tyler disappear.

As he lay on the rooftop catching his breath, a voice below shouted, "He went through the hole up there."

The rays of flashlights flickered through the small opening he had just been birthed from. In the next second, Tyler was on his feet, yanking on the thin wire he had just climbed. His palms were cut through and bleeding. He felt resistance on the line from below. Someone was holding the other end.

Tyler was not leaving any evidence.

He snapped the line as hard as he could, and from below he heard, "Shit! That hurts."

Even though there were guards below in the room, Tyler still hadn't heard any sirens. He looked up and realized he was standing in a full on blizzard. He could barely see across the street to where

Lucy was. He noticed two dim flashes from the flashlight. Guards were out and circling the building.

He had only one thing on his brain, *Do Not Get Caught.*

Tyler ran back carefully along the slippery rooftop to where he had ziplined across. He clipped a carabiner and a climber's pulley to the end of the zipline bolted into the wall, and with six of the world's most valuable paintings strapped across his chest, he slid over the edge and carefully released the line. If the bolt didn't hold there was a chance he could plummet to his death, or at least break one or both legs. Lucy watched in the darkness as Tyler began his slide downward.

Tyler could see flashlights below, swinging wildly as they searched for the intruder. The snow was falling hard. He waited until the two lights moving below him faded as they continued around the outside perimeter. The voices grew muffled in the silence of the snow. He had to go NOW!

He rappelled himself towards the ground. Halfway down, he spotted a light moving, about twenty yards away. He locked off the rappel line, and froze, literally, in position. He watched through the snowstorm as the light came closer, until it was directly below him. Tyler could just make out the silhouette of the person below. He waited in the cold, twenty feet up; the sweat from his exhausting climb started to chill him, his muscles getting stiff from the cold. A walkie-talkie crackled. Suddenly the light shone upwards, less than ten feet away from Tyler. Lucy watched as the light moved towards Tyler. The person with the light stood directly below Tyler. The light moved closer.

Tyler released the stop-lock mechanism on his harness and fell freely to the ground. It wasn't lost on him that in less than ten minutes he had made two free falls, one by choice, one not.

Tyler zipping freely downward broke the snow's silence. The guard holding the light suddenly looked up, the light aimed directly at Tyler, who was momentarily blinded. By the time the guard got the walkie-talkie up to his mouth and attempted to hit the push-to-talk button, Tyler slammed into him full force. He heard a thud and they crumpled to the ground together. Lucy watched through the binoculars as Tyler fell onto the guard. She gasped. Tyler needed help. She ran out of the apartment.

Tyler disentangled himself, and leapt to his feet. The guard remained motionless. Tyler started to move away, but then turned back. He rolled the guard over so he was face up in the snow. He realized it was the same guard he had spoken to a month before, while scoping out the gallery. He felt bad for knocking him out. He grabbed the guard's oversized flashlight and placed it under his head, so he was up out of the snow. Tyler slapped him lightly on both cheeks.

"Wake up," Tyler said.

No response. Tyler wasn't going to leave him here in the snow, unconscious. He tried again pushing down on the guard's chest trying to awaken him.

The guard let out a groan. "Aaarrrhhh" was all he could say.

The guard tried to focus but all he could see was a blurry black face with cutouts where the eyes and mouth should be. The eyes blinked at him as he tried regaining his wits.

"Wha hapen?" the guard asked weakly, and then he passed out again.

Tyler stayed silent. The guard came to. He's shivering.

"Izz culd...."

Tyler quickly took out his silver survival blanket and bundled it around the guard. He didn't want to chance the guard passing out in the snow so he grabbed the walkie-talkie.

"Man down on the perimeter. Call an ambulance immediately."

The guard lay in the snow, sliding in and out of consciousness.

"You'll be okay," Tyler said and then disappeared into the blizzard.

FIFTY-ONE

The storm was not isolated to the DC area. In fact the entire Eastern seaboard was blanketed. Airports were shut down. Trains stuck at stations. Highways were open only for emergencies. Nothing was moving. Not even Imasu, who was stuck in his Greenwich house. He was staring out into a white abyss instead of the usual view of Long Island Sound. His nerves were fraying, stuck in a house with his family was bad enough, but the conversation he was having with his two men, who were sitting in a large black SUV across the street from the National Gallery in DC, was moving him close to the point of doing something reckless. The two men were stuck in the raging storm unable to see anything, except that the guards from the National Gallery were out circling the building. Because of the white-out conditions they were unable to see Tyler flying down from the roof and landing on the guard. Nor did they see Lucy as she ran out of the building. They did however see an individual trying to run away from the building. No, they couldn't describe anything about the person, whether male or female, white (everything looked white they said) or black, nothing. Yes, there had been a call to the local police, but nothing specific, just that there was some sort of problem at the gallery.

Imasu listened, he was sure it was Sears, but trying to devise a plan for his capture was near impossible. There was only one option: "Do NOT under any circumstances let Sears get taken by the police."

"Yes, Imasu-san."

"Do what is necessary to get Sears, and my paintings. Understood?"

"Yes, Imasu-san."

Imasu's man sitting in the passenger seat turned around and opened a large case. It contained two micro-Uzis, two H&K MP5s with the shorter stock, two Beretta M9s, and half a dozen grenades—shock, tear gas, and smoke. Plus, enough ammo to make instructors at Quantico jealous. He turned back around. They sat and stared at nothing but white.

Across town, Rosenwater had just hung up on his call with Helmut Strell, head of security for the entire exhibit. Strell, being a good Bavarian, was direct.

"There's been a break in."

Rosenwater didn't wait for details. He hung up and dialed Chanel N°5.

"Our boy Sears just hit the museum."

"What! How do you know?" Chanel N°5 asked.

"Just get over there!" Rosenwater barked.

Tyler made his way through the deep snow across Constitution Avenue. The streets, thick with snow, were eerily quiet. He ran up the steps and across the plaza adjacent to the Canadian Embassy.

Tyler bolted up the back steps of the plaza when he heard a voice yell, "YOU. STOP!"

Paying no heed, he sprinted along C Street and turned up 3rd Street, his feet sliding in the snow with every step. The police station was just around the corner, on Indiana. Tyler could see his car covered in snow, the parking lights were on, the windshield clear of snow, the car running. Lucy rolled down the window.

"Get in! I'm driving."

Tyler jumped into the passenger side. He's soaked, a mess, and exhausted. He looked at Lucy who is staring straight ahead.

She put the car in gear, and pulled away from the curb. As she slowly moved down the street a police cruiser turned up the street. She waited. The cruiser suddenly turned on the siren and flashing lights and headed right at them. The cruiser slid in the snow. Lucy shifted into reverse and started backing up. In her mirror she saw another cruiser screaming up behind them, siren blaring. Lucy looked in every direction. Trapped. Lucy jammed the stick shift into first gear and spun the wheel hard left.

Tyler watched, panicked.

"What are you doing?" he stammered.

"Buckle up. It's gonna be a bumpy ride."

Lucy grinned as she stepped on the accelerator, jumped the curb, and aimed for the top steps of the plaza next to the Canadian Embassy. The Audi leapt from the top step and landed near the bottom, engine screaming. The wheels grabbed, as Lucy turned onto Constitution Avenue.

"That was lucky," Tyler said as he got slammed back into his seat.

Lucy smirked. She was focused.

The first cruiser followed the Audi.

"You gotta be fuckin' kidding me?" said the driver of the cruiser.

The second police cruiser reversed course and headed down C Street, to 6th Street, with the hope of cutting Tyler off on Constitution Avenue. The cruiser that followed Lucy off the steps hit the bottom steps hard and headed directly for a large, snow-covered, oak tree. The cop yanked the wheel to the right, but lacked traction on the snowy road and the back end of the cruiser swung wildly to the left and broadsided the tree. The car was crushed all the way to the wheel, and made a horrible screeching sound as it pulled away from the oak. The tree showed no damage.

Two other cars approached from the Capitol area. One of them did a 360-degree spin as it turned onto Constitution from Louisiana. The roads were treacherous at best. Cruiser number two was coming straight at them from the right. Lucy slammed the car into second gear and crushed the accelerator to the floor. The engine was racing at close to 6500 rpm and barely noticed the slick snow underfoot. It stuck to the road like a fly on a frog's tongue. Tyler stared at Lucy and smiled.

The police cruiser was closing in, and about to broadside them. Suddenly, a large black SUV smashed into the police cruiser. And knocked it cleanly away. Tyler turned to look out the back window.

"WHATTHEFUCKWASTHAT!" he yelled.

Lucy glanced in the mirror, as she slowed temporarily. The black SUV was turning around. Hardly a mark on the front. The police cruiser was crushed. Totaled.

"I saw that SUV drive by the museum about a half hour ago. I thought they were security. Who the hell are they?"

Tyler had a suspicion but held his tongue. No need to frighten Lucy. Besides, he might be wrong. *Doubtful.*

The storm had gotten worse as the wind picked up, making it appear to be snowing up, down, and sideways. Lucy saw flashing lights, ahead in the distance, and the wounded cruiser that chased them down the plaza steps limped after them. Police sirens seemed to be everywhere. Lucy moved cautiously and then stopped. The black SUV was gaining on them. The flashing lights in front were definitely getting closer. Lucy spun the wheel hard to the left, and jumped on the gas. She's headed right for the National Gallery.

"Now where are you going?"

"We've got to get off the road."

Lucy downshifted and revved the engine as she jumped the curb and aimed at the side of the building.

Tyler got tossed around as she sped over the curb.

"Where'd you learn to drive like this?"

"My Dad used to do winter rally racing… and I was his navigat—"

They hit the skating rink, unawares. The car started sliding.

"What the—" she said as she immediately took her foot off the accelerator and dropped the car into neutral. She held the wheel steady. The car steadied. Tyler stared at her, amazed at her driving skills.

Lucy gradually eased the accelerator back down and the car slowly began moving forward. When she hit the far side of the rink the tires grabbed terra firma, and jerked Tyler forward. The two cars in pursuit hit the ice rink, the cop car started spinning. The black SUV held—studded tires. Tyler watched through the back window. The black SUV aimed right for the cop cruiser.

BANG!

The cruiser was pushed with such force that it was knocked on its side. Lucy took a quick glance at the mirror. This time Tyler was certain.

"Who is that?" Lucy asked.

"Imasu."

The black SUV was gaining on them. Police cars had surrounded all possible roadways. They were trapped, hemmed in on all fronts. All viable exits were sealed off. They could hear a muffled voice barking through a police loudspeaker, telling them to stop and surrender. The SUV kept coming. The snowstorm was at whiteout conditions. Lucy shifted into second gear, turned the wheel, and headed into the winter forest. The black SUV gaining ground.

Imasu's man in the passenger seat pulled out the 9 mm Beretta gun and aimed it out his window. Shots fired. Their noise muffled by the storm.

"What was that?" Lucy asked.

The next bullet hits the trunk, and another crushed the mirror on Tyler's side of the car.

"Seriously! They're shooting at us?" she said.

Lucy pushed down on the accelerator, but the SUV was less than a car length behind. Tyler considered throwing the paintings out the window at the SUV, but before he could finish the thought Lucy turned the Audi's headlights off. As well as the dash lights. The Audi, Tyler, and Lucy, suddenly vanished into the storm. She rolled down her window and stuck her head out trying to navigate as she threaded through the stand of oaks. She aimed the car like a slalom skier cutting around the trees.

The black SUV lost sight of Tyler and Lucy, and as they sped up trying to see them in the storm, they smacked one tree and then two more before getting stuck. They tried freeing the vehicle. No luck. They fled the scene.

To avoid hitting a tree Lucy was forced to jerk the wheel. Tyler's head banged against his window, hard, as the car bounced off a hidden tree. Lucy slowed momentarily.

"You okay?" she asked Tyler.

"For now. Let's get out of here."

"Slow and steady," she said as she moved carefully forward, the lights still off. Lucy's face stung from the snow pelting her as she tried to steer clear of the oak village.

She silently slid past giant trees, the way ships slide by icebergs. Close enough to touch, and also to realize how dangerous a misstep could be. The SUV lights were no more. The car suddenly grabbed. Traction. They were back on pavement. Lucy turned the wheel to the right slowly. An enormous dark object loomed on her left. The Air and Space Museum. The dark object was gone. She guessed they were at the end of the building.

"Tyler, you okay?" Lucy asked.

"A lump and a headache."

"I need your help. Where are we?"

He tried to focus but his sight was blurry and bleary. He looked out her window, and then his.

"Turn left and you should be on a roadway."

She slowly pressed on the accelerator and turned the wheel as the car smoothly moved forward. She could sense the all-wheel drive system gripping.

Tyler guessed they were on 7th Street, and heading south. He knew that the expressway entrance at C Street would be blocked by the cops, so he told her to turn right. She was moving faster now. Tyler knew there was an entrance at 12th Street but it ran in the wrong direction, not exactly a factor at this point. It was total darkness as they passed by several large federal buildings, and drove into a tunnel. She stopped. She was worried about Tyler. His speech was slurred and he was slumped in the seat. There was no traffic, no sounds. No cops.

Suddenly headlights were coming straight at them. Lucy panicked. It was only a cabbie driving around trying to stay warm.

Lucy gunned it through the tunnel and emerged back into the snowstorm, visibility still nil. And then she saw the partially snow-covered sign for Interstate 395. Tyler saw it too and pointed.

"Up there," he mumbled.

Lucy aimed the Audi up the northbound ramp and accelerated as quickly as the slick, unplowed roadway would allow.

The best news was that no one seemed to be in pursuit. With all the lights of the Audi still dark they headed past the NSA building. Below them on the surface road were at least six, and probably more, cop cars with lights flashing. She drove carefully and steadily away from the lights as they faded into the storm.

Luck was on their side.

For the moment.

FIFTY-TWO

Tyler and Lucy exited the city while Chanel's boss, Rosenwater, worked his way through the snowy streets of DC in his armor-plated all-wheel-drive Mercedes. With his only directive, to his young military attaché assigned as his driver, being "HURRY!" the Mercedes was pushed to the limits of its German engineering.

The Mercedes pulled up in front of the DC courthouse, two blocks from the National Gallery. Chanel N°5 stepped out from the shadow of the building and climbed into the back of the car. She was cold and snow covered. The car was warm and dry. Rosenwater dispensed with any pleasantries and immediately asked for an update.

She briefed her boss on all that had happened as far as she knew. Starting with the guards roaming the exterior with large flashlights, and ended with a car, (no, no one got the license number), flying across the plaza in front of the Canadian Embassy, with police cars in pursuit. All of the vehicles ended up around the other side of the National Gallery building, at which point she lost visuals on all the vehicles. There was also a large black SUV that appeared to be helping Tyler, if in fact he was involved. A crowd had gathered around the injured individual—no, she didn't know if it was one of the guards or one of the intruders. An ambulance arrived a few minutes ago. And that was as much info as she had. Rosenwater made some sounds of displeasure and ordered the driver around to where the ambulance was parked. The Mercedes pulled up near the ambulance on Constitution Avenue, dropped off Chanel and Rosenwater, and then U-turned, and parked in front of The Capital Grille, directly below the still-open window that Tyler had exited less than thirty minutes before.

Rosenwater found a museum guard who was helping the EMT guys, he flashed his Interpol badge, and began barking questions. "What happened?"

"Someone broke in," said the guard pointing to the National Gallery.

"Any description?"

"Not really. The perpetrator was dressed completely in black with a black ski mask."

"Male or female?" asked agent Rosenwater.

"Well, Amos lying on the ground over there, says it was a male voice that spoke to him."

Rosenwater seemed perplexed by this news.

"Amos says he's the one who called for the ambulance."

"What!?" snapped Rosenwater in disbelief.

"Yeah, the intruder's the one who called on the walkie-talkie."

Rosenwater motioned for the head guard to stop talking for a second, as he and Chanel N°5 went over to where Amos, the fallen guard, was now being placed on a gurney.

Amos was still wrapped in the emergency survival blanket that Tyler had placed around him, as well as a wool blanket from the EMT guys. He also had an oxygen mask covering his nose and mouth.

Rosenwater flashed his ID card at the EMT crew. "I need to ask him a few questions."

"Make it quick. We need to get him in the ambulance and get going," replied the EMT driver.

Two EMT techs hoisted Amos up and into the ambulance. Rosenwater jumped in right behind them and sat on the supply footlocker that was bolted to the side of the vehicle.

"Can you hear me?" he asked.

Amos, lying on the gurney with an industrial-size ice pack wrapped around his head, nodded slowly.

The EMT crew moved quickly in the background.

"Can you tell me anything about the man who did this to you?" asked the boss.

"Heee whzz nze," said Amos through the oxygen mask.

Rosenwater turned to the EMT in charge and said, "Okay to remove the oxygen mask for a minute?"

"Sure, but be quick will ya," responded the EMT driver.

He leaned over and removed the oxygen mask from Amos. "Tell me what happened."

"He wuzz... nize," said Amos.

"Nice?" snapped Rosenwater, "I thought he attacked you."

"He fell on me... but then... he wrapped me... blanket... anthen... called fir—" said Amos, wheezing heavily.

"Wrap it up," snapped the EMT driver. "We've got to get him to the hospital, and with this weather we gotta move, now!"

"HOLD ON! So this guy knocks you out, and then calls for help?!" asked the Interpol agent, staring right at Amos.

Amos nodded but added in a light voice, "He fell... not... knock... wrapped me his blanket...."

"OK. We have to go now! Interview over," snapped the EMT driver to everyone.

They repositioned the oxygen mask on Amos's face and instantly the color came back into his cheeks.

Rosenwater jumped out of the van. "Where you taking him?" he yelled to the EMT driver just before the doors closed.

"GW," the medic yelled back as he closed his door and fishtailed the ambulance away from the National Gallery.

Chanel N°5, who had heard most of her boss's interrogation, stood silently as they watched the ambulance pull away.

A police car that lost Tyler in the pursuit returned to where the ambulance had just pulled away. The officers jumped out of their car and headed quickly toward Chanel and her boss. Rosenwater walked away from them and toward the spot where the guard fell.

"Hey! Hey hold on." The cop yelled.

Rosenwater ignored them and kept walking. Chanel stopped and showed her badge to the two cops.

"Wow. Interpol," said the younger one.

"The old guy deaf or something?" asked the older cop.

"No. Just focused," Chanel said, laughing.

Rosenwater looked around and then walked back. He looked at the cops.

"So, what happened?" he asked. The younger cop spoke first.

"We were in pursuit...."

"And we lost him" added the older cop.

Irving Rosenwater squeezed the bridge of his nose as though trying to ward off the incoming migraine. "How the fuck did you lose him?"

The older cop balled his fist up. He really wanted to hit someone from the night he's had, and Rosenwater was an easy target, and close. "If you hadn't noticed, it's snowing a shit storm out here. And that crazy motherfucker drove everywhere but on the road. On top of that, some bad-ass SUV took out two of my squad cars," the older cop spit out.

Chanel stepped between her boss and the two cops, trying to defuse the situation before they pistol-whipped him.

"Here's my card. Would you guys give me a call as soon as you get warm?"

They both nodded. Chanel N°5 gave the older cop a grim smile as if to say I feel your pain. The cops headed back to their car, and to someplace warm, and less hostile.

"Incompetents!" snarled Chanel's boss, as the cops drove away. He walked over to the footprints in the snow. He looked down at them and saw the name of the climbing shoe, and size 10 ½. As the snow fell, Chanel's boss began to laugh.

"What is it?" asked Chanel.

"Sears. It's definitely him."

"How do you know?"

"The same shoe, and shoe size that he wore when he hit the Prado. But it doesn't really matter if those idiots stepped all over the evidence," he said.

"Why not?" she asked, confused.

"Because. By the time the crime scene techs get here to take casts of the footprints, they'll all have been covered by more snow," he said, now shaking his head at the irony of it all.

"But it was definitely our boy Tyler Sears."

"How can you be so sure?" asked Chanel.

Rosenwater looked at her, trying to formulate in words what he knew instinctively. It had all the DNA of a Tyler Sears heist. Except something had gone wrong for Sears. A miscalculation? But where? And how? His gut told him it was Sears, but his brain said there was something wrong. Why had Sears risked getting caught to help the guard?

He stood there silently as the snow kept falling. There was a sudden explosion. They turned to see flaming debris falling all over his parked Mercedes, the driver racing away from the flaming car. The incendiary devices Tyler had set before he ziplined across the road had all exploded at once. Chanel stood transfixed by the inferno scene.

The flames were too much for even the best of German engineering. The Mercedes exploded in stages, beginning with the engine block, then the fuel line, followed by the gas tank.

Rosenwater hadn't moved, hadn't blinked. He just stood there watching his car disintegrate in flames.

"Sears. I just know," he said. "I just know."

FIFTY-THREE

Lucy wrapped gauze bandages around Tyler's hands. Both of which were cut through from climbing the wire. A bloodstained cloth, and a large tube of Neosporin were nearby. There's already a butterfly bandage up near his temple where his head banged against the car window. He looked like a war-wounded casualty. The Audi's rear quarter panel looked similar. The quiver holding six of the most famous paintings leaned against the car. The only light provided by a Coleman battery-powered lantern, set on the low setting. Lucy looked around at their darkened surroundings.

Two weeks before Thanksgiving, Tyler had rented a small airplane hangar. He'd paid three months' rent in advance, with cash. The entire transaction happened over the phone. Tyler had used a false name, and the owner of the small airfield was all too happy to pick up cash at the local Western Union outpost. The hangar could hold a small single-engine aircraft, so it could easily accommodate Tyler and his champ getaway car. It also provided shelter from the storm, although Tyler had not planned on that literally. Tyler had an aversion to roadside motels, as they were always the first place the cops checked. He had stowed enough food and water in the hangar for a five-day stay if necessary. He'd also packed a fresh change of clothes, a fake passport, fifty thousand in cash, a couple of burner cell phones, and a sleeping bag. He had not planned on giving away his emergency blanket.

The Audi was as solid as Gibraltar in a storm as Lucy had navigated through the blizzard, heading east on Route 50. Thirty minutes later they pulled off a deserted Route 50, onto an access road that led to a small airfield. She pulled the car into hangar number eight and together they slid the heavy metal door shut. Tyler, exhausted, drank a liter of water without stopping. His body craved food. He'd burned up all his energy in the last hour. Between having to climb a pencil-thin wire, then barely escaping through a blizzard, he was whipped. He was too exhausted to eat.

Tyler slumped against the car seat as Lucy finished wrapping his hands in gauze. Exhaustion rolled over him. He could feel his metabolism starting to calm down for the first time in hours, the adrenaline seeping out his nerve endings. He was beat, and worse, he got beat. He looked at Lucy, and then at the quiver with the paintings. His exhaustion turned to frustration, as it often does. How many bad decisions, how many things said in frustration would be better left to a decent night's sleep? And how often do we ignore the reasonable, to move as quickly as possible to the regretful when exhaustion is all that we are wearing?

"How the hell did I get caught? I triple-checked everything… God damn van Gogh—"

Lucy cut him off as she sensed his exhaustion was headed into the darkness of anger.

"Tyler. Not the curse… not now," she said.

She smiled, leaned in, and kissed his hands. He looked at her and his mood pivoted.

"Let's get some rest… at least for a few minutes."

Tyler tried to protest. Her smiled proved too potent. She held his head close. He closed his eyes, vertigo took hold, and he slumped in his seat. Lucy leaned his seat all the way back, and swaddled him in the sleeping bag.

"I'm gonna take a quick nap," he slurred, and then was out like a light.

What had happened? How had he been discovered? This unknown detail, the how and why, would play over and over in his head.

As he fell into total darkness, the last thing that floated through his brain was the face of Vincent van Gogh, staring at him with a look of doubt.

FIFTY-FOUR

Rosenwater was barking orders into his cell phone.

"I want round-the-clock guards on the injured security guard over at GW Hospital. And I want only *our* doctors and nurses tending to him.... I don't care, I don't want him talking to the press... when he comes to, you explain that he's to say NOTHING to his family about what really happened."

His next call was to Helmut Strell, a courtesy call to update him on what he had found out: half a billion dollars in art had just been stolen. This was going to be an ugly call.

While he was calling, he and Chanel waited in the freezing cold for another car to arrive from Interpol headquarters in downtown DC.

Standing in the freezing cold would be the least of their worries that night.

FIFTY-FIVE

Whilst Tyler slept, Lucy sat against the wall eating from a bag of trail mix. She had taken the quiver from the car and opened it to display six of the most famous paintings in existence. She lined them up against the hangar wall near her. Why eat alone. And what wonderful meal companions—Monet, Cézanne, Renoir, Manet, Degas, and of course, van Gogh.

She was humbled to be in their company. Even in the dim light the paintings were stunning. Their remarkable view of nature, society, and mankind stared back at her.

Half a billion sitting in a small plane hangar, just the canvases, free of their frames. There was a strange sensation of simplicity as she stared at them. Mesmerized.

The paintings seemed remarkably at peace, constraints cast off. Weirdly, she thought Vincent looked especially pleased to be free of his circumstances (hanging in a frame on a wall for the last one hundred years). She smiled, as he seemed to be smiling at her with a crooked grin.

"So, Vincent, is it true? You know, the "curse." And what happened at Saint-Rémy? You were never the same after that?"

Vincent van Gogh stared back at her, not giving up anything. Lucy shook her head as she waited. Nothing. She lay down on the bed pad and drifted off gazing at the paintings and their world of natural colors, brilliant brushstrokes, and incredible imagery.

FIFTY-SIX

Chanel and her boss had been up all night. She was convinced he never slept, and she felt guilty about the two hours of intermittent sleep she had grabbed on the couch in the borrowed office on the top floor of the Justice Department.

Rosenwater was one of a dying breed. He didn't use computers, and found "criminal justice" classes to be stupid. The only way to catch a thief was to outsmart him, he always said. His suit, a Men's Warehouse special, got more wrinkled by the day. The pants were a shade too short, and he wore standard issue white shirts (stained) with thin, black, clip-on ties.

He had little time for criminal psychologists, or sociologists. Lawyers were to him what houseflies are to the rest of us—a constant annoyance. "Bunk," he would bark, when forced to listen to some PhD blather on about the criminal's motive. To him, it was obvious. "It's about the money!" he would snap. "Criminals are criminals because of the money, and only the money."

A bit shortsighted, yes, but often closer to the truth then any of the new-style crime fighters would dare to admit.

He was on the downslope of his career. He'd already had a triple bypass, and his joints ached every morning. A hip replacement was awaiting him in retirement. He had been moved sideways from the CIA to Interpol as his old-school tactics, and lack of diplomacy in front of Congress had made him an agency liability.

Tyler Sears was in his sights, and he was determined to put him away for life. Three strikes and you're gone... for good. It would be his crowning achievement, in a long and successful career in criminal justice and espionage, which he thought of as one and the same. He was furious when Tyler was released on early parole, due to "good behavior." And the old man was determined to make Tyler pay.

His success came with the stigma of three failed marriages, and several children who barely spoke to him. He didn't just live to work, he breathed it. He loved his job, and he hated crooks, thieves, terrorists, drug dealers, the whole lot. He truly believed in Truth, Justice, and the American Way!

He was furious at the DC police for the botched job of the night before, and he was still fuming that the sonufabitch had managed to blow up his armor-plated Mercedes.

"If nothing else we've got him on destruction of government property. And he had to have accomplices on a job this big. Anything?" said Rosenwater to Chanel N°5 as he was put on hold.

"The gallery has been dusted. Nothing. And the tech guys said there were no prints anywhere on the SUV. No VIN. No plates. They did find a substantial arsenal in the back seat. But, again no reg. numbers, nothing," Chanel said.

"Weapons? Sears has an aversion to guns." Rosenwater pondered as he heard a voice in the phone. He listened for less than two seconds.

"Well he didn't fucking vanish into thin air. He's somewhere in your godforsaken state and I want you to find him," Rosenwater yelled into the receiver at the chief of the Virginia State Police, and then slammed down the receiver. Chanel N°5 was pretty certain her boss was NOT winning any popularity contests. Chanel looked away, stifling a laugh. Rosenwater, who by now was starting to act manic, was having no luck with either the Virginia or Maryland Police. So far they had all come up empty. And the staties were tired of his shit attitude. They had bigger problems with a full-blown snowstorm, than a few stolen paintings.

The news of the theft hadn't yet made the papers, which meant that Helmut Strell was doing his job—keeping a lid on information. As far as the *Washington Post* was concerned, a guard from the National Gallery had fallen on the snow-covered ice and hit his head, and that was the reason for the ambulance. Besides, the paralyzing snowstorm was front-page news, and digging out would occupy the capitol for the better part of a day or two.

Rosenwater knew it was only a matter of time before the truth came out. The other museum directors who had loaned priceless pieces would have to be notified, as well as the insurance companies. Leaks were inevitable.

And this evening was to be the gala opening for VIPs and press. It would have to be cancelled with some kind of bogus explanation. He could only hope that Helmut Strell, with his officious Teutonic attitude, could hold the press at bay for another twenty-four hours.

"It's not doing any good for both of us to be sitting here. We're accomplishing absolutely fuckall.... I want you to head to New York and wait for him there. And get his mug shot to every toll booth, train station, bus depot, anywhere he might stop."

"How can you be so sure that's where he'll end up?" she asked.

"Just a hunch," he replied.

Chanel stared at him for a moment and walked over to look out the window at the surrounding federal buildings lacquered in snow.

"Well, if it was him," she began, "and you seem pretty certain that it was, then we know his only movements have been up and down the New York-DC corridor, with one known stop in Wilmington. His MO, and it has never varied, has always been to stay within designated route patterns."

He cut her off.

"So, you agree. He's back in New York City."

Chanel, slightly flustered with her boss's impatience, put her hands up in front of her in a STOP motion.

"All I'm saying is I don't think he's anywhere near Virginia. It's out of his designated range. And yes, I think he'll be trying to get back to New York. The question is when?" Chanel stated with more authority than her boss was used to. He realized she was probably right, at least more right than any other theories he'd heard in the last ten hours.

"So where do you think he is?"

Chanel walked over to the map of the mid-Atlantic region and studied it. She pointed her finger along Route 50 and followed it out towards the Chesapeake Bay Bridge.

"My guess is, he's somewhere along here. I don't think he's foolish enough to try and use the Interstates, and Route 50 can provide plenty of cover. There are lots of small towns to hide out in, and it's a long expanse that flows all the way up to Wilmington. Plus, it's hard for police to cover because of all the entrance and exit ramps." Chanel jabbed her finger at Route 50 East at almost exactly the location where Tyler and Lucy were in fact hiding out.

"Your theory's a good one, but I disagree on his actual route. Fifty has almost no traffic, especially after a night like last night, so, any vehicles will be easy to identify. I think he's switched vehicles and is somewhere on I-95 northbound, trying to blend in with all the normal interstate traffic," said Rosenwater.

And with that, Tyler was given a reprieve.

FIFTY-SEVEN

Tyler was unable to move. The artist with the bandaged ear kept moving towards him, swinging his brush in wild strokes. Tyler's leg felt bolted to the floor. The closer the mad painter got, the more immovable Tyler's leg became. The madman started singing in some strange language. Tyler wanted to push him away, but his hands and arms were stuck at his sides. He began to panic as he thrashed around, trying to escape the psychotic painter. Something was pushing on his arms, holding him down.

"Tyler, wake up. TYLER!" Lucy said as she shook him awake.

He woke with a start. He'd fallen into a deep sleep in the car, and had rolled up against the gearshift and hand brake. His leg was totally numb. His body ached from being in such a twisted position. His heart was racing. He untangled himself from the goose-down bag. Lucy helped him sit back up. He took a few deep breaths, squeezed his eyes tight, and tried to pull himself together. He stared at his surroundings: a dark hangar, stale air, a chill that fogged his brain, and, leaning against the wall, staring straight at him, was the very artist who was trying to attack him in his dream.

Oh cursed one!

Carefully he swung his legs out of the car and tried standing. The exhaustion of the last several days hit him like a lead weight, and he fell back into the car seat. He took another deep breath, and then carefully Lucy helped him up into a standing position. He checked his watch. The next day. Not possible. That meant he had slept almost twelve straight hours. He peeked through the small door at the back of the hangar. Total whiteness.

He slogged down a couple of power bars, some water, and a handful of aspirins. He looked at the paintings.

"Couldn't help yourself?" he said to Lucy.

"You were asleep, and I got lonely," she said.

He smiled.

"Besides I wanted to see them before we return them."

This time he raised an eyebrow. Lucy noticed, even through the darkened hangar.

"We are returning them, right? That was the deal."

Tyler just stood quietly absorbing the paintings and all that they meant to him, and….

He nodded, "Yeah, we'll return them. When, I don't know?"

Lucy went quiet. Tyler continued to stare at the paintings. He had no idea when they would be returned, because he wasn't sure he'd even be alive in the next twenty-four hours. And with that thought came Imasu. Mom. Alex. Interpol. And as grateful as he was to have Lucy by his side he had to figure out her exit, from this whole mess.

"We need to get moving," he said as he stashed the sleeping bag and swapped license plates on the car for a set Ricardo had given him. Lucy carefully rolled up the canvases, giving each a last look, and slid them into an aluminum cylinder that said Sage fly rods along the side. Just a sportsman traveling the Eastern Shore, planning some late-autumn fly-fishing.

Tyler slowly slid open the hangar door. Everything outside was draped in a thick sheet of fresh snow. A final check around the hangar. He looked at the Audi, with its dented rear quarter panel. He looked at Lucy.

"How about I drive today?" Tyler said.

She shrugged, and tossed him the keys.

He drove out of the hangar, slid the door closed, and headed east on Route 50. He'd have to move quickly and contact Imasu soon or there'd be hell to pay.

But where to?

As Tyler pondered the next few hours Lucy's phone chirped. They both looked at each other. Lucy wasn't sure if she should answer it. Tyler nodded. She hit the talk button.

"The exhibition's in lockdown. Closed indefinitely." Snapped the agitated voice.

Lucy looked at Tyler and mouthed "my boss." Before she could respond he spoke again.

"What have you heard? What's going on?"

"Nothing. What happened?" Lucy responded.

"That's what I want you to find out. No one's returning my calls. This number is my home number. Call me as soon as you hear anything."

"Okay. Let me call—" she started to say, but he'd already hung up.

Lucy sat stunned. She looked over at Tyler.

"He knows, but he doesn't," Lucy said as she instinctively turned to look at the fly-rod container holding the half a billion in cargo.

"Interpol's keeping a lid on it," Tyler told her.

Lucy looked out the window. She was struck by the bleakness of it all.

The trees were covered so heavily with wet snow and ice that their branches hung almost to the ground. No other cars. No sounds. Not even the sound of their car on the snow-covered pavement. It felt like they were the only living things out on the highway, out in the world. The end of the world covered in snow. Tyler slowed as the early-winter cold blew in through the open window. He exhaled and watched his breath. The cold air made Lucy shiver. With the window now closed, she felt woozy. The last twelve hours hit her hard. Overwhelmed. Overpowered. She slumped back in her seat. Tyler listened as her breathing slowed. What had he done drawing her into his fight. His life. He knew it wasn't fair to her, but selfishly he was glad she was sitting next to him. As he drove through the white abyss staring out at nothing, he missed hearing the jet-helicopter that was above the hanging cloud bank heading to New York City. Instead a poem by John Keats floated through his head:

Ode to Autumn
Steady thy laden head across a brook;
Or by a cider-press, with patient look,
Thou watchest the last oozings, hours by hours.

He drove silently on Route 50 East, crossed over the Severn River Bridge, and continued over the Chesapeake Bay Bridge. The water was more roiled up than usual. Things weren't normal. There were no boats anywhere to be seen. He crossed over to Kent Island, and at the turnoff of Route 301 he turned south, instead of heading north towards New York City. He knew this was a mistake, but his instincts were running the show as he had abrogated rationale thought. He'd have to move quickly and contact Imasu soon or there'd be hell to pay. Lucy slept. Peacefully, he hoped.

FIFTY-EIGHT

"Commercial travel's a mess so you're going to New York in the jet-helicopter," Rosenwater shouted over the buzz of the incoming Bell 407 helicopter.

They were standing atop of the Justice Department building, near the heli-pads. The rotors got louder as the chopper began its descent. Snow blowing everywhere. "You'll rendezvous with Nigel Harrison from MI5, and Jorge Galcèran, his counterpart from Spain. Galcèran was directly involved in Tyler's capture in Madrid," her boss barked over the deafening sound.

Without a lick of hard evidence, he was certain that Tyler was his boy on the National Gallery heist. And Rosenwater knew the longer it took to catch Tyler, the less chance they had of getting the paintings back.

"I'll call you as soon as I make contact with the other two agents," Chanel said, her breath frozen from the near-zero temperatures.

"I'll come up tomorrow, or sooner, depending on how things go with Helmut Strell and the various museum directors," Rosenwater said.

She nodded, unable to hear a word he said. The chopper's rotors muted all other sounds.

She climbed aboard the helicopter, buckled herself in. The first thing she noticed was how warm it was in the chopper. She looked out the window at her irritated boss giving her a thumbs-up in the freezing cold. She was tempted to give him a single-finger salute. His obsession with Tyler Sears was not rational, a shrink would say unhealthy, but as hard as she pushed, her boss never revealed why he was so focused on Tyler, to the detriment of other investigations. Chanel could find nothing in Tyler's file to explain Rosenwater's obsession.

The chopper rose quickly, and the last thing she saw was her boss shouting, "Find me Tyler Sears and my paintings."

And in less than a minute she was flying directly over the Capitol Building, draped in snow, and beelining it to New York City.

FIFTY-NINE

"Yes."

"Imasu-san, it's—" Tyler said into the untraceable phone Bart had given him.

"I know who it is. I trust all is well?"

"Yes… and no."

"I do hope it's nothing… tragic?"

Silence.

"I'm in my office if you'd like to come by."

"There was a minor problem—"

"How minor?"

"Things didn't go as smoothly as hoped—"

"I expect to see you this afternoon. Otherwise I'll assume you've violated our contract. And that would be most… tragic.

"I'm trying to expl—"

"Today. With all my goods or a serious penalty will be called for. Am I clear?" Imasu said with the calmness of an assassin just before he squeezes the trigger.

"Please, let me—" Tyler realized the line was dead.

Tyler stood on the top deck of the MV Cape May ferry as it pulled away from the dock at Lewes, Delaware. It was so bleak out on deck that not even the seagulls were making an appearance. The few other passengers were bundled up down below in the warmth.

Lucy sat in the car watching Tyler. After his unpleasant call with Imasu, Tyler hoped the brisk air would help clear his head. As the land receded he felt more isolated than ever. The stiff breeze off the Delaware River went unnoticed as he stared out at the white-capped river, trying to come up with a solution. Something, anything, that didn't involve his, or his family's demise.

Alone on the top deck, his face began to sting from the cold. He barely noticed as his internal rage took hold.

"Fuckingcursefuckingcursefuckingcursefuckingcurse!" Tyler was screaming over and over as he pounded on the deck railing. Lucy watched and became concerned. Tyler was coming unhinged. And then suddenly he stopped beating the railing and started laughing uncontrollably. Now she was really worried.

Tyler realized he had made the biggest mistake of his life, and as he stared out at the gray water he stopped laughing. And just as suddenly, he knew what to do.

Curse be damned.

SIXTY

The driver of the black town car with the tinted windows peeled off from the curb at the downtown heliport near Wall Street, and headed straight for United Nations Plaza. Chanel N°5 settled into the plush leather seat trying to solve the puzzle that was Tyler Sears. It didn't add up. The pieces fit together worse than a Picasso portrait. It'd been almost two full days since the Thanksgiving heist. Her phone rang.

"Any sign of him yet?" Chanel's boss barked into the phone.

"Nothing yet. We've got his apartment, the bar where he worked, and several of his accomplices from previous heists all under surveillance."

"Damn it! Where could he have gone?"

"I think he's—" Chanel tried to finish.

"Who the hell is he working for? He must have had help."

"I'm working—"

"Jesus! Work faster! Check his phone records, his bank accounts, anywhere he might have been in the last thirty days. Check with that derelict bar owner that gives him refuge. Put the screws to the bastard. Get me some answers, and get—"

Chanel N°5 had had enough of her boss's ranting. "I'm working on it and the sooner I get off the phone, the sooner I can get back to headquarters and monitor things more clearly. I'll check in every hour, or sooner if I have something."

"I want the sonuvabitch." And the line went dead.

Chanel settled into the backseat and considered what she knew about Tyler Sears. Why hadn't he returned to New York City? Where the hell was he? The break-in itself was far too sophisticated for one person to accomplish. Who were his accomplices? This was an expensive endeavor. Who was underwriting the project? Who was the final customer on the deal? Why had Tyler risked getting caught to wrap a guard in a Tyvek emergency blanket? Who was in that black SUV with the small arsenal? And why had they left the weapons behind? Why had he transferred his brother to a different facility only weeks before? And where did he get the money to pay for his brother's twenty thousand a month ranch rides? The Town Car was crossing under the Brooklyn Bridge, heading uptown on the FDR. Chanel checked her makeup in her compact mirror, as she was pondering all these things.

As she stared back at herself layering on a fresh line of lip gloss she wondered: *And how come he turned me down in DC?*

SIXTY-ONE

Tyler drove their bruised and battered Audi S4 off the ferry at Cape May Landing and noticed the only other car in the parking area was a local Cape May police cruiser. The engine was running but no one was in the car. Tyler's survival instincts were on high alert as he slowly drove past the cruiser and pulled up near the exit. Snow was piled everywhere.

"Why don't you go in and ask if the roads are clear heading north," he said to Lucy.

Lucy walked into the small ferry office building, which had a small wood-burning stove keeping the inside toasty. The cop was leaning against the counter chatting up the youngish female clerk. Lucy didn't want to intrude so she looked around and then stood near the end of the counter by the copy/fax machine. Lucy looked down for a second and noticed some paper in the fax tray. She was about to interrupt when she focused on the fax tray. On top of the tray was a picture of Tyler. A mug shot.

"Can I help you?" The clerk asked Lucy.

Lucy was transfixed by the picture of Tyler.

"Hi, can I help you?" the clerk said a little louder. Lucy snapped out of her trance. She looked up.

"Ladies room?" Lucy asked.

The clerk just pointed down the hall. Lucy moved away as the cop started in jabbering again. Lucy eyed a back exit and beelined it for Tyler. She casually got in the car.

"Drive. Carefully, but get moving."

Tyler didn't question her. He realized for better or worse Lucy Phillips may be the best accomplice he'd ever had. Loyal to a fault. And gorgeous. Neither of which any of his previous accomplices have ever possessed.

He drove slowly along Lincoln Boulevard and then swung right onto Seashore Road, crossing over the Intracoastal Waterway towards the Cape May lighthouse. He followed this until he saw the snow-covered signs for Cape May State Park. He crept along the snowy street and spotted the park entrance, up ahead on the left. The trees were all covered in an icy sheen. He pulled into what he suspected was the car park area. The place was completely deserted.

"You okay?" he asked her.

She didn't respond. She was just staring out. She was shaking, and not from the cold. She was frightened. He reached for her hand. She pulled it away. It had finally hit her just how much trouble they were in. The thrill had been replaced by sheer panic, which plagues every normal law-abiding citizen when they have crossed that line into criminality, whether by choice or by accident, or usually a combination of the two. The image of Warren Beatty and Faye Dunaway being riddled with one hundred and thirty rounds of ammunition from assault weapons, shotguns, and pistols flashed in her brain. Her jaw tightened. What a mess. She wanted to scream. She wanted to be back in Boise and the warmth of her family—the ultimate safe haven. Her eyes welled up. She started crying, sobbing out of control.

Tyler was helpless. He knew exactly what she was going through. He'd been there and he felt like a total shit for exposing her to his world. He leaned into her and whispered, "It's going to be okay. I promise." He kissed her forehead and her sobbing slowed.

"I need to make a call. I'll be right back." He squeezed her hand.

He left the car running, and hopped out. He pulled out the cell phone Bart had given him, punched a number, and hit send. The number flashed on the screen of the smaller device. He waited about ten seconds and suddenly the number stopped flashing. This device was able to throw his location to another phone up to a hundred miles away. The number Bart had given him was for a pay phone at the Philly train station.

There were never any pleasantries with Barthold. "What the hell are you up to!?"

"What are you hearing?" Tyler asked.

"I'm hearing from an old source at Interpol, and he's pissed. It took me a long time to convince him I had nothing to do with it."

"Bart, I'm exhausted, and really twisted. I need an out, and I need your help."

"Forget it. You're in deeper than even I can imagine, or help. You're fucking toxic. Pure poison. I'm sending your money back. I'm hanging up now, and denying I ever knew you."

"Bart, please I'm begging. It'll be your last payday. Add five more to what I already donated…."

There was a long silence.

"Talk" was all Bart said.

Tyler quickly explained his dilemma. Bart listened in silence. When Tyler was done, Bart gave him the address of one of his studios where Bart hid out and worked, without worrying about the authorities, or an angry girlfriend.

"It'll take me about a week to get everything together," said Bart.

"You've got twenty-four hours" was all Tyler said.

"FUCK. You're joking right?"

"I'll double the price. Ten mill. Deal?"

"Deal, but they won't be Bart perfect. You're out of your fucking mind, and way out of your league."

"Thanks. I appreciate your confidence. Just get me what I need."

Bart told him that everything he'd requested would be at the secret hideaway by the time Tyler arrived, but he'd need at "least" twenty-four hours to pull everything together.

"Hey Ty."

"Yeah?"

"How's Philly?"

Tyler smiled and the line went dead. The good news was the scrambler was working.

He knew the next call would be much more difficult.

"Imasu-san—"

"Ah, you're early. Excellent. I'll wait in my office."

"I'm not there, and I won't be coming by your office," Tyler said.

Absolute silence. Tyler had learned from an old Wall Street pirate that in the world of negotiations, the first one to talk, loses. Tyler said nothing.

After Tyler had enough time for the drop of nervous sweat to roll down his chest Imasu finally responded.

"Then I'm afraid you've incurred your first penalty," Imasu said.

"Penalty, what penalty?"

"You didn't really think you'd just walk off with my money, and my art, without paying a penalty?"

"Look, I'm delayed a little bit. I'll be there tomorrow."

"Excellent, then you'll only face today's penalty. I look forward to your call tomorrow."

"Imasu, please...."

Tyler thought he detected a laugh.

"Tomorrow." And the line went dead.

Tyler looked out at the icy, unforgiving Atlantic Ocean. The windshield was steamed over from Lucy's breathing. His own anger rising.

What a mess. This was far worse than the Prado job. At least that time he could blame the accomplices, who after Tyler paid them cash, holed up across the street from the Prado at the The Ritz. They had the loudest, most raucous party ever seen at The Ritz. The local cops were called, and then when they found two small-time thieves with a million euros in cash, well, the jig was up as they say. It was either jail, or finger Tyler. As the two men watched the naked beauties being hustled out the door, and realizing a future without women awaited them, it was a simple decision. Tyler had been yanked off an Iberia flight to Casablanca, and promptly hustled into a Madrid jail cell. Even though he returned the art, he'd refused to name the buyer. He had received five to twelve, out in four for good behavior.

Somehow the parole board was convinced of Tyler's remorse (Imasu's payoffs), and the board figured his cell could be put to better use with a hardened criminal. So eighteen months later he was out and washing bar glasses for Max at the Art Bar. This was one of the reasons Chanel's boss was so focused on Tyler. Good behavior was one thing, but out after eighteen months, well the old man knew the fix was in. What he didn't know was that Tyler had nothing to do with it. It was Imasu's payoffs to the parole board members and the warden that had turned the wheels of "justice" in Tyler's favor.

Unlike the Prado job, this was all on him. No one else to blame. And now he had dragged Lucy into this debacle. His arrogance had brought him to this place. His anger and fear boiled up. What was Imasu planning? He worried about Alex, but knew he couldn't contact the clinic. And his mom was sailing somewhere off the coast of Corsica.

It was time to roll the dice. It was all or nothing. The only way out was to create an untenable situation for everyone. He grabbed his phone and made the call he was hoping he wouldn't have to make. He needed serious help.

"It's me."

"Call me at this number in sixty seconds," said Ricardo as he recited a new number. Tyler did as he was told. Sixty seconds later.

"I need your help" was all Tyler said.

"You've been busy," said Ricardo.

"I'm worried about my brother," said Tyler.

"Your mother and your brother are fine. Although he spends a lot of time with a horse."

"How did you—"

"I told you, you and your family would be safe. Now tell me how I can help."

Tyler relayed the basics and explained his dire dilemma with Imasu, and about his plan involving Bart's studio, and Imasu's threat of a penalty. He also mentioned Lucy. The voice at the other end listened without speaking. Ricardo said he'd see what he could do about helping him with his bigger problem.

Tyler walked back to the car, his breath coming quickly in the cold. He knew his adrenaline was at max output, and he'd have to calm way down before he jumped back in the car and headed back to New York City for what might be his final day on Earth.

SIXTY-TWO

Tyler couldn't help but worry about the penalty Imasu had threatened. Maybe it *was* just about the money? He'd withhold the other fifty million? According to Ricardo his brother was safe, and his mom was hopefully sailing along the Corsican coastline. What else could it be? It had to be the money. Fuck it. It wasn't about the money anyway. It was about the art. And about staying alive.

And now he'd promised Lucy he would return the art.

Once the art landed in Imasu's hands, who would ever see it again? The Vermeers, cut from their frames at the Gardner in Boston, hadn't been seen in over fifteen years. Would they ever see the light of day again? He looked back at the fishing-rod case holding six of the most famous paintings in the world. A museum in and of itself. He had a more pressing immediate problem.

Driving away from Cape May State Park he was determined to control the situation as best he could, or at least die trying. He drove out of the park, snaking his way back to Seashore Drive. Lucy had drifted off, exhausted from all the emotions that had overwhelmed her. As he passed the local Cape May County airfield he noticed a sign for H&R Used Cars with an arrow to the left. The storm had shorted out the sign, and a weak glow emanated from the point of the snow-covered arrow. Tyler decided to take a chance and swung left onto Bayshore Road.

"We need to get a new set of wheels," he said to Lucy as she was waking up.

A quarter-mile past the end of runway 1-9 was H&R Used Cars, as advertised. Tyler pulled up across the street from the car dealer. A guy in a pickup truck with a plow attached was trying to clear the snow away from the late-model American beauties lining the fence. There didn't seem to be anyone in the office. The place looked deserted. Just the plow and the driver.

He knew his botched exit made it only a matter of time before either Imasu or Interpol finished him off. Calculating risk was no longer a factor. Now it was simple survival. Do whatever's necessary to survive, and stay alive.

The shark's motto: keep moving forward.

"Sit tight. I'll be back in a minute."

The snowplow continued its careful clean up around the cars, Tyler walked across the street. He waved at the plowman.

The guy threw his truck in park and rolled down the window. It was too cold to get out of the truck, especially for some stranger. The guy was probably just lost and needed directions.

"Hey, how's it going?" Tyler asked.

"Lotta snow for November," said the driver, looking past Tyler at all the snow piled up.

"Is anybody in the office today?" Tyler asked.

"Nah, I'm one of the mechanics. I help out with jobs like this when they need me."

Tyler just nodded.

"Do you need something? Want to leave them a message?" asked the driver.

"Yeah, I want to trade my car over there," Tyler said as he pointed at his trusty Audi, "for that Ford 150 pickup truck sitting there," Tyler said.

"What do they want for it?"

"Gee, I think around $8,995, but I'm not positive. Besides no one's here right now. But I could give them a call."

"That's okay. You mind turning the truck off for a minute so we can talk?" Tyler asked, smiling.

The driver switched off the ignition and jumped out of the truck. He was a good two inches taller than Tyler, and had fifty pounds on him, most of which appeared to be muscle.

"Vincent," said Tyler extending his hand.

"Bobby," said the driver.

"Bobby, I'm in kind of a hurry, and my car's had a slight accident, and my wife's kinda pissed about it. Too much fun last night. You know how that goes," Tyler said, looking over at the Audi with its obvious dent in the rear quarter panel, and Lucy sitting in the passenger seat staring straight ahead.

Bobby nodded with a slight grin as he started across the street with Tyler right behind him. Bobby squatted down to look at the extent of the damages. He felt around the dent, and then put his hand up under the wheel well. He then looked at the back end of the car, with the S4 badge. "This the one with the Porsche engine?" Bobby asked.

"Yup." Tyler opened the driver's side door and popped the hood. Lucy gave him a nervous look.

Bobby lifted it open, and smiled. "Sweet" was all he said.

Tyler smiled inwardly at Bobby's comment. Lucy couldn't see them, blocked by the up-raised hood.

"So whattya say, an even swap?" Tyler said, hoping.

Bobby rubbed his hands together trying to stay warm.

"I don't know... it ain't for me to be making deals when the boss isn't around."

Tyler needed new wheels, and he had to get going. "Tell you what, you keep the Audi, I'll give you ten large, cash, you give me the truck and a set of plates, and I'll be outta here."

Bobby knew this was too good a deal to pass up, and his brain wasn't developed enough to ponder the intricacies as to why some guy in a fifty thou car suddenly wanted to trade down to a crapped up Ford pickup. All he could think was lottery ticket. He'd be able to off-load the Audi for an easy thirty grand, and explain to the boss that some guy was in a hurry and gave him cash for the pickup. He knew old man Harrison was willing to take seven for the truck so he'd give'm eight cash, and everyone would be happy. Bobby grinned at Tyler and then put out his hand.

"I'll go get ya' the keys" was all Bobby said.

Tyler pulled the Audi into the used-car area, parked, and walked into the H&R offices.

In less than two minutes Tyler was starting up the pickup truck, Lucy in the passenger seat. It didn't hurt matters any when Tyler handed Bobby an extra ten grand cash, and suggested he take an immediate two week vacation. Bobby knew he might have to face some music for making this deal with "Vincent"—but not until he got back from Cancun. Besides, he'd blame the lost dealer plates on Harrison's nephew Eddie, the "director" of sales as Eddie liked to tell anyone within earshot. Eddie was one of those types that couldn't screw in a lightbulb without checking the box for directions. Bobby sat adding up his good fortune, a thirty-grand foreign job, twelve large in CASH, as he watched the stranger and his wife, drive off.

Who said snowplowing didn't pay?

SIXTY-THREE

Local roads were the best bet Tyler knew as he headed north on Route 9. Interpol would be hunting him but there was no way they'd involve local law enforcement. Interpol wasn't about to answer a lot of questions from the sheriffs of Essex, Camden, Cherry Hill, or Somerset about some heist that might or might not have happened. Tyler knew Interpol would try to keep a lid on what had really happened for as long as possible.

The local surface roads had almost as many lights as the Milky Way, but Bart had said his place wouldn't be ready until tomorrow, so no need to rush. Lucy finally turned to Tyler, her shell-shocked look had given way to a healthier, more normal look.

"What? No heated seats?" is all she said as she reached for his hand.

Tyler smiled as they passed the Shore Gate Golf Club and approached Petersberg, where they forked onto Harding Highway and the MacNamara Wildlife Preserve. The preserve was completely blanketed in white. The trees, the marshes, the hawks' nests, even the sign to the entrance. The storm had hit harder the farther north they traveled. The trees were iced over. A lone goose flew in front of them, from left to right, descending for the frozen marsh as they wound their way around the backside of the wildlife refuge. Tyler remembered reading somewhere that the goose was the one creature known to scientists to mate for life. He looked over at Lucy as she watched the goose land on an open patch of water. The spray flickering some color up into the whiteness.

"Was it a good picture?" Tyler asked.

Lucy looked at him with incredulity.

"It was a mug shot… not your best look," Lucy said.

Tyler looked disappointed. Lucy looked annoyed.

By taking the local southern Jersey route, Tyler bypassed the major interchange stops at the Maryland border, the Delaware Memorial Bridge and the Philly interchanges—all spots guaranteed to have his old Interpol photo posted. He motored through the automatic ticket booth, merging anonymously onto Interstate 95, northbound. A full tank of gas, a nondescript pickup.

Next stop Fort Lee.

SIXTY-FOUR

It was getting dark when Tyler parked in the back of the Bridge Motel in Fort Lee, New Jersey. The guy behind the bulletproof glass didn't ask for ID. The sign on the wall said, Cash is all the ID necessary.

Tyler paid a week's worth upfront.

Tyler pulled open the back curtain. They were looking out onto a cemetery, the Madonna Cemetery. The George Washington Bridge was beyond the cemetery. A whip-sawed chain-link fence separating them.

"Why don't you take a shower and get some rest. I'm going to run across the street to get some food, and something to drink," Lucy said.

"Grab some newspapers if you see any."

Lucy just stared at him. Tyler looked at her, not sure what he'd done wrong.

"What's the magic word?"

Tyler paused for a second.

"Be naked?"

Lucy shook her head as she exited.

Tyler stood in the steaming-hot shower, just hanging onto the showerhead. He didn't want to think, or do anything. He wanted the water, the heat, the steam to cleanse all the shit of the last twenty-four hours off his skin, out of his soul.

He was wearing a pair of jeans and a clean T-shirt, sitting on the bed waiting for Lucy to return. He grabbed the remote and flipped on the TV. He ripped through the dial. The Fort Lee Motel which made claims to cable, in fact had your basic channels and a couple of porn channels (one of them in Spanish). No late-breaking stories on the art heist. Kudos to Interpol. Tyler was tempted to call the *Times* and report a rumor of a theft at the National Gallery. It'd create chaos, which might aid his escape, but it also might make the next twenty-four hours even more difficult. No, he had to play the hand dealt him, especially since he was the dealer. He'd made the mess, and he'd have to clean it up. He was getting restless just sitting on the fire-retardant, style-retardant bedspread. He wanted this to be over, but at the same time he knew the next twenty-four hours would be critical to his (and Lucy's) survival. He flipped the dials one more time. The usual shootings, burning buildings, and a car rammed at an intersection. He cruised to another channel trying to quench his unease. The burning building story was on again. Must be a helluva fire, he thought.

"LIVE BREAKING NEWS."

The news cutie was standing in front of a smoking building that suddenly looked familiar to Tyler. He got right in front of the screen. SHIT! It was Maggie's building. He turned up the volume.

"A massive explosion in a top-floor apartment. According to our sources someone may still be trapped inside. The police have yet to confirm this. The fire is believed to have been caused by a gas explosion. We'll keep you informed as we receive more information. I'm Louise Flash, live from lower Manhattan."

Tyler stared at the screen in disbelief, horrified. He was watching, live, as Maggie's building, her apartment, was engulfed in an inferno. Transfixed by the blaze and unable to do anything about it, he sat in stunned silence. His helplessness only made matters worse. Imasu? It couldn't be. It had to be.

Tyler stared at the raging fire his eyes welling up. He was overcome with every emotion from rage to despair to helplessness to fury.

This was Tyler's first penalty from Imasu.

SIXTY-FIVE

When Lucy walked back in carrying bags of takeout, Tyler was staring at the TV zombielike. The remote dropped on the floor. He didn't move, didn't blink, barely breathing. She dropped the food.

"Tyler. TYLER. What's the matter?"

He turned toward her and his eyes were red and tears pouring out. She took a quick glance at the screen and wasn't sure what he was looking at.

"Ty, please talk to me."

"Maggie... that's Maggie"

"Who is?"

"Her apartment... Imasu."

Lucy stared at the TV and saw the fire, the story, the smoke. She got it. A wave of grief rolled over her. She grabbed the remote and turned the TV off.

"I'm so sorry."

"She was innocent. Sweet. Why'd he have to hurt her?"

Lucy pulled him in, tight. His eyes flooded. Dams burst. She held tighter. Even from the window of the shit-bag motel Lucy could see the black smoke from the horrific fire rising and floating up the Hudson River towards them.

SIXTY-SIX

It was his farewell drink to Maggie. Lucy decided to get him out of the room, so they headed to Trudy's Bar, near the bridge. A couple of shots of Patrón, with long-neck Bud chasers, seemed a fitting toast to Maggie. Lucy worried about the mental anguish of the last day and the possible detriment this might cause to Tyler's decision-making. Having gotten this far Lucy didn't want to risk losing Tyler to recklessness. In her mind, as she sipped her beer, jail was a better alternative for Tyler than death.

Tyler drifted in and out of a fitful sleep aided by the shots of tequila. He dreamed of his childhood. Alex, already a daredevil, swung out on the rope over the pond and let go, his last words being, "C'mon Ty, don't be chicken!"

Young Tyler reached out to grab the rope swing. He stood on the edge of the slight precipice, unable to jump, but unable to let go of the rope. Finally, he jumped off the ledge and swung out over the pond, which now looked ominous compared to the safety of the high embankment. He let go too soon, only to discover the pond was gone, replaced by a dark abyss. The ultimate black hole. The darkness took over his sleep.

The clock read 5:45 a.m. Tyler's head was numb. He was drenched in sweat. He showered, dressed, and headed to the Red

Oak Diner, about a half mile away. He let Lucy sleep. It was still dark outside as he entered the diner. He barely swallowed some toast and coffee. He was on flat-out automatic. No thoughts, no hunger, pain deadened, a single focus, driven purely by survival.

Darwin at its best.

Leaving the diner he saw piles of snow left over from the storm but they were beginning to subside, or at least turn that hideous shade of gray-black that comes from a mix of highway salt and city pollution. His breath was visible as he glanced over at Manhattan.

Lucy was awake and dressed when he came back. A worried look on her face. Tyler looked at her.

"I'm okay… I promise."

"I just wondered why you didn't bring me any breakfast?" Lucy said with a slight smile. Tyler smiled, for a moment.

"He's got to be stopped," Tyler said.

"Ty, try to be rational. He's a billionaire. He'll be untouchable—"

"His weakness is thinking he's untouchable…. I have to make a call."

Tyler left before Lucy could say anything. She realized it was futile to try and stop him. She could only hope that he didn't try to leap off the high board into an empty pool.

Tyler was furious with himself for what happened to Maggie, and now he regretted drawing Lucy into this madness. He needed to think clearly, as it was now a lethal chess match. His only hope was to catch his opponents (Imasu and Rosenwater) off guard, and at the same time. He picked up the pay phone and tossed in the quarters.

"It's me" is all Tyler said. He listened carefully as Ricardo outlined the only possible move to make on the board to get the other "players" to move as needed.

"I hope we meet again" was the last thing Ricardo said before he hung up.

Tyler took a deep breath and then dialed his fate.

"WHAT!?" the gruff voice snapped.

"It's me," Tyler said.

"I'm sorry, who?"

Rosenwater jumped out of his chair, and motioned for Chanel N°5 to get on the call. He scribbled T-R-A-C-E on a sheet of paper, and showed it to the others in the room.

"I heard you've lost something. I may be able to help you recover it," Tyler said.

"I'm not sure what you're talking about."

"I'm hanging up now."

"WAIT!"

"No. I'll call you back in a few hours with the meeting point," Tyler said as he counted the seconds on his watch.

"You destroyed my car you fucker!" is all Tyler heard as he hung up.

The line went dead. Rosenwater stood up and looked at the other people in the room. Not enough time to get a successful trace. No one wanted to meet his gaze. He grabbed the phone off the desk and threw it across the room. It bounced off the tinted bulletproof glass like a super ball.

Tyler dialed.

"It's me."

"Ah, Sears-san I'm so glad you—"

"You killed my friend, so now we do it my way."

"That is not our arran—"

"Don't talk. Listen. You want your goods. I'll call you back in four hours with the meeting point. And I want ten million cash, small bills, untraceable."

"Sears-san, even I am unable to—"

"Make it three hours," Tyler said as he slammed down the phone.

SIXTY-SEVEN

The morning rush hour was just cranking up, as Tyler and Lucy headed out on foot. He was wearing a baseball cap, pulled down low. Tyler hadn't shaved in close to a week. Lucy was makeup free, something that wasn't lost on her. She was wearing a beanie with CAPE MAY on it. They cut behind the motel parking lot and walked along the back fence of the Madonna Cemetery. They were careful to stay below the massive highways, and out of sight of any of the tollbooth lackeys, or any of the bridge and tunnel cops who might be on the lookout for him. They cut up Bridge Street, made their way up the escarpment, and climbed over the railing to the steps leading up to the walkway to the bridge. They looked like a couple of stragglers as they crossed the bridge. Tyler had the fly-rod container slung across his back. He figured no one would be looking for someone walking into Manhattan with close to half a billion in stolen art. Halfway across Tyler stopped and looked down river at the Manhattan skyline. He thought about Maggie.

They crossed over the Henry Hudson Parkway and past the public housing projects, and headed down the steps of the subway entrance at Fort Washington Avenue. On the subway they sat with their heads down amidst the early-morning commuters. Tyler felt surprisingly focused, considering all that had happened in the last seventy-two hours. He thought that if he was still alive this time tomorrow, he would consider it a good day. He had to decide what to do about Lucy. He had to get her away from the madness that was about to unfurl. By the time they reached 125th Street the train was filling up; by 96th Street the car was packed with the full cadre of commuters—immigrant daycare providers, students, Wall Streeters, Midtown mid-levelers who hadn't yet rated a car service, nurses, doctors, technicians, the true melting pot of America.

With the subway car stuffed to capacity Tyler was no longer worried about being followed. Even if they spotted him they wouldn't be able to reach him in this crowd.

Lucy sat close to Tyler. She held tight to his hand. She knew he would try to get rid of her. To make sure she was safe. She wasn't going to let him go. She didn't know it at the time but she was operating in a way she never had before. Something totally different from anything she had ever done before, or would ever do again. A way that felt completely natural. Too normal.

They jumped off at Canal Street, climbed the stairs to daylight and headed east. As they crossed Houston Street, Tyler grabbed Lucy's hand and headed into the Remedy Diner.

A waitress who looked like she'd had a rougher seventy-two hours than Tyler and Lucy tossed a menu on the table, and without speaking, poured cups of coffee. She merely pointed to the sugar and cream. Speech was not her strong suit. He put the backpack and the fly-rod canister on the adjacent chairs. Tyler knew he had to talk to Lucy. To force her out of his world of madness. Where to begin.

"I need to talk to you about something. About us."

Lucy didn't say a word. She waited. Tyler took a breath, stared right at her.

"What's about to happen, or… look, I never should have gotten you wrapped up in this mess that's my life," he said.

Lucy still didn't say anything. Nervously, Tyler continued.

"I… I am glad that you were there, that you're here, I just can't risk you getting hurt, or worse. It's not fair, and it's not right. You can leave now if you want, and I wouldn't blame you, and I promise I'll never contact you again. This is my problem. My fight. There's about $100,000 in the backpack," he said as he slid it towards Lucy. "It should be enough for… I just want you to have it. I promise no matter what happens I will come and find you, unless you don't want…. I just can't let you go any further. I want, I need to know you'll be safe."

Still, not a word out of Lucy.

"Well, say something. Anything," Tyler pleaded.

Lucy looked at him very seriously and said, "Are you done?"

Tyler nodded.

"Okay, then let's go and get this finished," she said as she pushed the backpack back at Tyler. She stood up, and put her arms around his neck. Tyler held her tight.

"We don't get to choose who we fall in love with," she whispered to him just before she let go. Tyler smiled. He grabbed her hand and they headed out the door, together.

SIXTY-EIGHT

"Where we going?" she asked.

"A friend's place... as soon as we get there I'll explain everything."

She nodded at the fly-rod container, "How's the fishing?"

"Amazing," he said laughing.

They walked quickly in silence, their fingers interlaced.

Alphabet City territory. A run-down abandoned apartment building at the corner of East 7th Street and Avenue B, across the street from Tompkins Square Park. Lucy noticed that all the buildings had the same burned-out look. Tyler led her around to a side entrance of the building. He punched in a key code and when the small door with the chicken-wire-glass window buzzed, they slipped in. It was dark. Lucy grabbed his arm.

Tyler fished a Mini Maglite from the backpack and switched it on. He followed the hallway around to a huge warehouse door. Next to them was a warehouse elevator. Tyler pressed a button on the wall and the elevator gurgled to life, the gears grinding as it started down. It lurched onto the ground floor. Tyler pulled on the greasy strap on the floor and the massive door slid upwards. They walked in and Tyler pushed the button marked PH. Lucy started to laugh.

"This gives new meaning to the concept of penthouse."

"Only the best for you," Tyler said.

The rusted-out elevator creaked and shook its way skyward. The entire building appeared to be vacant—no lights and no noise except for the screechy elevator as it came to an abrupt halt.

Tyler pulled the strap and the door slid up to reveal what looked like an abandoned artist's studio with easels lying against the wall, and canvases stacked haphazardly. The place smelled of gesso, and the heavy oil of paints, which were splattered all over the walls and floor. There were windows high up along the back wall.

Lucy wandered in amazement until she came to the wall of windows that looked out past the East River. "Jesus, what is this place? Where are we?"

"A friend's loft. It's a place he hides out at when he needs to work."

"What's he do?" Lucy asked.

"Don't ask."

The giant loft had been divided into makeshift rooms. The bulk of the space was given over to an enormous painting studio. The rest consisted of a small bedroom, a tiny kitchen with a small fridge, a double-burner gas stove, and a microwave.

There was a small living room/dining room. It held a typical small Parisian bistro table, a couple of chairs, a couch that had seen better days, and an oversized comfy chair that had a sheet draped across it.

Tyler began to unwrap his prized cargo. She turned around. Tyler stood stone still staring at the six canvases, unframed. It was the first time he'd seen all six in broad daylight. With the wall of windows providing maximum daylight, their magnificence was revealed. All the nuance, the richness of the age-old oils still bursting off the canvases that had seen nothing but artificial light for the last hundred years. The courage, the daring, the amazing talent of Manet, Renoir, Cézanne, Gauguin, Monet, and of course Vincent. Six of the most recognizable paintings in the world sitting in a dilapidated loft in broad daylight. Even in such surroundings, their beauty shone through. True genius. In any environment their beauty would lift the plight of man and his ability to think, act, and try to raise the level of humanity. All right in front of Tyler and Lucy.

A wave of remorse poured over him.

Lucy walked over to the canvases, and began to examine them closely. She stepped back next to Tyler. She was unable to blink.

"Tyler... ," was all she could manage.

Tyler just stared.

"You're returning the paintings... right?"

He nodded. Their hands touched. They stood staring like that for several minutes.

"Have you got a plan?" Lucy finally asked.

"Sure... sort of," is the best he could do.

"Do I want to know? Or do I already know too much?"

"Yes to both...."

She didn't smile. She just walked over and looked very closely at each of the paintings. "Hope it's a genius plan," she said.

A glimmer of hope washed over him, followed by a flood of relief.

With renewed energy, Tyler laid out his strategy, a plan so reckless that it just might produce the necessary outcome.

His survival, and Imasu's downfall.

And Interpol out of his life for good.

He turned to Lucy who then helped him put the final pieces in place.

SIXTY-NINE

"I'm so glad you called, Sears-san. I was afraid you might incur another penalty," Imasu said. "Shame about your friend."

Maggie's face floated through Tyler's brain. He wanted to reach through the phone and strangle the son of a bitch.

"Imasu-san, what you did yesterday was unforgivable; therefore you too will be penalized for your lack of trust. As of today you have lost one painting."

Tyler waited. No response.

The silence lasted so long Tyler thought they might have been disconnected.

Finally Imasu said, "Sears-san, you do not want to anger me."

"Likewise, Imasu-san. I suggest a truce. No more penalties from either side."

"Sears-san, where are you?"

"I'm close, very close. Meet me at Tompkins Square Park. At the statue at the Avenue A and 7th Street corner. Be there at 12:10. Do not be late. And YOU need to be there. Deal's off if you only send your hired goons. Are we clear?"

"I will be there," Imasu said into the phone.

"And don't forget the money. No cash, no paintings. Understood."

"Sears-san, I will keep my end of the bargain."

Tyler heard Imasu say something in Japanese in muted tones.

If Tyler could have understood, he would have heard him tell two of his Yakuza goons to get to Tompkins Square Park immediately, grab the paintings, and dump Tyler in the East River off the end of Pier 70 near Stuyvesant Town.

Tyler had anticipated what Imasu had in mind. Two moves ahead.

His next call was to his old nemesis, Irving Rosenwater.

"WHAT?" barked the dinosaur of international spies.

Tyler wanted to make wise, but he knew time was at a premium, because in thirty seconds they'd have a trace.

"How are you, Irv?"

"Miserable, you son of a bitch. I want those fucking paintings back."

Tyler had the angriest dog at the end of a taut leash on the other end of the phone. "I'm great, thanks for asking."

"Listen you fucking pissant, when I get done with you, you'll be coming out of Leavenworth in a pine box."

"You want help solving your problem… or are you just gonna keep running your mouth, 'cause Irv, you're about two syllables away from losing one billion in art. So which is it?"

This time there was only silence.

"Meet me at the northeast corner of Tompkins Square Park, the 10th Street and Avenue B corner, at high noon. Don't be late."

"Tompkins Square Park. Noon. Roger. You'd better have my paintings."

"Like you're in a position to be making demands," Tyler responded and flipped his phone shut.

"Now what?" asked Lucy.

"Now we prepare for the worst, and hope for the best."

"Ever the optimist, Tyler Sears," said Lucy trying to smile.

Tyler dialed one more number. "It's me Ty.... As best as can be expected." He listened to Ricardo Alvarez for a minute and then responded, "The Yakuza and Interpol... ten minutes apart... the Interpol boys first... yes, as per your instructions... you're sure this will work?"

Tyler listened for another minute.

"Thanks for everything. And I hope I see you again, someday."

And Tyler hung up.

"Who was that?" Lucy asked, completely perplexed.

"That was our angel of mercy."

"I thought that was my job."

"Everyday but today," Tyler said with a grin.

"Tyler, can I ask you something?"

"Anything," he said, waiting.

"Good, then I'll wait till tomorrow."

SEVENTY

High Noon

Tyler looked down at the Square and observed a black Ford sedan with tinted windows pulling up to the north side of the park. Two agents stepped out, followed by a grizzled-looking old man in a rumpled suit. Irving Rosenwater. The old guy was wearing a permanent scowl. The other two wore white shirts, skinny black ties, trench coats, and standard issue Ray Bans, the geekster model.

Tyler punched in a number that the old crank had given him yesterday.

"What?" growled Rosenwater.

"You really need to work on your phone etiquette, Irv."

"Go fuck yourself."

"Today's your lucky day. See the building at the south side of the park?" The old guy looked to his right.

"The other way," said Tyler shaking his head. "That's better. Go around to the Avenue A side of the building. Look for the steel door. Buzz and you'll be let in. Take the elevator to the penthouse. Got all that?"

"Yeah slimeball. I got it. Enjoy your last moments of freedom."

"Who was that?" asked Lucy as she could hear growling through the phone.

"That was the angriest man on the planet. He's the guy that nabbed me in Madrid. He's a truly nasty piece of work."

Tyler watched as the old man talked into his shirtsleeve. He and the other two agents moved quickly toward the side entrance.

Tyler guessed that the last call was monitored and he surveyed the rooftops.

Suddenly snipers appeared along the rooflines of all the buildings surrounding the park. He noticed that all the snipers had trained their sights on the building Tyler was watching from. It sent a chill up his spine. Fortunately, the tint on the large windows blocked direct line of sight.

"Step one is in motion."

Lucy nodded.

Imasu was on time, with three of his goons in tow. The goons wore long overcoats, probably covering some long-barreled weapons. He punched in Imasu's phone number.

"Greetings Imasu-san. I hope you have not been too inconvenienced?"

He was watching Imasu through his binoculars.

"Sears-san, no inconvenience if it brings our arrangement to a successful conclusion."

"Please open the cases so I can see the money. And have your boys rifle through it so I can see it's all there."

Imasu instructed his men to open the oversized Louis Vuitton cases. Tyler could hardly believe what he was looking at.

He was staring at ten million dollars in fresh bills.

"The building just south of you."

He watched as Imasu turned and stared at the building. Tyler noticed all the snipers had pulled back and were no longer visible.

"Yes, that one," said Tyler. "Go around to the Avenue A side and you'll see a small steel door. Buzz and I'll let you in. Take the elevator up to the penthouse."

Imasu was already in motion as Tyler finished giving him directions. Each Yakuza goon carrying one of the cases. By Tyler's estimates each case weighed close to 150 lbs. Lucy watched through the corner of the windows. "Nice touch using Louis Vuitton."

Just as Imasu turned the corner out of Tyler's visual, two Apache Longbow Attack helicopters appeared out of nowhere, and circled overhead. Tyler looked through his binoculars to get a closer look. Each helicopter was equipped with sixteen Hellfire missiles. Eight per side, and a pair of 30 mm guns. There was enough firepower attached to the two choppers to invade Connecticut.

"Jesus Christ, I'm an unarmed art thief, not some international narco-terrorist," he thought to himself. He swung the field glasses around the rooftops. He could just make out the men on the adjoining rooflines, all looking through high-power scopes. This probably meant there were agents on his building as well.

The buzzer sounded.

Tyler looked at Lucy. "Okay, now it's time for you to get out of here, and to a safe place. Leave through the back stairs and you'll get out undetected. I'll call you when all this is over."

"Tyler, last time I let you out of my sight you pulled a runner, and I didn't see you for three years. That's not happening again."

"Lucy, you're leaving. NOW. I mean it. This is serious."

"So am I. You decided to trust me, and now, I'm trusting you. From now on we're in this together… for better or worse." Lucy held her ground.

Tyler shook his head and stared at her gravely. "Then you do exactly as I say."

Lucy nodded.

"When this gets going, you stay out of sight in the bedroom, and no matter what you hear, or how bad it sounds, do not show your face. If you hear a shot fired, you exit immediately. Do not hesitate. Do not deviate from the plan. We clear? We'll meet at the rendezvous spot, understood?"

"Yes Tyler, we're clear."

The buzzer buzzed. Tyler walked to the door and pushed the button, allowing the downstairs door to open. He watched on the tiny wall screen as Captain Cranky of Interpol and his two field agents entered the building.

Tyler studied the small video screen and noticed one of the agents had a Heckler & Koch MP5K peering out from under his trench coat. The weapon of choice for international police forces, standard issue for NATO, Interpol, GSG 9-the German antiterrorist force, and the New York and LA SWAT teams. The H&K MP5K is a submachine gun that can be used in very tight quarters, single shot, or three quick bursts. Nothing disrupts a drug deal like a couple of rounds from an MP5K. Tyler noticed the agent had the modified French stock, so the weapon could be swung up, and handled like a handgun.

This was going to be a "take no prisoners" operation from start to finish. The elevator screeched as it made its way back to the ground floor.

The buzzer sounded again. Tyler checked the small monitor. It was Imasu and his Yakuza goons. He waited until he heard the elevator moving again, and then he buzzed in Imasu and his Yakuza friendlies. The door he was standing behind was a solid sheet of six-inch steel. An antitank missile would barely make a dent. Bart, in his paranoid state, had commissioned the door during his days of heavy debt, and heavier drug use.

He turned back to Lucy.

Lucy tried wearing a smile but it looked lopsided. "So I guess it's official. I'm Bonnie to your Clyde."

Tyler smiled.

"Yeah, but with a different ending, hopefully. Now help me finish getting ready."

She slipped the small chain with the alligator clips on the ends around Tyler's neck. She then attached van Gogh's *Self-Portrait with Bandaged Ear,* to the ends of the alligator clips, careful not to touch the actual painting, only the edges of the canvas.

"How do I look?"

She stood back to gaze at him and couldn't help but smile. He looked like a bum on the street with the most expensive sandwich board ever.

There was a pounding on the door, and muffled yelling. And then the elevator came alive. The party was about to begin.

"Showtime," he said. Lucy kissed him. He returned volley. She retreated to the small bedroom.

SEVENTY-ONE

"Hold on!" Tyler yelled through the stainless steel door.

The choppers were still hovering. The snipers were staring down from every rooftop, aiming at his windows. If the windows hadn't had a special reflective tint, Tyler would've been able to feel the laser bead smoking a hole through his forehead. Thank God for Bart's paranoia. Tyler had a whole new appreciation for his friend's thoroughness.

"Stand back!" he yelled. He then used the remote to unlock the door. Slowly the handle turned, and the door opened.

The younger agents came through first, followed by Rosenwater. A grizzled shit of a man. The guy was old-school meat and potatoes, and looked it. His forehead had the wrinkle design of a Shar Pei, and his nose was redder, and more bulbous, than Ted Kennedy's. His suit looked like he'd slept in it, which he often did. And to top it off his tie had some brownish stain on it. This was in contrast to the younger agents who at least made a sartorial attempt. They looked neat, pressed, well kempt.

The agents and their boss moved into the loft apartment quickly, holding their gaze on Tyler Sears and trying to work out why he had van Gogh's painting, *Self-Portrait with Bandaged Ear*, hanging around his neck. Behind him were all the other canvases, all world famous, all worth hundreds of millions. The old man grinned.

"Gotcha," sneered the old man.

"Not exactly," replied Tyler, as he pulled a small acetylene torch from behind his back and lit it in one quick motion.

The younger agents swung their submachine guns up from their hips before Tyler had a chance to finish his sentence. Both carried the same Heckler & Koch MP5K submachine gun. The old bird was holding a Glock 33 Pocket Rocket, which Tyler knew was a handgun less than seven inches long yet capable of exploding a .357 mag at a rate of 1330 feet per second. Tyler stared at the mass of destructive weaponry. He noticed the safeties were all off. If there was a war they were planning on winning it.

"Boys, you're looking at close to a billion dollars in paintings. A bullet through any one of them or a melted or charred canvas will end your careers before you even leave the building. Correct?" Tyler said, looking directly at their boss.

"Stand down," Grumpy snapped at his pets. Guns were lowered.

"Whaddya want Sears? Your options are pretty limited."

"How about we all chill for a minute and wait for the rest of the party to show?"

"What the fuck are—"

The door flew open. Guns were raised. Standing in the doorway was Komate Imasu, with his Yakuza guards in tow, carrying the cases with the money.

"Please enter, Imasu-san," Tyler said.

Imasu entered with his goons, all three with weapons locked, loaded, and ready for game day. The first one in was wielding an Uzi submachine gun pistol. The Israeli super-weapon. A gangster's favorite. Yakuza number two had a Benelli M2 SuperNova shotgun with the barrel altered. It was normally used as a tactical weapon for law enforcement, but in this guy's hands, at such close range, it'd be able to make a hole big enough to fly the Apache through. The extending stock of the shotgun was already in position and his hand was wrapped around the pistol grip. The last one in was the young, bald bodyguard Tyler had met at Imasu's office a few months back, when all this madness had started. True to his youthful, gangsta image, the young Yakuza thug was wielding a pair of Smith & Wesson .357 revolvers, the 500 series, with the long barrels, and pearl inlaid grips. The guy was all show pony, at least that's what Tyler hoped.

"Gentlemen, welcome. First off, how about you all toss your phones in a pile right here," Tyler said to everyone.

"And Irv, how's about you and your boys toss their GPS trackers in as well," Tyler said.

The two agents looked at their boss. The GPS devices would allow the snipers to determine which of the moving bodies in the penthouse were agents, and which were not. Reluctantly the old man reached in his pocket and tossed a small electronic device on the floor. He signaled for the other two agents to do likewise. Imasu and his men tossed their phones onto the pile.

"Excellent," said Tyler, as he quickly reached down holding the torch with its bluish flame on top of the devices. The pile of electronics fried up quicker than a marshmallow at a Boy Scout cookout.

The shooters surrounding the rooftops all readjusted their positions, not quite sure what to do having just lost their direct signal. The Apache Attack helicopters did circling 360s trying to hone in on the defunct signals.

"Sears-san, it is most unfortunate for you that we have uninvited guests," Imasu said.

"The more the merrier," Tyler replied. "Safety in numbers and all."

"Your boys carry permits for those weapons?" snarled the Interpol boss.

Imasu didn't respond, didn't flinch, didn't even acknowledge the old crank's presence. The young, bald Yakuza hotshot flipped the old man a grin and opened his black leather trench coat to reveal a Lupara twelve-gauge, sawed-off, double-barrel shotgun, strapped to his leg. The two Interpol agents stood frozen, not sure what to do.

"Enough chit-chat," said Tyler. "Here's the deal. Imasu hired me, blackmailed me actually, to pinch the paintings. So technically he's your mastermind, and the new owner," Tyler said looking directly at Imasu.

"So, I'm delivering as promised—"

"You're a few paintings short of our deal," Imasu cut him off.

"Well see, that's where my friend Irv, from Interpol, comes in."

"Fuck you Sears," the old man growled.

"As you can see, Imasu-san, he's a cranky son of a bitch so I thought you could pay him the outstanding balance you owe me, and he'll be able to hand you the rest of the paintings," Tyler said motioning over his shoulder to the other canvases.

Tyler took a quick read on the room. The Yakuza boys were only focused on the trigger fingers of the Interpol agents. They didn't even give a glance to the several dozen agents that lined the rooftops surrounding the building, much less the hovering attack helicopters. Everyone was frozen in place.

"You see, old man, I know you're close to retirement so I planned this little party for you. And like any party there are presents. And this one's ten million cash, to you, and your helpers.

Imasu-san please ask your men to open the cases and leave them open over here on the floor." There was a hesitation but Tyler aimed the acetylene torch at a lower corner of the van Gogh hanging around his neck. Imasu immediately barked out some Japanese, and his thugs did as they were instructed. Everyone was now staring at the fresh-wrapped hundreds sitting in the cases.

"That's ten million to you, and whatever you choose to share with your trainees is your business." The young field agents shifted in position. They quickly glanced at each other, and then stared back at the cash. Ten million.

Tyler took a small microcassette recorder out of his pocket. He punched the play button.

"For now, your brother is spared. I will not stand for any more of your insubordination. Are we clear?"

"You owe me. You do this job and you're free."

"I'm sorry? I owe you. Owe you what?"

"Sears-san, it was I who got you out on early release. You didn't really think you got out because you were a model prisoner? You got out because I paid for your freedom, and that greedy warden cost me an extra hundred grand. And now you will do as I say. Understood?"

"It was you, Komate Imasu, who arranged my early release?"

"That is correct Sears-san."

"As grateful as I am for your generosity I must reluctantly decline your proposal."

"You have no choice if you value your mother and brother's life."

"With all due respect Sears-san, you're in no position to negotiate."

It was Imasu admitting that he had paid off the parole board and the warden. Tyler had recorded their entire conversation. He stopped and looked at the grizzled old goat.

For once the old man was speechless, sort of.

"Sears, you didn't bribe your way out of jail?"

"Exactly. It was Imasu. This whole mess is on him."

Imasu stood motionless. The young, bald Yakuza was rubbing his left thumb along the grip of the long-barreled revolver.

The old man was actually growling. Tyler decided to move the pieces on the board now.

"Here's how it'll work. Imasu gets the paintings, except for the one around my neck, which I intend to use as an insurance policy for my safe exit. And you old man, you get all that cash sitting—"

"NO!" Imasu said cutting Tyler off.

Outside, the noise of the helicopters circling disrupted the normal pattern of the pigeons that called Tompkins Square Park home. A flock flew straight up from the lower ledge of the building and straight into the face of the sniper in a prone and ready position on top of the adjacent building. The sniper swatted at the birds as they flew into his face and in that split second with his finger in the ready position, he accidentally squeezed the trigger. The crack of the M403A sniper rifle was heard on all the other rooftops. Radio silence was broken.

"HOLD FIRE! REPORT!" crackled over everyone's earpiece.

By the time the head of the swat team finished saying the word "REPORT!" the 30-caliber Barnes X solid-copper, heat-treated bullet, traveling at over 1000 feet per second, had cracked the large loft window and impacted the right shoulder of one of the Yakuza thugs. The bullet, known for its razor sharp edges, flared backwards on impact, tore through his chest cavity, taking most of his scapula with it on exit.

Imasu ducked down, and pulled out the small H&K P2000 subkompakt handgun he always carried. The old man dove behind one of his field agents. Tyler fell to the floor.

The wounded Yakuza brought his Uzi up with his good hand squeezing the trigger. The Interpol field agents swung their MP5Ks up, and were already firing. The other two Yakuza boys dove for cover, with their fingers squarely on the trigger.

Outside along the rooftops, all anyone could see were the continual flashes of gunfire from inside. It looked like Chinese New Year gone wild.

"All shooters, if you get a target take it, otherwise use caution," was heard through the headsets of the shooters along the rooftops.

Inside, it was getting ugly quickly. At such close quarters it was bound to. The Yakuza firing the Uzi got his head blown clean off by a quick double round burst from one of the MP5K, fired by an Interpol agent. Instinctively, the beheaded Yakuza, his arm still gripping the Uzi, swung it wildly up, and blew away half of Manet's *A Bar at the Folies-Bergère*. His torso fell backwards into Cézanne's *Apples and Oranges*, the blood gushing from his neck cavity onto the painted table holding the fruit.

The young-buck Yakuza with the long-barreled Smith & Wesson revolvers was doing his best John Wayne at the Alamo, strutting with guns blazing, knowing this was his last stand. The Interpol agent shot him repeatedly with his assault weapon, but the young buck kept coming. He staggered and haplessly shot the Interpol agent in the lower abdomen, disemboweling him.

The third Yakuza was firing his Benelli shotgun randomly. The blasts looked like roman candles blowing out the end of the barrel.

Tyler leaped for the kitchen area, and almost made it, but felt a sudden stinging pain in his right ear. Rosenwater had gotten off a lucky blind shot from behind the table and nicked Tyler's ear. He looked back into the living area and saw two of the canvases riddled with bullets. The third, Cézanne's *Apples and Oranges*, had a headless body lying on top of it, blood pouring out of the open neck cavity. Tyler could hear someone yelling in Japanese.

Outside, the snipers all had fingers on their triggers, awaiting instructions.

Chanel N°5 watched it all through field glasses from a building rooftop directly across the park. Transfixed.

Everything inside was beyond madness. Tyler had to make a move. The young Yakuza triggerman was staggering towards Rosenwater, his sawed off shotgun hanging on his hip. Just as he was about to pull the trigger a 30-caliber sniper bullet flew through the loft window, and pierced the young Japanese warrior through the frontal lobe tearing away everything except his lower jaw bone. With no brain to worry about, his fingers froze on the twin triggers of his Lupara shotgun, and shells screamed helter-skelter from the barrels. He staggered like a monster from *Night of the Living Dead*. One of the rounds hit the old man in the ass as he tried crawling away from the headless onslaught. A second cut through his lower leg, which exploded the old gizzard's calf muscle and Achilles tendon. He rolled in agony across the floor. Imasu was in a fetal position cowering behind his dead bodyguard, trying to grab the case with the money.

He was screaming in Japanese. Tyler didn't wait to find out what he was saying.

Outside, the commander of the operation had a decision to make. What was supposed to be a simple grab and go was turning into a chaotic firefight.

"Apache One and Two off."

"Apache One and Two returning to base."

And with that, the twin helicopters banked in opposite directions and headed south down the East River.

"High Hat are you in position?"

"Roger that," came through the earpiece.

High Hat was the rocket-propelled grenade launcher that was sometimes used by SWAT teams.

"Do you have a visual?"

"High Hat has visual."

"Stand by."

Chanel lay on top of the building, dumbstruck by what she was watching through her binoculars. This routine arrest was turning into one of the deadliest firefights in agency history, with hundreds of millions of dollars of art caught in the crossfire.

"Sears! I want my paintings," was the last thing Tyler Sears heard.

Tyler was in agony from the bullet grazing his ear. It was time to move. "Lucy NOW!" he screamed. Lucy ran in from the bedroom and stared at the bloodbath.

"Don't look! Help me up!" Tyler ordered.

Too shocked to say anything, she silently helped him up.

"Help me push the stove away," Tyler yelled over the confusion.

Together they pushed the stove as hard as they could and moved it away from the wall, revealing an old garbage chute, and accidentally knocking the gas stove from the intake pipe. Gas was now quickly filling the loft.

Tyler smelled the gas and barked, "Now!"

The fear in her eyes was palpable. Lucy was paralyzed by the scene. Tyler didn't wait. With what little strength he had left, he picked her up, and stuck her feet through the opening. And in a flash she was gone.

"High Hat, smoker only, on my count... 3... 2... 1. Fire!" could be heard through the earpieces along the rooftops.

"High Hat smoker away."

And instantly a smoke grenade was launched at the firefight taking place in the penthouse loft. The commander hoped the smoke bomb would cause enough of a distraction that his men would be able to enter and secure the building. He was unaware of the open gas valve spewing highly combustible unstable natural gas in every direction of the loft.

Tyler could hear the unmistakable whooshing sound of the rocket-launched grenade. "SHIT!" He realized what was about to happen.

Plans changed dramatically at that moment. Tyler wrapped Vincent around him and dove headfirst into the open garbage chute, just as the smoke grenade entered the loft. The grenade landed just inside the living room where Chanel's boss and Imasu were still clinging to slivers of hope, hidden behind underlings turned into corpses. When the grenade exploded the free flowing natural gas had a thermal party. An enormous cloud of flames blew out the wall of windows in the loft, with shards of glass flying in every direction. The ten million in cash followed the glass bits as charred hundreds filled the sky like a perverse ticker tape parade. The explosion knocked the remaining windows out of the building, rattling all the buildings surrounding the park. If the noise of the lethal chemical explosion hadn't been so loud someone might have heard the human screams as the remaining bodies immolated. The reddish-black chemical cloud that was released left all those watching from the rooftops speechless.

The SWAT commander said nothing. Chanel could actually feel the heat being thrust from the building.

Tyler flew headfirst toward the basement, Vincent covering his ass, he felt the heat from the gas permeating the air. The shaft he was traveling through, at sixty feet per second, was heating up. He hit the mattresses he and Lucy had piled up, head first. He rolled off the mattresses and quickly moved to a far corner. The flames shot down like a bolt from Zeus, the mattresses burst into flames. Tyler fell to the floor as the gas spread and collected on the basement ceiling.

"LUCY!" he barked. "GET OUT. NOW!"

Upstairs was far worse. The open gas valve continued to feed the inferno. Heat levels were approaching 600°F. Carnelley's Rule was kicking in. The aluminum window casings were losing their molecular structure. The oils on the canvases were bubbling off the paintings. Fingers were fusing directly onto the steel triggers. Chanel's boss's polymer-handled Glock had melted right into his hand. The pain in his lower leg disappeared since his entire lower body had vaporized when the grenade exploded near him.

Imasu was no longer able to scream since his vocal cords had melted into his esophagus, which was in the process of jellification. The heat continued to build.

Outside, along the rooftops, all anyone could see was a giant fireball, followed by a blackish cloud growing around the loft. The occasional flame burst through the black fog. No one had ever seen anything like it. They were all frozen at the horror they were witnessing.

"Ground report," barked the commander.

"Sir, massive heat is escaping from every opening of the building. It's too hot to send anyone in. And we've already evacuated all our men that were on the rooftop. We'll need at least a couple of fire brigades to get things under control."

The commander spoke very carefully.

"Are there any survivors?"

"Sir, we attached an external heat gauge to one of the windows on the back of the building, and it raced through three hundred degrees in seconds and then exploded. I can't believe anyone survived either the blast or the continuing fire."

"Son of a bitch!" the commander said.

"Get your men away from the building and coordinate with the fire brigades when they arrive."

"Roger that."

Across the park, Chanel was watching in shock as she listened to the negative survivor report. She was lying in a prone position watching the madness through her field glasses when a hand came around her face from behind, and before she could react a cloth filled with ether was covering her nose and mouth. She tried holding her breath but her initial gasp was all it took for the ether to enter her bloodstream. In less than five seconds she was out cold. And she stayed like that for the next twenty minutes. Ricardo's man left the rooftop undetected.

She missed the fire trucks arriving, trying to get the building-on-a-spit under control, and she missed the couple leaving through a small basement door on the adjacent building. They were covered in soot and looked like two homeless souls. Their clothes hung on them like rags. Her hair was a bedraggled mess, and he walked with a ragged cloth wrapped around his ears, and a long cylinder slung over his shoulder. The SWAT team members didn't give them a second look. Chanel N°5 would definitely have given them a second look. Especially the long cylinder which contained all of the original paintings Tyler had lifted, including the van Gogh, which now boasted a singed corner courtesy of its time as Tyler's protective heat shield as he dove down the chute just ahead of the flames.

SEVENTY-TWO

The Following Week
NEWS REPORTS:

Washington Post
Dec. 3, 1999

WASHINGTON — The Hundred Greatest Paintings of the Last Thousand Years exhibition opened today at the National Gallery of Art. The opening was delayed one week due to technical problems with the new security system. Due to administrative customs problems van Gogh's *Self-Portrait with Bandaged Ear,* on loan from the Courtauld in London, had to be replaced by van Gogh's *Self-Portrait,* part of the Whitney permanent collection at the National Gallery. There was a morning VIP tour attended by the President and the First Lady. By afternoon when the exhibit was open to the general public there were long lines. The exhibit is scheduled to remain open until February 1. A review of the exhibit will appear in the Sunday Style section.

Santa Fe Times
Dec. 1, 1999

CHIMAYO — Two men of Asian descent were found dead, floating in the Rio Grande River about three miles downstream from Chimayo. The bodies were discovered within ten yards of each other. Both men had suffered severe head trauma believed to have been caused by falling onto the rocks along the riverbed. The men were dressed in almost identical dark suits, and it is believed they had engaged in a double suicide. The bodies were discovered by a local Chimayo man, who was fly-fishing on the river. Neither man had any identification. No further details were available at press time.

The reporter didn't know that the location of the two dead Asian men was just down the hill from the Double H Ranch where Alex Sears was living. Nor did she know about the gentleman from Juarez, Mexico who had been keeping a careful eye on Alex, at Ricardo's request. And she certainly wouldn't have known that it was Ricardo's associate who "encouraged" the Japanese killers to take a swim in the Rio Grande. Sadly, each of them missed the water, bouncing off the rocks several times, and then being dragged into the water by the current.

Corsican authorities were mystified that the Japanese man who they dubbed "Jacques Hardón" lying in the morgue had no identification of any kind. They were equally baffled that his fingerprints were not found in any data bank. Since no one could be contacted there was no need for an autopsy. Death was ruled to be a massive heart attack. Corsica is a small island with limited resources, so instead of waiting the obligatory thirty days, they were forced to cremate the body after fourteen. His ashes were dumped into the ocean unceremoniously.

The New York Times
Metro section
Nov. 30, 1999

A drug deal gone bad caused the police and fire departments to block off an entire city block near Tompkins Square Park on the Lower East Side.

According to authorities, rival drug lords were involved in a firefight in an abandoned Lower East Side building. Police sources say the building caught fire, and the fire department was unable to bring it under control until most of the building had burned. There were no survivors, and the police are withholding the names of the victims pending an investigation.

The New York Times
Obituaries
Dec. 1, 1999

Komate Imasu died today in his Sixth Avenue office. According to his personal physician, he suffered a massive heart attack and was pronounced dead on the scene by paramedics.

He was the chairman of the board of Trans-Pacific Holdings Group, a multinational conglomerate. He was best known in the New York City art world for his love of modern art, and for his encouragement of young artists.

He was on the board of the Metropolitan Museum of Art and The Guggenheim, and he supported many downtown galleries.

He also organized a large art exchange between the Tokyo Museum of Art and the Met. He leaves a wife, a son, and daughter. A memorial service will be held at the Met, and the body will then be transported to Japan for final burial.

A complete description of his efforts in the art world will appear in the Sunday *Times* Arts and Leisure section.

There was no mention of the death of Irving Rosenwater, the old Interpol agent in any newspaper. Nor was there any mention of the Japanese assassin sent by Imasu to kill Max, Tyler's friend and owner of the Art Bar, on his boat. It was to be Tyler's second penalty.

Max heard water lapping against the sides of his sailboat as he was trying to sleep. He heard someone quietly climb on board. When the Yakuza thug stepped below into the cabin area with a piano wire wrapped between his two gloved hands, Max let loose with the fire extinguisher and sprayed the assassin in the face. Unable to see, the Yakuza stumbled, blind, back out on the deck.

Max escaped through the front hatch and while his Japanese killer was bent over trying to rub his burning eyes, Max let fly with his seven iron, always his club of choice. He caught the assassin square in the groin. He then reared back for a final swing, and caught his would-be killer across the left temple. In severe pain, the killer fell forward over the lifeline, and into the Hudson River. Max quickly revved the engine of his old wooden sloop and started forward. He threw his would-be killer a life preserver, as the assassin grabbed hold, Max sped up the engine. The sailboat was now moving directly into the middle of the Hudson River, with the Yakuza assassin hanging on for dear life, about ten yards behind the boat. In the dark Max could see the lights of a tugboat, with a barge, moving south, down river. He cut well in front of the tug and cut the killer loose at the same time. The young Yakuza was sucked under the tug and the barge.

No body was ever recovered.

The late November wind was biting cold, so Max decided it was time to head for sunnier climes.

Max welcomed the new millennium sitting at the Admiral's Inn outdoor bar in Nelson's Harbor, on Antigua.

As for Bart, he left the day after the firefight on a private jet for St. Barts, where he had decided to spend the winter. This was all paid for by the funds he'd received from Tyler for creating the almost-perfect fake masterpieces, all of which perished in the fire.

EPILOGUE

July 4, 2000

Heading south on Main Street out of Saranac Lake in the Adirondacks is Branch Farm Road. Follow this to the end and you'll find a dirt path, which leads to the banks of a decent-sized lake, one of the many pristine lakes dotting the Adirondack region. At the edge of the lake is a large ramshackle original Adirondack "cabin." It's rumored to be the cabin where Paul Smith housed his lover of twenty years, until she was brutally murdered via axe, next to the enormous fireplace, by Mrs. Paul Smith. Charges were never filed. The original insanity plea.

The cabin never sold and it fell into disrepair. Rumors of it being haunted made its sale all but impossible. In January 2000, this historic relic was purchased and by summertime, it had been beautifully restored. Even the grand living room with its enormous floor-to-ceiling fireplace made from surrounding river rocks had been returned to its original splendor.

A dozen or so guests had gathered on the outside porch, enjoying a July 4th barbecue. Antique kerosene lamps were lit. The crickets were close by, and lightening bugs were flashing along the water's edge. A perfect midsummer evening. The booms and distant flashes were beginning as the town began its annual fireworks extravaganza.

The host discreetly slipped away and headed back into the house. He ignored the beautifully rebuilt floor-to-ceiling fireplace in the living room and headed straight for the master bedroom, which was in the back of the house on the first floor. He slipped into the bedroom and looked around. He could hear the oohs and ahhs from his guests out on the lawn, as the fireworks dazzled across the lake. He turned and looked over at a painting held in a simple frame above the dresser. It was Manet's *A Bar at the Folies-Bergère*. He stood and stared at the painting. He didn't notice the bedroom door crack open, and he was too mesmerized to notice that his wife had entered the room. She walked over to him and stood next to him. She reached up and lightly touched her husband's slightly scarred right ear.

"She's gorgeous, even for a fake," Lucy said.

Tyler just grinned a Cheshire cat grin....

"Tyyyllerrr?" Lucy said, questioning.

On the same 4th of July, in the morning, an oversized package was delivered to Chanel N°5's residence in the Adams Morgan section of Washington, DC. The Hispanic deliveryman said no signature was necessary. All prepaid.

He got back into his stolen, unmarked white van, drove several blocks, and left the van, after wiping away any prints. He jumped into a black Corvette and headed back to Ricardo's farm north of New York City. Chanel N°5 carried the oversized package inside. There was no card, no identifying information.

She tore the heavy brown wrapping away. With the contents revealed, she began to laugh.

She was staring at Van Gogh's *Self-Portrait with Bandaged Ear* with a slightly singed corner.

ACKNOWLEDGEMENTS

The notion of a writer sitting alone creating fiction is a myth. It really takes a village, a village of friends, family, and a boatload of pros.

First there's Susan Grode, protector of all things creative, who introduced me to Marion Rosenberg, who in turn, urged me to take the leap of faith required to begin this novel. Then there's Brooks Dexter who goaded me into finishing it, after I'd stopped at the halfway mark believing Sisyphus had an easier task.

Thank you also to Peter Sears, Bob Sabbag, and Jesse Kornbluth—three of the best at what they do.

Also thanks to Bart Gulley and Jorge Caunedo, for art inspiration, and Erin Cox, for her eternal optimism. Thanks to Michael Gauthier for his technical expertise and friendship.

All kudos to Judy Sternlight, editor extraordinaire, for spinning straw into gold, and to Charlotte Sheedy for introducing me to Judy.

Thanks to John and Nyna Weatherson at Trokay Restaurant, who allowed me to commandeer table fourteen for days on end, as I navigated my way through the edits.

Thanks to Crystal Patriarche and the gang at BookSparks for their never-ending professional support.

A shout-out to my early readers (you know who you are), thanks for your wide-ranging comments.

To my sister, Christina, who's the best bookseller on the planet, thanks for everything.

Meg Baldwin for always pointing me toward true north.

My daughter, Willie, who has always been the brightest star.

And finally to my wife, Jane Prior—cheerleader, critic, and the one person who believed in this book even when I doubted it—thank you.

Paul Hoppe
2014

About the Author

Paul Hoppe worked as a lobbyist in Washington DC, a stockbroker on Wall Street, and a screenwriter in Hollywood before writing his first novel. He has lived on four different continents and currently splits his time between the High Sierras and the beaches of Australia.

About SparkPress

SparkPress is an independent boutique publisher delivering high-quality, entertaining, and engaging content that enhances readers' lives. We are proud of our catalog of both fiction and non-fiction titles, featuring authors who represent a wide array of genres, as well as our established, industry-wide reputation for innovative, creative, results-driven success in working with authors. SparkPress, a BookSparks imprint, is a division of SparkPoint Studio, LLC.

To learn more, visit us at www.sparkpointstudio.com.

CPSIA information can be obtained at www.ICGtesting.com
Printed in the USA
LVOW11s1340080914

403018LV00005B/371/P